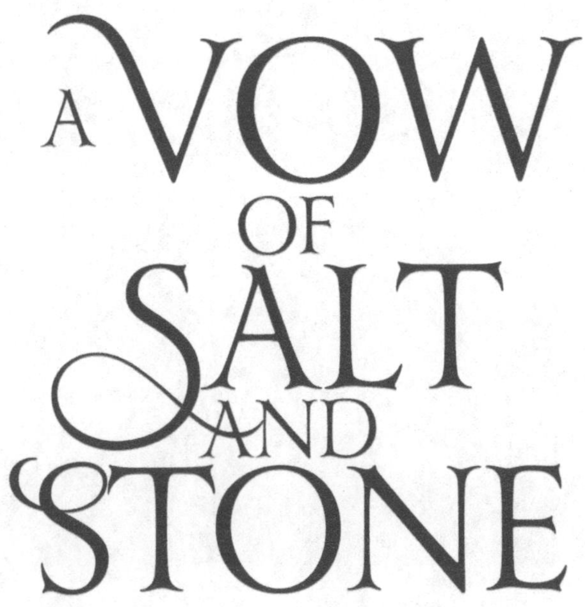

A VOW OF SALT AND STONE

A BLOOD AND BLOOM NOVEL

SANTANA SAUNDERS

For those bravely healing their childhood wounds and searching for their stars.

Keep going.

It will all be worth it.

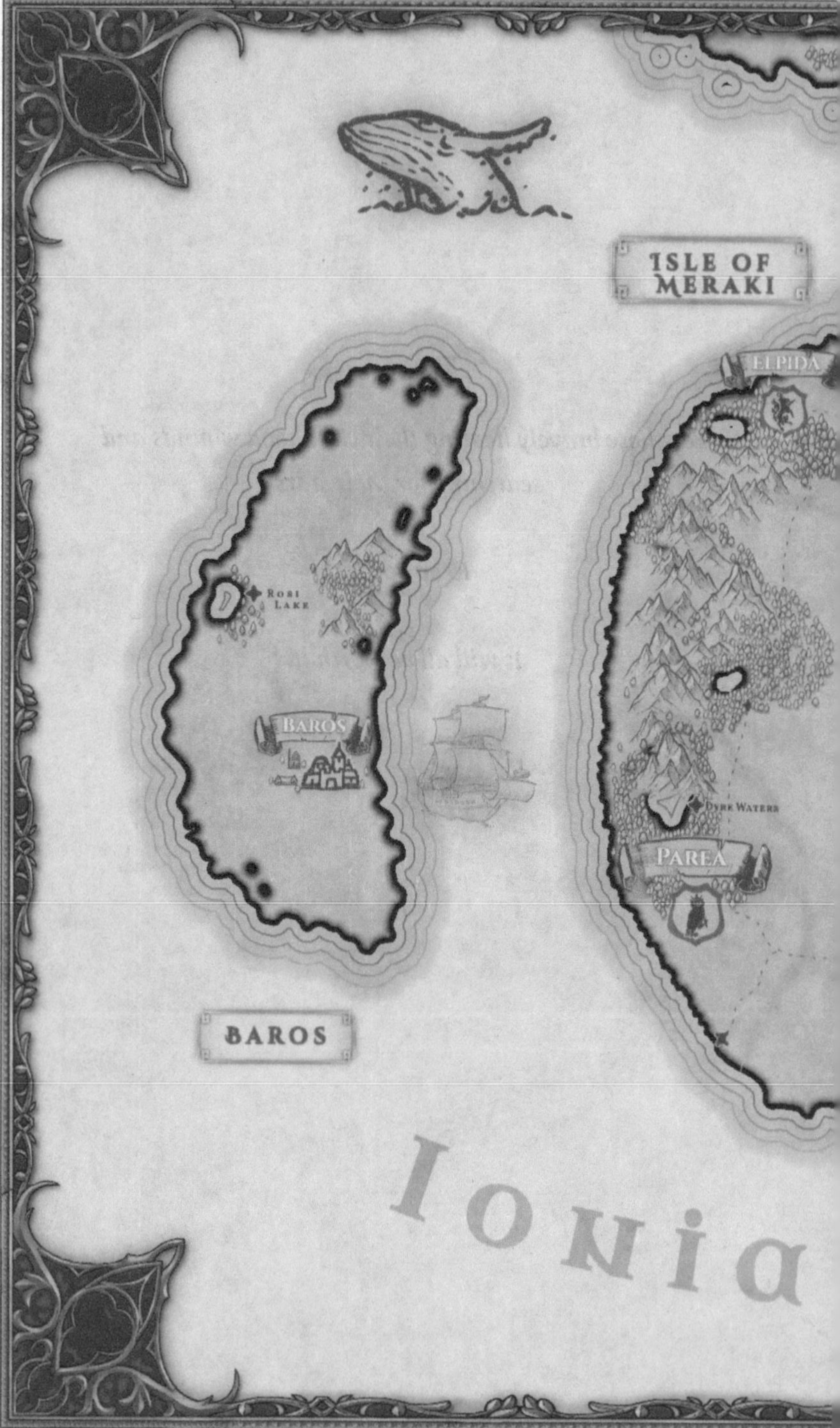
ISLE OF
MERAKI
ELPIDA
ROSI
LAKE
BAROS
DYRE WATERS
PAREA
BAROS
IONIA

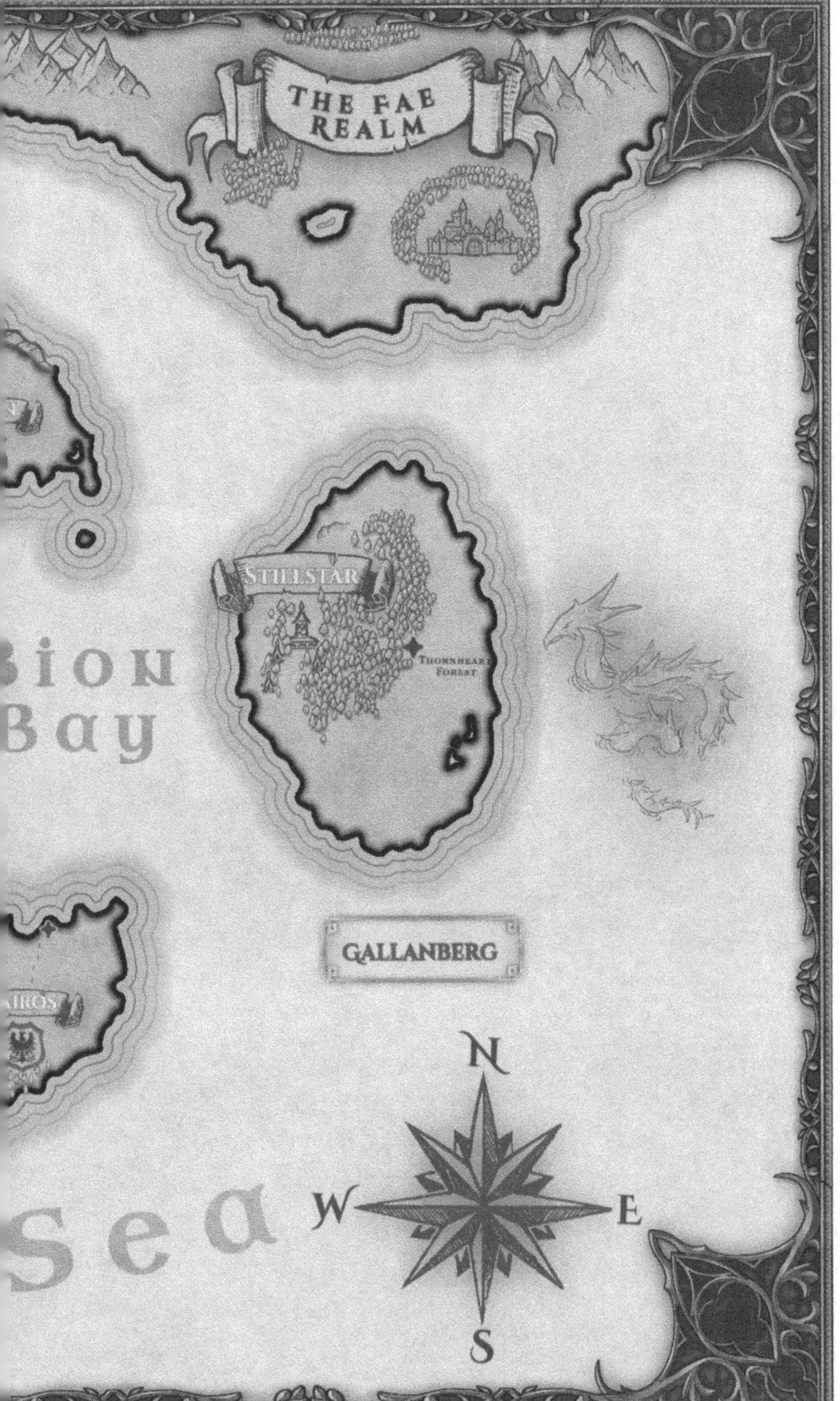

THE FAE REALM
STILLSTAR
THORNHEART FOREST
BION BAY
GALLANBERG
AIROS
SEA
N
E
S
W

In the heart of the forest, where shadows play,
Beware the Fae, as they come your way.
Their magic's a dance, both dark and bright,
With fire and water, they'll steal your night.

Oh, the Fae, they weave a wicked dream,
In a promise of air and earth, it seems.
With whispers and charms, they'll lead you astray,
In their mystical realm, where wild things sway.

Their fire's a spark in the cool night breeze,
A flickering temptress, a dance to tease.
Water flows like a silken thread,
Binding your soul where secrets are spread.

-The Song of Warning
The Meraki Chronicles

1
EVANTHE

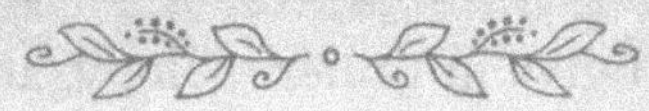

Drowning is nothing like I had imagined it would be.

It's worse.

My body slams into the solid rushing force of a river. I do my best to dodge shards of wood from the ship spinning through the currents around me, but there are too many to avoid. I try to make sense of what is up and down. Flailing my limbs desperately, I try to claw my way back to the surface, but I can't seem to break through. I hold out as long as possible until a singular erratic breath drags a mouthful of the deadly, cold water into my lungs, and the panic sets in. It burns like molten lava. The searing pain is viscous and unrelenting until it's not at all, the once violent, dark surge turning to a tranquil, orange hue. Much like a sunset. Pleasant. Warm. Weightless.

My arms and legs go limp as I stare at the soothing sight. And all at once, it goes pitch black.

All feeling fades away until it's as if I had never existed. The fighting force that stirred inside me only moments ago is seemingly gone, and I think, *It wouldn't be so bad to stay in this quiet place*, the dark nothingness consoling me like a mother singing her child a lullaby as she drifts away. I give in to her melody, and the darkness lifts to white.

Stark white.

Then I'm only a girl once more, back in my aunts' feather bed. The familiar scent of sage and lemon waft in the air, dancing along to the faint sound of singing voices. A song I know all too well. Their bare feet shimmy and slide over the old stone floors, their chorus growing louder as they approach. The door bursts open with a fit of giggles as my aunts raise their jars and plop down next to me. I lift the water to my lips—moon water spiked with spirits, lemon peel, and herbs. They pull me from my room, and we run naked through the barren streets of Parea, down the dirt trail and into the meadow, where we roll in the grass, plucking snapdragons all through the night. I look down at the colorful blooms in my arms and recall how the windowsills will be full of them through the duration of the spring and into the summer until it gets too hot for them to survive. It is my favorite time of year. I lie down, the earth cool on my bare back. Looking up at the full glowing moon, I lift one of the snaps and pinch the sides of its pink mouth, giving the illusion that it is swallowing the celestial orb. My Aunt Maria scoots closer to watch me and points up at the night sky. "She may swallow the sun, but tonight, the bloom swallows her." She wiggles her eyebrows, and I chuckle.

"Wouldn't that be something?" I ask, waiting for a reply, but she only smiles, her face fading away. Throwing the flowers to the ground, I reach out for her. Running with all my might, a voice screams inside me, or maybe I *am* actually screaming. I can't tell. Then she's gone. The starry sky disappears, and the burning in my chest returns, making me curl in on myself. I wince at the pain, pinching my eyes shut and hurling the fire from my mouth until there seems to be nothing left. With a cough, my eyes flutter open to see Aero crouching over me, his eyes wide with worry and his hands outstretched, dripping with water.

"Eva! Eva, can you hear me? Are you alright?" he asks.

My head still reeling, I squint, looking down at my body. My vision is hazy, but there appears to be rivets of diluted blood from those sharp pieces of wood running the gamut of my arms and legs. Although it's gruesome, nothing seems to be broken, so I nod.

"We can't stay here. It's too exposed. Get her up," Phira urges with an angry whisper.

Aero's face hardens at the fiery-haired female's words.

"Give her a moment. She nearly drowned," he growls.

"That will be the least of her concerns if we don't move soon," she snaps.

Aero clenches his jaw with a scowl, but bites his

tongue. Having been one of Liri's right-hand warriors for years, Phira isn't making any room for error. We are in their world now. A bunch of humans following them blindly into this new place. But, like it or not, we should take heed to her warning.

Leaning against a tree behind them, Shade Addington, deity of seduction and wine, looks out in the distance and sighs. He nonchalantly moves closer and reaches his hand out to me. "She's right. You're not in Gallanberg anymore."

His demeanor may be calm, but the warning tone of his voice is clear, sending a shiver down the nape of my neck. Aero, not letting him get any closer to me, moves between us, shaking the water from his hands and letting it splatter onto the male's face. Shade clenches his jaw but knows better than to pick a battle at a time like this. A low-pitched rumble sounds in the distance, and we all pause, holding our breath as not to risk drawing any attention our way. Liri leans in, placing a finger to her mouth, signaling that we must remain quiet, then points toward the forest behind us. Hera, Feliks, and the others quickly follow her lead.

Without a second thought, Aero scoops me up in his arms. "I can walk on my own," I quietly balk, still feeling weaker than I'd like but will never admit to it. He scoffs, continuing to trudge forward. I press my hand against his chest, trying to push him away, but another bout of water comes surging up my throat and gurgling out of my mouth in a coughing fit.

"I'm sorry. I thought I had gotten it all out," he apologizes, and I realize he must have used his power to pull the water from my lungs. That explains why his hands were sopping wet.

Liri looks back at our group and nods toward a small opening in the thick woods ahead. Cirrus gasps at the sight, falling to his knees and kissing the ground beneath him. Diaspor, Phira, and Bel also pause in awe, seeming to find the same relief being back in their homeland.

My eyes clear now, I take in the terrifying new world. Everything is somehow familiar yet completely different. The sky, less blue than the one back in our realm, is an empyrean turquoise, its gaze making every leaf and blade of grass appear that much more green, purple, or blue. Entering the thicket, an aroma of musky pears and sandalwood fills the air. The trees are giant, at least ten times the size of those on Meraki. Oddly, their branches grow away from their trunks in spirals, lifting into heaps of flora like I've never seen. Humming and fluttering insects of the most dazzling, metallic colors dance around us.

Feliks, with his usual childlike wonder, bounces from one side of our uncharted trail to the other, exploring. He snatches a few round pieces of yellow fruit from an offshoot nearby and begins juggling them with hopes to entertain Hera. Based on the rather irritated look upon her face, I'd say he is failing miserably. Although I hate to admit any common ground with the clown, I, too, feel myself falling for the intrigue of this place. Like a youngling told not to touch something, the danger only makes it more appealing.

Curiosity bringing life back to my limbs, I leap from Aero's arms to get a closer look when a massive, beautiful bird flies right over my head and lands on one of the looping branches above us. Its feathers are the deepest royal blue and fuchsia, arranged in an enthralling pattern I can't seem to look away from. In awe of its beauty, I step closer and reach out toward it. But Liri snatches my wrist, pulling me back. "Don't get any closer. That is a sqrieth."

"She's stunning," I gasp, finding it impossible for such a gorgeous creature to be dangerous. Liri shakes her head.

"Stunning, yet deadly. You see that shiny substance lining the rim of her beak?"

I nod, staring at the yellow iridescent border, the way it cups her bill with its mesmerizing gel. Liri darts her gaze back to mine and grips my chin for dramatic effect.

"It's poisonous. Even the tiniest snip, and you won't just lose some blood. You won't take another step."

Hera and Feliks look in my direction, their maws wide open in horror. Swallowing the large lump in my throat, I return the gesture. I knew that the Fae could use their lethal magic against us, but I hadn't considered the gifts their creatures or plants might have. What's most frightening is knowing that if Liri hadn't pulled me away from her, I doubt I would have had the willpower to resist the bird's lure on my own.

Seeming convinced that we've been frightened enough, Liri continues with a hushed voice. "Just don't touch anything unless I tell you it's safe, and keep your wits about you. There are more things here that will kill you than those that won't, and I won't be able to babysit you the entire time."

I wince, the insinuation that I'm like a baby here in her realm stinging. She turns back to the front of the line and whispers something into Cirrus's ear, only adding insult to injury—as if they are the wise ones, and the rest of us are not privy to their knowledge. I left everything I know to come here and save them. Even though my people in Meraki will reap the benefits as well, she doesn't need to be so condescending. After all, I just learned of my Fae lineage. And now I have to be their Final Guardian. I didn't ask for this. I think back to the way the featherbed in my aunts' home felt. How much easier things were before all this. What I wouldn't give to take it all back.

The forest canopy is full, leaving little light along the floor, but I can still see where the sun sits through the foliage, and it seems to be just where it would have been in the human realm.

"Is it the same time of day here as it is in Meraki?" I ask, hoping the question doesn't sound too juvenile.

Shade falls back to hike beside me. "Good observation, Evanthe. Our worlds may be quite different, but in many ways, they do mirror one another. This is just one of them. We have one sun, one moon, and they both rise and fall at the same time those of Meraki do."

The corner of his mouth curls with a glimmer, drawing that connection from my realm to his—as if that means anything. I feel a warmth trickling in, and my stomach clenches. I can't tell if he's using his magic on me or if my body is trying to tell me something else about this place. Either way, I know better to be safe than sorry, so I shut my eyes and muster up a barrier between us.

The night is even more dramatic than it is in the light of day. Luminescent sprouts of shrubbery sporadically enliven the ground as radiant, glowing grubs burrow in and out of the dirt below. I take it all in, my senses overwhelmed and the twinge in my stomach still ever present. I try to ignore it. Liri and Phira will be back soon with something to eat. Surely, it will go away once satiated.

Higher in the understory, I watch Diaspor leap from limb to limb, stretching the massive, rubbery leaves from one tree to the next. He plays with the greenery, smiling from his core, the plants his long-lost friends. I climb up the winding branches to get a closer look. With the flick of his finger, the vines heed his command, tying one end to another tree.

"What's the point of all this?" I ask.

He wipes the sweat from his brow and observes the cradling leaves between us. "They're beds."

"We're going to sleep in these?"

He lifts his brows to insinuate I'm a bit slow to catch on. "Yes. Trust me when I say you do not want to sleep on the forest floor." I look back down at the busy ground and decide to take his word for it. They do look rather comfortable. If anyone is accustomed to sleeping in a tree, it's me.

Diaspor returns to his work but calls out to me over his shoulder.

"Get over here and help me. You're an earth Fae. Time you started using your gift for something useful."

Grateful for the chance to prove myself, I place a hand on the trunk of the tree I'm perched upon and determine the easiest way to navigate my way to him. He's at least two trees away. I don't dare step on one of the leaf cots he's crafted, assuming they'll break with my weight applied, but the closest branch to the next tree is at least three Aero-lengths away. I try to imagine taking the leap, but I make the mistake of looking down—the so very long way down. My chest tightens, and my balance seems to be floating away, along with my head. Diaspor chuckles. "Use your magic, you fool."

Hera and Feliks, sitting on one of the branches below, call up. "Just don't fall on us when it doesn't work."

Assholes. Gripping the trunk tightly, I shut my eyes and gather my courage. I focus on the bloom strapped to my thigh, the rough crystal feeling consistently warmer than it did in the human realm. I swear I feel it humming in these new surroundings, like it's nuzzling up to me, thanking me for bringing it closer to home.

This will be the greatest trust fall I've taken with my gift, and I'd like to have something to show for it. At least Aero left with Bel to fetch us some water, so he can't try to step in and save me again. Looking up and all around me, I spot a thick vine overhead. It's too far up to grasp but sturdy enough to carry me. I might be able to swing across. I close my eyes again, using the tactics Diaspor taught me back in Gallanberg. A euphoric humming starts in my core and expands, like the first bite of a warm meal after days of eating nothing. The tingling energy builds, shooting up from my toes and out of my body, reaching for the vine. My eyes still pinched shut, I feel it rapidly pulling closer until, all at once, I know it is done. I open my eyes, expecting to find the vine dangling right in front of me, but there is nothing. Hera chuckles, whispering from below, "Great Divine, look down."

My gaze falls, and I gasp. Diaspor, holding in his applause as not to draw attention to our group, silently throws fists of celebration into the air. At my feet lies a bridge of intricately woven vinery sprawling all the way across to the precise location I had imagined swinging to. I look down at my trembling hands, somehow knowing the force inside them is ready to cast in any given moment.

The power is greater than I have ever felt.

Stronger than I know how to wield.

Swallowing a nameless dread, I take a step.

2

AERO

"**A** canteen for each will be plenty," Belanor argues with a skip in his step.

The male is everything I have always despised. Quite full of himself. He moves as if the world is only there for him, everything happening to him and for him. His white-blond hair is the same pale color of his brows and skin. He's nearly a foot shorter than me, but just as wide, stomping around like his weight is earth shattering. I look back at the stream beside us. Despite the light dwindling and their depth beneath the rushing water, the white stones at the bottom still glisten. I place my hand in the stream and watch it run over my calloused fingers, every line and crevice of my palm still in plain view, the water seeming crystal clear. Not even a speck of dirt. It's unsettling how it all defies the way of nature I'm accustomed to.

I can feel Bel's eyes on me as I fill the last few vessels with water from the bubbling stream. His arms crossed, he steps back as I place the last one at his feet.

"I see that you feel it too."

I furrow my brow. "Feel what?"

"Your magic. It's stronger here, right? I know I've only wielded the water with you once on the way to the veil, but you moved that water into those canteens with lightning speed. It must feel different. I know mine does."

I look down at the canteens and try to recall any difference. My body reacted as it always does. Maybe more rapidly this time, or maybe I just want to get this task done with.

"No, I don't think so. I don't think our abilities are the same," I reply.

He places his hands on his hips. "Probably not. I'm sure only us Fae benefit from being back where we belong. Too bad for you, buddy."

Something tells me that was meant as an insult, but I can't be sure it wasn't just another way for him to boost his ego. I always thought Feliks was my opposite, but I was wrong. Bel runs his mouth like his life will end if he stops—and not the same way Feliks does. Feliks speaks from an innocent heart. This male has a much more selfish motive. All the rambling is only for the sake of himself.

But then he leans over a cupping bud and draws the pool of water from inside it directly into his mouth, and a strange twinge of kinship takes hold of me. His bond with the water stirs something up, softening the dislike I carry for him. He's everything I'm not and everything I am at the same time. It's fucking miserable.

I should tell him our journey here is a waste if we return with only these few canteens, but it's getting late, and I want to get back to Eva.

"I suppose this will be fine. We can always pull water from the plants later if someone runs out."

He rolls his pale-blue eyes. "We only do that if we absolutely need to."

I clench my fists, the irritation for him boiling over. "They're trees. I think it will be fine."

He abruptly stops, slapping his hand on my chest, and I want to rip it from his body. "We are not in your realm anymore—or whatever realm you deem to be yours, deity. We only take what we absolutely need here. Nothing more. The forest is alive, just as you and I."

My stare holds his as I concentrate on reining in my temper. *He's on our side. Don't hit him. He's a fucking douche, but he's on our side. Don't hit him.* Finally, he removes his hand from my chest, and I take in a calming breath, proud of myself for not knocking him through one of his beloved trees.

I imagine what must be going through Eva's mind as we hike back to the group—if she feels the same dread crawling beneath my skin here, or if the part of her that's Fae feels right at home. I don't want her to suffer, but a selfish part of me hopes I'm not alone in my paranoia. This place is the embodiment of a temptress. Her luscious colors and smells. The soaring heights of her woods distracting you from what lies behind her dark shadows. I can hear Phineas's warning in my head: "*Your instincts will betray you for the spell she casts. Even when it becomes apparent that she has used you for her own gain, you will refuse to see her ways. It's the innocent look in her eyes. The way she denies such a treachery. You see, my boy, she wouldn't be able to help it. It's in her nature.*" But those words were meant to warn me of the women of Meraki, and look at how wrong he was about them. Eva might have her ambitions, but she's never deviated to trick me. Yet, here I am, in the realm of her father's kin, hearing the voice of the man whom, although I took orders from him, I never truly respected. I spent my life looking to him as I've been expected to. The way a man should look at his father. Especially a father who is king. But he is not my father. And he won't be king for long.

A small scaly creature leaps from its perch on a log, its long narrow wings taking air, spinning above its head with a buzzing hum. It hovers uncomfortably close in an attempt to land on my shoulder, sending me into a fit, slapping it away. Behind me, I can hear Bel laughing at my expense.

"What the Hades was that?" I ask, still keeping a look out for any other pests that might try getting too close.

"A jafslink. One of the few creatures here that are completely harmless."

Swallowing my embarrassment, I clear the way with

my sword to hear the voices of the others overhead. I look up, searching for Eva and Feliks, but all I see are mammoth leaves swaying back and forth among the canopy. Then Feliks's bright face peers around the side of one.

"Get up here, brother," he calls down quietly.

Heaving the satchel of canteens onto our backs, Bel and I start climbing up. In the lowest rung, Hera, Feliks, and Phira lie, each nestled into their own leaf beds side by side. Feliks, pleased with his predicament, smiles, waving me on.

I climb up to the top row to find Diaspor, Shade, and Eva filling three of the four remaining nooks. Shade, on the other side of Eva, flashes a malicious grin in my direction when she isn't looking, and I'm tempted to knock him right off that cot and toss his body in the river. Instead, I focus on Eva, who doesn't seem to care whom she's lying next to after the events of the day. Uncertain about the construction of these things, I cautiously step onto the foliage. Eva rolls her eyes. "It will hold you. You're not *that* big."

"Oh, but I am," I chide, awkwardly falling into place and rolling on my side to face her. "Where are Liri and Cirrus?" I whisper.

She points to a nest in the cranny of a large branch above. "They're up there." I don't miss the disappointment within her voice. She and Liri had grown close back in Stillstar. I can't help but notice how distant the princess has been since we've arrived here, but I don't want Eva to think I'm trying to put a wedge between her and the Fae.

She doesn't fully trust me yet. I need to prove myself, show her that no matter how much she pushes me away, I am hers. I glance over at Shade, his conniving, icy eyes locked onto her as she falls asleep. The endless ways he imagines touching her, tasting her, lying with her. Rage thunders down my spine, lighting every inch of me on fire. I can't let him win. He won't win. There is no way, even in this dark world, that the powers above will let him bond to her. Something so right could never be fated to something so wrong.

As if he can hear my thoughts, his gaze shifts to mine. I lock onto it, casting every ill wish brewing in the back of my soul his way. He holds my stare for some time but eventually flinches just the slightest bit, and I know I've gotten to him. I smile.

The smirk of an opponent who knows he has already won the battle.

3
EVANTHE

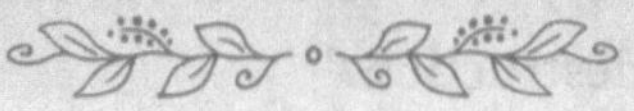

The sweet air is thick in the midday sun as we move farther into this jungle, like we are wading through a pool of sticky syrup. I wipe the sweat from my brow and look back at Hera. Her cheeks are beet red, and her hair is just as slick as mine from the labor of her efforts. She peers out into the seemingly never-ending wood and shrugs her shoulders with defeat. I, too, have my questions.

Liri, still leading the way alongside Cirrus, hasn't even looked back to check on us since we started early this morning. We can't expect them to have an exact route as much has changed since they were last here, but this just feels wrong. Like we are wandering aimlessly. I take a look at the rest of the group, and sure enough, they all barely move one foot in front of the other in a heated daze. This is ridiculous. I march forward, past Aero and Shade, until I'm in front of Liri.

"Where exactly are we heading?"

The princess's violet eyes meet mine with the slightest bit of hesitation. "Like I said before we set out, I won't know for sure until we get closer. It has been a long time since we were privy to a vision of our realm, and the war has done much destruction."

I hold her gaze, feeling the words that have gone unsaid. They linger there, stuck in the gooey air around us, taunting me. Does she think I'm a fool? That I know so little of her not to notice when she is keeping something from me? I look back at Cirrus, but he cowers. Something isn't right.

"Why do you lie to me?" I ask, sounding more hurt than I intend.

Liri's brows lift with concern as she shuffles her feet back and forth in a dance, deciding if she should be honest with me. *Yes, you should. What are you hiding?* Folding my arms together, I remain strong. Unyielding. Shade clears his throat. "Honestly, the Fae cannot tell a lie."

I shake my head, not understanding his statement. It doesn't make sense. I've told many lies and I'm Fae. I know she is keeping something from me. She isn't the same as when we arrived here. It's not just the danger around us. The other Fae wouldn't feel so joyous to be back here if that were the reason. Surely, they would be sharing her fearful demeanor. Aero moves beside me, glaring at the other male deity as if it were sending salty blades into his flesh.

"If that's so, how can you prove it?" I ask, challenging him to find suitable evidence, because he can't. He steps closer, completely disregarding Aero's presence, and leans down so our noses nearly touch.

"You will just have to trust me. Think about your time with us. Can you remember a time that we lied to you? Has any full-blooded Fae, like Princess Liri, ever lied to you?"

I narrow my eyes. "*You* are not full-blooded Fae."

Leaning back, he nods. "That is true. I didn't say that I couldn't tell a lie." He looks back at the other Fae in our group. "But they cannot. That much is true."

Aero moves toward Liri, his fists clenched at his sides. "Then why do you hesitate? If this is true, you can't tell a lie. What is it that you want to lie about? It seems that is the issue at hand."

For once, appreciating the pressure he's applied, I don't stop him from speaking for me. The princess looks to Cirrus, reaching out for his hands, her eyes weary from this weight she carries. The blood reader returns the sentiment, nodding, giving her permission to share their secret. Drawing in a deep breath, she cautiously approaches. I feel the worry behind her gaze. Whatever it is, it can't be this bad. Not after all I've been through. She stops right in front of me and folds her hands together.

"Evanthe, when you first arrived in Gallanberg, we didn't know what to expect. The prophecy read that, once bonded with a deity, our Final Guardian would save our realm. But we didn't know that you would also be human —a human whose Fae lineage would be traced back so far. Yet, here you are, your magic somehow just as powerful, if not more powerful, than other full-blooded Fae within your elemental family." She and Cirrus look at me as if I may know what they are getting at. I try to think of every possibility.

"Is this when you tell me I'm not human at all? That both my parents were actually Fae?" I ask with disbelief.

Liri winces, shaking her head. "No, Cirrus's gift allows him to see what you are comprised of, and you are just as much human as you are Fae, if not more so. That's the problem. With that amount of human lineage, the Fae part of your blood should be so much more diluted. Your magic shouldn't be nearly that strong."

Cirrus steps closer and reaches out for my hand. He glides his thumb over the finger where he drew my blood that first day when we were pulled from their forest and taken to Stillstar.

"Historically, to have such magic would only be possible when an ancestor's soul has been reborn through them. That particular soul wouldn't retain their memories of the life they already lived, but they could carry over any darkness along with them." The blood reader's voice is shaky, as if saying the words aloud makes them truer. What dark soul could stir such fear in them? There's only one Fae family that has ever been brought to my attention.

"You think this is about the Brackens?" I ask in disbelief.

Liri nods in the same sad way she has looked at me since we crashed through the veil and into her realm. I recall the tale of my lineage written on the scroll she read to me back in Stillstar.

King Eldar Bracken of the Fauna Court sired three sons—

Bim Bracken, a very gifted earth prince.

Luthais Bracken, his eldest and powerful heir to the throne.

And Athryc Bracken, not so gifted in any way, shape, or form.

Athryc, jealous of his brothers' abilities and birthright, made a deal with Gossom Mortia to betray his father, but Luthais overheard his treacherous plans and warned him. When Athryc, who fell under Gossom's influence, refused to reveal the Underrealm king's conduit, King Eldar banished him to the Underrealm and made Bim the First Guardian of the Fae Realm, and so the Court of Shield & Shadow was formed. This court was unique in that it did not hold a specific kingdom or a castle. It lived with the people in the mountains, the shores, and the valleys. It moved in the shadows, with no glory or praise. It existed simply to protect us.

Bim spent his life trying to find the conduit that Gossom had used, but he failed to do so. After nearly driving himself mad, he made the bloom and encased it to be passed down his family line just in case a conduit was ever revealed. It is said that the bloom will poison the Mortias, ending them once and for all. You, Evanthe Sideris, are his kin.

If this is true, they wouldn't fear Bim or Luthais Bracken's souls living through me. They would fear...

"Athryc Bracken?" I ask, the horror sinking in.

Their silent sorrow tells me all I need to know. They think I might be Athryc. I pull my hand away from Cirrus and break from the group, pacing back and forth along the path behind them. This can't be. Liri had been so relieved when Cirrus told her I was the guardian they had been waiting for. She cared for me. Cherished me. She begged me to come with them here. To end the Mortia. Pivoting on my heel, I snap back, pointing at the princess.

"You really think the Mortia could influence me like it did Athryc?" I ask, my voice shaking.

Liri lowers her head. "I have to consider the possibility for the safety of every Fae. For the safety of all of us here."

If something so evil does lurk inside me, it puts everything at risk. What if she's right to question such things? What if it deceives me from bringing the bloom to its rightful place? The Mortia would go on destroying our realms at the hands of King Murrick. But how could she keep this from me?

"Why the concern now and not weeks ago back in Gallanberg?" I ask.

A knowing way about her, she looks down. "It wasn't until you had completed your training with Diaspor that we realized your ability. I've carried the burden ever since. I stayed up for nights, contemplating if the risk was worth the reward. If I could bring you into our world, knowing what may live in your veins, or if I could leave you behind, knowing the Mortia may destroy us. I had to follow the voice inside me. The one telling me that, even if it is Athryc inside you, you might be strong enough to fight him. That the promise you made to your mother to take back the throne and your love for the people of Meraki might overcome the darkness."

Fury rolling off his skin, Aero turns to Diaspor. "You knew about this?"

My mentor holds up his hands, looking to me. "No, I swear it. Princess Liri had me report back to her with your progress, but I thought it was only to ensure you would be prepared for the war ahead." His gaze holds mine, pleading for me to understand. To believe him. I blink back the tears threatening to fall from my eyes when Liri steps to his aid. "What he says is true. Cirrus and I are the only Fae who know of this. We didn't realize the potential risk until Diaspor started reporting back to us."

I narrow my eyes at the princess and lower my voice. "All this time, welcoming me to the last feast in your grand hall, telling me stories of the Fae Realm as if it were my own, going out of your way to make me feel a part of your realm...it was all an act. A ploy to get me here."

"If I had told you then, would you really have come with us?" she asks, more a statement than a question.

I throw my hands in the air. "You didn't give me a chance. Did you every consider that maybe the soul belongs to Bim Bracken? In case you've forgotten, he's one of my ancestors too. He created the bloom with his magic. The bloom that I carry. Did you even consider that?"

"Of course I did. That would be my greatest hope, but hope alone won't save our realms. The Mortia are masters of manipulation. Even the strongest of Fae have fallen prey to their ways."

The pain inside me shifts, turning red. My fingers curl into fists, flames of anger licking through me like a wildfire. I do my best to contain the heat, stepping back to silently scream into the thicket. Pulling at my hair, a whirl of every decision I've ever made crashes over me. Stepping into the Dyre Waters and making a deal with Hale Mortia. Letting Despina's offer to drink of her blood linger in my mind for so long, truly tempted by the thought. Letting Sorrow fend for herself so I could fight a single battle. Stepping into the thicket that Noonsnight, drawing my mother's attention away from Athena and watching her take her last breath in my arms...

My aunt Maria told me that my father had hid the bloom from me for all those years because he didn't want me to carry the burden that comes with it, but what if he saw a darkness inside me? What if, despite the legacy, he feared placing it in my hands? Shadows follow me everywhere I go. They touch everything I touch. Can I really blame them for thinking the soul of Athryc lives on inside me? Can I really say it isn't him but another? Someone better? Someone good? I didn't want those horrible things to happen, did I? I didn't wish for them. Surely, that has to mean something.

I feel Aero's arms wrap around me, and I look down to find myself in heap of shredded foliage, rocking back and forth. My fingers, shaking and red from ripping at the leaves, draw away from the mess as I turn to find Hera and

Feliks standing between us and the other Fae, like a protective wall keeping them from causing any more damage. Diaspor calls out from behind them, "I'm so sorry, Evanthe. Please don't let this ruin everything you've worked so hard for."

I want to believe him, but I can't. And it's clear that whatever lives in me could break our group apart. It could divide us, leaving us vulnerable in this treacherous realm. I never should have come here. They'll never trust me again, and I'll never be able to trust them. Not now. Not after this. I belong in Meraki, with my people. Not here, looking for some part of me that doesn't matter—that might not really exist. How can they be so sure that I'm their Final Guardian? That I can defeat the Mortia? The bloom may have simply wound up in the wrong hands. A cool sensation runs the length of my thigh where the token rests, trying its best to sway me. But I'm not sure I can trust myself anymore.

Liri attempts to move toward me, but Hera and Feliks step even closer together, forcing her to speak from a distance. Her face is soft and earnest, but all I can see is a facade.

"Evanthe, I don't know what your soul is made of. I don't know what our future will bring. But I don't think we can do this without each oth—"

A rushing wind whips from the wilds behind us. My heart stops for a beat, frozen in time. The hearty laugh of a male echoes from the same direction. Every eye in our group widens in full alert. Feliks, his body shaking, reaches for his sword, but the metal hilt slips from his fingers. We all watch, frantic with fear, as he fumbles with the weapon, slipping from one shaken hand to the next.

Until it falls.

Crashing onto the rock beneath him.

The only rock I've seen in this forsaken forest, and it appears in the worst possible place. The clamor rings out into the air around us. An undeniable alarm for our enemies. The wind that once whipped now roars behind us, pushing any cover out of view, exposing our group. Still frozen, I watch as they make a mad dash for the closest concealment. I need to move. I need to protect myself. They will rip me apart. I look down at my hand, expecting my mother's dagger to be tucked inside my fist. But it's not a blade. It's the bloom. Vibrating in my grip. Screaming in the only voice it has. A pressing heat urging me to take action.

Pulling myself together, I look for the closest tree and tuck myself behind it. I clutch the bloom to my chest and squeeze my eyes shut, trying to mute Cirrus's voice still ringing in my head. *"To have such magic would only be possible when an ancestor's soul has been reborn through them. That particular soul wouldn't retain their memories, but they could carry over any darkness along with them."*

The sounds of metal clashing, flames blazing, and air lashing through the thicket resonate louder as the battle ensues around me. The river. The veil. It can't be too far. We couldn't have gone too far. I could go back now. Be there by nightfall. If I ran, they might not be able to catch me. I peer around the side of the tree at the storm of elements devouring the wood. In the distance, Aero slays one of the Fae warriors with a fury of water. Back to back, Hera and Feliks remain strong, fighting off another. They don't need me for this. Aero will protect them. An aching pain fills my chest with the thought of leaving them, leaving him. But my aunts need me. Meraki needs me. It's where I belong.

Choking back tears, I break away from the tree, pushing myself away from it. My legs begrudgingly move as fast as they can take me, back in the direction I came from. To the river. Back to the veil. The bloom, still clutched in my fist, rapidly dips from its life-bringing warmth to a sharp, stabbing cold, piercing my palm with disapproval and sending a bracing chill down my spine. Still, I run. Back to my home. Back to the place I know. My feet swiftly move along the forest floor until my boot catches on something, and it sends my body crashing onto the ground. I pull my face from the dirt and find two small boots dangerously close. Frantically, I pull myself upright.

"Where do you think you're going?" Phira asks, her voice full of fire.

"Nothing to bother yourself with. We both know you'd rather I wasn't here, Phira. Let me go, and I will no longer be your problem," I reply.

She draws in a furious breath, her nostrils flaring and wrinkling up at my scent—surely the very intense sense of smell she used to track me down so quickly. "So this is what you do when the road gets a little bumpy? You run away, like a coward? Go on then, Evanthe. Prove me right." Her eyes narrow as her lip curls with disgust. I shiver, the chill of the crystal bloom now spreading through my body so quickly. The female Fae gives me one last glaring look and stomps back toward the battle. I go from teeth chattering to screaming out a war cry. Not for the Fae. Not for the people of Meraki.

For the part of me that can't walk away from either of them.

4
EVANTHE

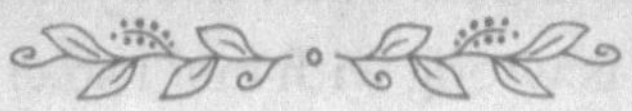

My magic rumbles from deep within my bones amidst the slashing chaos, pushing and pulling the earth in every direction, a quaking horror I don't quite know how to control made even more unpredictable by my racing heart.

A male leaps from a cloud of smoke, locking his eyes onto me. His next victim. A blue flame curls from his fingertips as he sizes me up. His gaze trails from the sword I carry up to the crook of my neck, and a grin forms. He steps even closer. "You're different." Before I can object, a spark shoots from his hand, just grazing my left ear.

"Those are rather rounded, my darling," he sneers, lunging at me with his full force. I dodge his attack just barely, lifting the ground beneath him, but before I can strike, he's gone. Vanished into thin air. I gasp, suddenly feeling far too exposed. Pulling my sword in tight, I turn in circles. He could be anywhere. Hera finds me through the haze and pulls me aside. "This is fucking insane. They can do all kinds of unnatural shit."

Her eyes bore into mine, wide with terror, and something twists in my stomach. It's my fault she is here. Not a drop of Fae in her blood. And I nearly left her with them. What the Hades is wrong with me? I steel myself and grab onto her shoulders, letting my fingers dig deeply.

"I'm here with you. We are Stone Holders of Meraki. Get your shit together," I shout.

Pulling her sword from its sheath, her mouth draws into a straight line, and she follows me back out into the fray. It's a blur of snarl and groan as the forest floor becomes slick under the turquoise sky. A spray of blood shoots through the air, finding its way into my mouth. The vinegary taste makes me gag, but I don't stop. My magic moves so freely I barely have to think of the way I want it to happen. I only need to feel it. Throwing vine and root. Slashing and splintering as the throng of Murrick's warriors smash into us. Fast and hard, over and over, until they are all nothing but corpses, lying in a mess of their making. Of our making.

Aero finds me, his eyes searching me for any signs of injury.

"I'm alright," I say beneath my breath. A sigh of relief escapes him as he turns to face the destruction around us.

Barely standing, our silver blades gleam with the red dew of our enemies. None of us perished, but a sadness fills the air. Those who share the same elemental gifts seem to find the deaths of these warriors a loss of their own. Liri falls to her knees beside the fire Fae who had disappeared before my eyes. Quietly, she whispers words I don't understand and moves his hands to his chest into a resting position. Feliks, afraid he's done wrong, crouches next to her.

"Did you know him?" he asks.

Her solemn gaze looks up at the young man. "No. And yes."

Feliks's mouth falls, unsure if he's killed a friend turned to the wrong side. Diaspor, knowing Liri doesn't have the energy to explain, steps in.

"Feliks, we all took lives today. And we are all connected—even to those who attacked us and those who will attack us. All lives are sacred. What's happened here is a tragedy."

The corners of Feliks's mouth fall, and he nods. "I'm sorry."

Aero throws his sword to the ground and places his hand upon his brother's shoulder. "You have nothing to be sorry for, Feliks. You did what you had to do to survive."

Picking up on the cold edge of his voice, Diaspor narrows his eyes. Shade, picking pieces of wood from his golden hair, lifts his brows as if he knows where this is heading. Standing behind him, Phira's paper-thin lips pull tighter than usual. But for once, I don't fault Aero for his brooding way. He's right. Feliks was only doing what he had to. He shouldn't have to feel sorry about it. Placing my sword back in my sheath, I join Aero next to Feliks and address the other Fae.

"We've come here to end the Mortia. You all know that means blood will spill. We can't afford to have an elemental ceremony every time this happens. It's a waste of time. Now, someone tell me where we are heading."

Without a second thought, Diaspor charges forward like a bull that's lost his temper, until we are eye to eye.

"I understand you are upset with Liri and Cirrus, but you don't get to make demands here. This is our land, and we won't be disregarding customs that go back long before your humankind ever existed simply because you think your time is more valuable."

His commanding voice leaves me shook. I want to shout back into his face. Tell him all the ways he doesn't understand. How this is different for us. But I'm too shocked by his cruel tone. It leaves a dull ache in my chest. He's never spoken to me this way. He is my mentor. The one Fae I thought would always have my back.

Blinking back her pain, Liri pulls herself from her knees to face me. "Until you're able to better understand the direction your bloom needs us to take, we move toward my court. The Court of Ember."

"And what happens when I do hear the bloom's voice clearly?" I ask, as if I'm calling her bluff.

"Then we take your orders—the bloom's orders," she replies.

I study her for a moment, waiting for a sign to tell me she's lying again. Her tone is level, leaving no indication of deceit. But I know too much now. I know what they're capable of. And I'm not so sure what I'm capable of. This isn't the time to let my guard down. Regardless, it is a relief to know I still have some control over all this—or the bloom does, and it belongs with me.

None of them can change that.

I've just settled inside the nook of a tree base when Aero peers around one of the large, lifted roots. He extends his hand, offering me a palmful of nuts. Too weary from the day's journey after the battle, I accept. The oily morsels take me back to the place outside Parea where chestnut trees grow in abundance just below Mount Mooring. Sellers from the market would spend days picking them each winter to take back roasted heaps of them packaged up in paper cornets. The aroma would drift into the streets, inviting everyone to make their way to city center for a treat. What a simple time that was.

Liri told us that the journey to the Court of Ember wouldn't be easy. That she doesn't know what we will be met with along the way or when we will arrive, but it is the only place to start. It's there that any of her allies might remain, or clues to where they may be if any truly exist anymore.

My attention is drawn to the movement of Aero running his fingers over the root between us, attempting to choose his words carefully.

"We don't have to stay here if you don't want to—if you don't feel it's right," he says.

It's a funny thing to hear from his mouth: *we*. To think of him and myself as a *we*. Funny that I am in another realm with Hera, a competitor to the throne, who would have taken my head only weeks ago if given the chance. Liri, who has deceived me into thinking I'm one of them. Who made me think that she cares for me. And Aero. The man who makes me wonder what it would be like to have more—also the man who wants my isle and was willing to let me think his intentions were innocent. My enemy by blood. The prince of Baros.

It would be so much easier if I were drawn to Shade the same way and not under the influence of his magic. Sure, he is sly as a fox, and I could never fully put my trust in him, given his abilities. But he doesn't want Meraki. His interests clearly lay here in this realm, and he doesn't strike me as one to want more than the simple pleasures of life. Plenty of wine and good sex, and he's satisfied.

Aero wants more. He wants the land. To merge our people. He wants me. *All* of me. I can feel it in the way he holds me. The way he looks at me. He would never accept the watered-down version of me I've offered to others. He would see past it, and if it went that far, I might offer him all of me. What if I want all of him? I can feel the color draining from my face, fear throbbing inside. I'm afraid our bond will burn too bright, consuming me until nothing is left. I look up into his speckled gray-blue eyes, waiting for me to speak. I take a swallow of water from my canteen, drowning the dangerous thoughts.

"I wouldn't still be here if I didn't think it was the only way," I reply.

A cool, damp breeze blows through the nook, stirring a chattering of my teeth. Aero moves from his side of the tree, pulling his cloak from the satchel, and crouches down to lie beside me. With a half-assed attempt to object, I shoot him a glare. Ignoring me, he scoffs.

"You're shaking, Eva. I won't let you freeze to death out here."

Still shivering, I glance down at my figure and sigh at the way my trousers bag around my legs. I've grown thinner. As much as I want him to be wrong, I know he's right. I wouldn't last long out here alone without cover. I look back out into the thicket, searching for the others, to find that even Hera has opted to curl up with Feliks in a hollow spot beneath a bush. Liri and the other Fae have made a nest of their own with fallen leaves and twigs. It seems I'll have to get used to sleeping next to someone else if I'm going to survive this place.

Aero's warm body slides behind mine, his hand tucking in around my waist, pulling me closer, until I can feel every powerful part of him against me—some parts a bit harder than others. I can feel his breath draw in and out, his heart beating onto my shoulders. A moment of silence passes, Aero seemingly deep in thought. My own mind...empty. No thoughts left after such a day. Just the primal need to feel him next to me. I let my eyelids fall shut, and his deep voice breaks through the quiet, the scruff on his jaw grazing my neck and his breath tickling over the burn on my left ear.

"If a time comes that you change your mind, just say the word. I'm with you, Eva."

5
AERO

Inside my leather boots, my swollen feet tingle, completely numb from the absurd amount of ground we've covered over the last couple days. The sweetness in the air seems to be thinning, along with the fullness of the forest, replaced with a smoky aroma and a smattering of tall barberry-looking shrubbery. Their unruly hedges are decorated with yellow flowers, thorns the length of my fingers, and blue berries that are apparently poisonous as Diaspor smacks one out of Feliks's hand when he lifts one of them to his mouth. A scowl on his face, he leans over to me and whispers, "What's the point of living someplace where everything wants to kill you?"

Wishing I had a better answer, I reply, "That is a great question, little brother."

Unable to let it go, he shakes his head with frustration. "I don't feel right about this place, and neither does Hera. Last night, I woke up in a cold sweat, my heart pounding, my hands shaking. Hera thought we were under attack until she realized I was just losing my mind. I'm telling you, we don't belong here, and something is trying to warn me."

Most older brothers would tell him that it's going to be alright. That we have each other. But Feliks was born with far too wild an imagination for such ploys. It's both his greatest strength and his greatest downfall. He can drift away to another place in his head when he needs, but it has no limits. The best of the best can happen in the worlds he creates, but today he is living the worst of the worst. If I tell him everything will be fine, he will tell me that I don't know such things. I can't see what he does. And often, he's right, so instead I tell him something I know to be true.

"Then we listen to the warning, and we remain prepared as best we can. But no making any sudden movements. These Fae have lived hundreds of years beyond ours, and this is their territory. We have to be wise, Feliks. It takes courage to face our fears. Lucky for me, I have you by my side." I smirk.

Rolling his eyes, he carries on down the unbeaten path and through the narrow clearing ahead where we are met with what I can only imagine is the Court of Embers.

Or what it once was.

My eyes widen at the devastating sight as Liri steps closer to the charred bones of her once grand kingdom. I can't help but recognize the way she moves, in the same way Eva walked toward the strand of Sorrow's hair on the beaches of Gallanberg when her closest friend was taken by Despina. Her feet slowly step on a fog of fear to face what she's dreaded most: to find that her court, the one thing that has kept her going, is no longer. It's the only reason I sailed to Meraki in the first place. So, one day, I wouldn't have to find my people ruined this way. So they won't have to suffer like this.

The princess, struggling to conceal her shock, lifts her hand to cover her mouth. Cirrus moves closer, lifting up on his tippy toes to wrap his arm around her, and she finally finds the strength to speak.

"This was the Court of Ember. My family's court for generations."

Her voice cracks, hollow and empty. Without another word, she takes off, running into the meadow surrounding the rubble. Keeping our heads on a swivel, we follow her, right up to the outer wall. Bits of stone still crumble from the ashen parts that were destroyed. The bronze gates, barely hanging onto their hinges, are as tall as mountains. When Liri pushes them open, a loud creaking echos through the empty streets. It startles a large flock of black birds. They leap from their crumbling rooftops, taking flight, making my heart jump in my chest. Eva, seeming to feel the same fright, remains silent, latching onto her dagger as we make our way farther into the city, stepping over scorched stone and pieces of burnt fabric.

The scenery distracting her, Hera unknowingly steps onto a pile of bones. The cracking sound makes Phira stop in her tracks. The female Fae's face wrinkles into a scowl as her chest rises and falls with rapid, angry breaths. Hera quickly moves off the remains, throwing her hands into the air, admitting her wrongdoing. "I'm sorry. I didn't mean to."

"Tread carefully, human," Phira sneers.

"Shh, quiet back there," Liri warns, continuing to lead us closer to the tallest structure near the farthest part of the city. It's one of the only left standing and clearly the castle she would have called home all those years ago. The once rust-colored blocks of stone appear blackened now, most likely from the flames of the fire Fae who did this. But that doesn't make sense. Princess Liri was a fire Fae herself. Based on the way she reacted to the deaths of those in her elemental family back in the forest, I can't imagine they would so easily be at war with one another. Eva seems to have the same question and clears her throat. "Who did this?"

Liri pauses and looks up at the ravaged castle. "Fire Fae. I can't be certain who exactly, but there had to be many. And they had to be desperate, forced into such violence against their own."

She clenches her fists, and her eyes well up with tears. Seeming to share her heavy heart, Eva nods and follows her inside the grand tower. The soaring, curved walls are lined with seared tapestries, each displaying different shapes and colors. Liri walks the perimeter, looking up to each with a revered gaze.

Red with flames.

A deep blue with crescent waves.

Emerald green with a rooted tree.

The lightest of blue with white barbs of wind.

She stops in front of the last one, reaches up, and rests her fingers on the fabric. Black as a starless night, a silver shield and the bloom. The same dark-amethyst bloom that Eva carries. Downward-curved petals sitting on top of a black stem, adorned with sharp thorns. But this one isn't trapped inside a crystal. Eva gasps and steps closer.

"It's the bloom."

Liri nods, taking Eva's hand and placing it on the tapestry as she does. She traces the artwork with her finger, as if she were touching the actual bloom.

"This one belongs to your court. The Court of Shield and Shadow. One of each court hangs in the high tower of every royal castle in our realm. Or at least, they used to," Liri's voice falls, saddened to see how much has changed since she was last here. With a sigh, she reaches high to where the tapestry is nailed in place.

"Do you want to take it with you?" she asks.

Eva pauses to consider the offer and shakes her head. "No. If the others remain here, so will mine."

The princess's brows lift with surprise, and she respectfully nods, pleased with her decision. "It seems there is nothing more for us to find here. If any of my Fae survived this, they would have journeyed deep into the Repenlow Wood. That is where we will go."

Eva awkwardly jumps a bit and reaches down the length of her trousers, pulling out the bloom. The slightest smile spreading across her face, she holds it out in the middle of our group. "Can anyone else feel that?"

Each of us cautiously reaches in and touches the rough exterior of the crystal. No one seems to understand what it is that she feels, and her smile falls. Cirrus cups her fingers tighter around the bloom. "It is only for you to feel, Evanthe. None of us will ever be able to feel it like you."

Her mouth draws into a tight line, and she places it back in her garter. "It grew hot when Liri told us to go into the Repenlow Wood. Based on my experience so far, that's good. It tends to feel warmer when I'm moving in the right direction and cooler when I'm going the wrong way. At least, that's my theory."

Liri smiles, I think for the first time since we arrived in this realm, and places her hand on Eva's stomach, then her chest. "If you feel that right here, then your theory *is* right. We will go where you tell us. Where the bloom tells us."

Eva looks up into the princess's eyes, searching them for what, I can't be sure, but I'd bet she's looking for an unsaid truce. One that will allow her to go on, knowing Liri will not betray her and allowing her to see herself the way I see her. Wounded, yes. But also virtuous and exceptional in every way. Shifting from one foot to the other, I wait impatiently for Liri to give her what she needs. And the princess caves.

"I'm sorry for thinking less of your soul, Evanthe. I'm sorry that I didn't tell you about the possibility sooner. I see now the unnecessary pain it has caused. Can you forgive me?"

Fuck no. You don't owe her anything, Eva. Take the apology and walk. Eva grabs her hand, removing it from her chest, and lifts her chin. *That's right. Good girl.*

"I can accept your apology so we may work together. For the sake of my people. But I won't forget, Princess."

My chest swells with pride. That's my girl.

6

EVANTHE

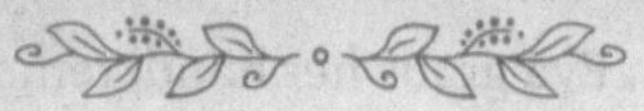

"She said it is just beyond this bit of forest," Aero says, picking up his pace.

When he offered to teach me how to swim, it sounded like a great excuse to get away from the other Fae for a while, but I'm starting to think I've made a mistake. I've seen what roams these woods, so I can only imagine what might be lurking in the water. The woods start to thin, and the lagoon comes into view. My legs get a little wobbly, and I reach out, grabbing his wrist. "You know, we don't need to do this today," I say.

Without hesitation, Aero pulls his tunic over his head and drops his trousers alongside the still, green water. I try to look away, but it's impossible. My gaze follows the smooth lines of his body, astonished by the way it swells and pulls taut in all the right places. Some of them must have been inflicted by others—battle scars, perhaps. His throat clears, and my eyes flutter back up to his face. He nods as to imply it's my turn.

Swallowing the lump in my throat, I awkwardly remove one article of clothing at a time. Feeling his gaze upon me, I fumble with the laces of my trousers and the buttons of my tunic until I finally drop the last garment onto the ground. The hair on my arms stands at attention, wildly aware of how exposed I am.

Still standing in the same spot, Aero's heated eyes find mine, then drop lower, trailing the length of me, making my thighs clench together. My heart hammering in my chest, I look down to find my nipples pebbling beneath the thin, white undergarment. My stomach leaps into my throat, and I lift my arms, attempting to cover them. This was a terrible idea. I look back in the direction we came and then to Aero. He shakes his head as if to tell me *no turning back now* and takes a couple steps into the pond.

Chewing on the inside of my cheek, I watch him scoop up some of the water, bringing it to his head and running it through his dark, wavy hair. It falls down his neck, the slope of his shoulders, and over the partially completed bear tattoo across his back. Still taking in the sight of my nearly naked body, he extends his hand.

"Come in. I won't let anything happen."

I'm not sure what *thing* he means, but I don't think he's talking about me drowning again—not from the hungry, unsure look in his eyes. I don't think he can trust himself any more than I can. Choking back my fear, I step into the pond. The soft, cool mud seeps between my toes. His chest rising and falling heavier, he pulls me into him. His hand wraps around the small of my back. My stomach somersaults as I grab onto him, and he pulls us in deeper and deeper until my toes no longer touch the earth below, and I'm completely at his mercy. The panic rising, I hardly notice he's so close until his nose brushes the tip of mine.

"Your heart is racing," he observes, looking down at my heaving chest. Unable to stop my lower lip from trembling, I nod.

"I'm going to let you go, but I want you to calm yourself first." He tilts my chin up to look into his speckled eyes. "Take one hand and place it on your chest. Breathe in. Now out. Again."

I follow his instruction without question, feeling the air fill my lungs to the brim, then emptying completely. Once my heart stills, he moves his hand from my back, only holding onto my arm. *No, don't let me go.* I don't trust myself. I don't like being ungrounded. Seeming to feel the worry returning, he circles his other hand beneath the water in front of me. "Give in to it. The water. Move with it. Use it as you need."

I pinch my eyes shut and slowly begin to kick my legs. The cool water glides over the bottoms of my feet. Then his hand slides down my arm, slipping away until only our fingertips touch.

And then nothing.

And my legs don't carry me. I'm sinking. My arms thrash around. I open my eyes, wildly searching for the closest shore and try to direct myself toward it. A huge gulp of water goes down my throat and into my nose. Choking it down, I fear I might vomit, and his hands find me again, wrapping around the small of my waist.

Gasping for air, I ball up my fists, slamming them into his wet chest. "Is this fun for you? Watching me suffer? You sick fuck!" I spit with another punch.

He grabs my wrist, shaking his head. "It took *everything* in me not to reach for you right away. You have to learn, Eva." His gaze is stern, hovering over the red spots on his chest where my knuckles impaled him. He deserves worse. My temper flaring, I feel the venom bubbling up and spilling out before I can stop it.

"Maybe I'm just not made for this," I say.

Maybe the water and I don't belong together. As if he can hear my thoughts, he winces at the poison lingering behind my words. But something about his pursed lips still balks at the suggestion. Then he tilts forward, forcing me to see the seriousness behind his eyes.

"Every part of you is made for this. If only your head would catch up with the rest of you." He thumps my forehead with his finger. I lash out, trying to grab it, but I'm too slow. He chuckles. Infuriating ass.

"How can you be so certain?" I ask, challenging his confidence.

The corner of his mouth curls, and he points down. My eyes follow to find his hands slowly sweeping across the surface of the water between us. No longer holding me. I gasp. "You let go!"

Amazed, I watch my cupped hands continue moving through the water, my feet softly fluttering beneath me. I can't believe it.

I'm not drowning.

I'm...I'm swimming.

I begin moving faster, pushing the water to one side of me until I've spun in a complete circle. "I can't believe I'm really doing it," I gasp.

Aero smiles, his face radiating warmth and pride. My legs slow at the sight, letting the water catch up with my chin, but he draws me into his arms before I sink below the surface.

"You had no reason to be afraid. I would never let anything bad happen to you."

Every muscle in my body tenses, frozen in his arms. Lost in his grey, speckled gaze. But only for a moment. Any longer would be dangerous.

"Thank you, but we should probably be getting back to the others," I say in a hushed voice.

Diverting his gaze he lets out a groan. "Probably."

Without another word he whisks me back to shore. Both surprised that he didn't push closer and a bit disappointed that he didn't, I quietly watch him dress as I wring the water from my hair.

***

We've only been in the Repenlow Wood a few days, but my feet are throbbing from the rough paths we have crossed. I shift from one foot to another as I move through the thicket.

"I'm glad the others left to hunt. We haven't had much time alone. You've grown strong here, Evanthe," Shade says.

He holds one of the baskets out that Diaspor and I weaved together earlier as I pull at the scalloped, leafy bunches of green with my magic. I watch as their thick roots spring from the rich soil with the nod of my head and follow my order to move onto the pile he carries with ease. He's right. I barely have to think about it in the Fae Realm. This earth moves with me as if it can predict my desires before I even know they exist.

I've always envied those whose talents seemed to come easy for them. The women, like Hera and my mother, who were born with the brawn and stamina to battle with little to no training. Those women have endless possibilities. The world is theirs for the taking. I've always had to work harder than them. I may be hard on the outside, but even that has been built over time. Years of practice guarding my secrets, letting them think I'm weaker in some areas than I actually am, but never letting them see the soft spots inside that could be my downfall.

Seeming to find my silence charming, Shade lets out a shallow chuckle and places the basket of lettuce on the ground. "I know you feel it, the warm, familiar simplicity that comes with this place. I feel it too," he says.

I'd be lying if told him there wasn't some truth to his words, but there is still a part of me that doesn't belong here. The part that misses the human realm. Aero understands this. Half of him belongs back with his people too. Still, just as I'm not a full-blooded Fae, neither is Shade. I have to consider it's possible he, too, can imagine what I'm going through, and I'm relieved that he isn't trying to use his seductive power on me.

"I feel it sometimes, but this has never been my home. For all the simple, easy magic in this place, there is just as much pain for what I've left behind. Don't you feel that? Is there not some place a deity belongs that calls to you?" I ask.

A strand of his straight, blond hair falls over his brow as he steps closer to me. His fingers trail the sides of my arms, sending a shiver down my spine. I feel the weight of his body, hovering over and around me, wrapping me up in an embrace that can't be seen. But he still refrains from using his abilities to sway me. Smart male.

"I've never truly wanted a home. I don't need one. I don't need a place. My place, my fate, is everywhere with you." He shrugs as if the idea is clear for anyone to see. Everyone but me, apparently. And Aero.

Never flinching, he waits for my response. I swallow the massive lump in my throat and turn back toward camp. His confidence is unnerving. How can he be so certain? How can anyone be so certain of anything? Surely, beneath his smoldering, ice-blue gaze is the tiniest bit of ambiguity. There has to be. The Fae are not immune to free will. Even if he is my fated mate, I could still choose someone else. Or no one at all. But according to the prophecy, the only way I can defeat the Moria is if I'm bonded with a deity. It is either him or Aero. My mind spinning, I pick up the pace.

"You do realize that I wasn't raised to believe that someday I would meet a deity, travel to the Fae Realm, and become the Final Guardian of this place, right?" I don't give him time to answer. "Shit, I wasn't even raised to believe the Fae were real at all! And if they were, they were the monsters that came to claim all that was precious to me. A hideous, horrifying creature that couldn't be trusted. That's what my people will think of me if they learn who I really am. You, on the other hand, have spent your days walking in the light of this glorious prophecy. Some of us were not blessed with knowledge of our future, but I wouldn't take it as such." I stop in my tracks, planting my feet into the ground. "You're not guaranteed the legacy you deem to be yours."

Catching my breath, I watch his every feature, searching for any sign of resentment. For the slightest twinge of anger, but I'm only met with his same unstirred, direct expression. The kind that comes from far more years of life. So wise and unimpressed with my outburst. My cheeks burn within the unassuming gaze. I should make the earth open up and swallow me whole. Why do I keep doing this? I can't stop testing them. I just want to know that one day I will trust them. That I will truly belong... somewhere. Hot tears begin coursing down my cheeks before I can stop them. His face falling with empathy,

Shade lifts his hands, wiping the tears away with his thumbs, and clears his throat.

"All this grief for nothing. Sure, there's a chance you will choose to spend your life denying your mate, watching every world you've known crumble before you. But I don't believe you will do that. I know you won't. You care too much about those people and those places. You *will* choose one of us. And then we will know who it was all along."

I want to tell him he's wrong. In the past, I probably would have done the opposite just to spite him. But I've already lost so much. My mother, Sorrow, even my father. A sharp pain grips my chest.

I don't know if I can open myself up just to experience another loss.

7
EVANTHE

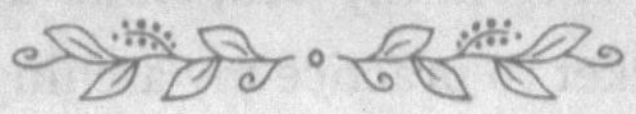

I wake before the sun has sprung, the Repenlow Wood still a smattering of oversized trees, shadows of various forms, the occasional set of glowing eyes, and looming limbs stretching across the moonlit sky. Unable to fall back asleep, I sit up, making my bed of leaves sway a bit more than I'm comfortable with this high up. I reach down into my satchel and pull out my book of nautical tales, but the moonlight isn't quite bright enough to make out the words, and I can't seem to shake the feeling that I'm being watched.

Narrowing my eyes, I scan the thicket around me. Nothing out of the ordinary. Well, nothing my half-human mind can decipher. Then I feel it again—the skin-crawling feeling you get when someone is staring at you. I look left toward the other cots, and sure enough, all the way across,

I find Bel, lying there wide awake in a sad way. The same way he's appeared since we left the Court of Ember. Seeming to find my attention intrusive, he looks away. And I don't mind one bit. I have my own issues to tend to. I'm in no way to soothe his worries. I'm just relieved to find that my stalker isn't a real threat.

I quietly crawl from my bed, climb down, and tiptoe through the thicket to practice my arching skills. It's been too long since I've used my bow, and my fingers have grown too soft. The thrum of the string leaves a burning sensation along the tips of them, but I don't stop until I've consecutively hit my mark several times. Even then, I don't feel satisfied. It's only been a few days since we were last attacked, but my body feels on edge, a wound-up ball of nerves ready to snap at any moment.

I look down at my palms, and images of Aero's callused hands running along my midriff take shape, curling around the edges of my tautly strung mind. The way they grazed along the seam of my leathers, dangerously close to touching my skin that night curled up under that tree. The way they wrapped around the small of my back, pressing my wet body to his bare chest in the temperate waters of the Giltona Lagoon. The sensation sends an aching twinge down my middle.

Dropping my bow to the ground, I close my eyes and run my fingers below my navel, imagining they are his. His body pressing against mine. The scent of salt, sage, and an earthy essence that only belongs to him drawing me closer. His fingers, *my fingers*, traveling lower. The touch excruciatingly slow, then faster and faster until my chest is rapidly rising and falling. My body tensing, I fall back into the tree behind me, pressing into the rough bark. The heat in my core rises, building and finally bursting. Pulsating, rippling, melting. My mouth falls open, letting go of the faintest gasp—

"Eva? Is that you?" a groggy female voice calls out from behind me.

My other hand clasps around my mouth, grazing my cheeks that feel hot to the touch. I peek around the trunk to find Hera standing in the distance, a hand on her hip and her brows furrowed.

"What the Hades are you doing out here?"

Her eyes suspiciously trail down by frame until stopping right where my trousers begin. Still flushed, I look down and scramble to grasp the leather strings and tie them shut. Hera snickers.

"I had to pee," I mutter.

"That's all? You look a little winded for such an easy task. You know, if things aren't moving along like they should, the Fae might have something like licorice root around here to help get things going."

I nod with relief. Letting her think I'm constipated is much more favorable than the truth. I can only imagine how long she would badger me about that. I gather my bow and walk back to camp with her. A squawk sounds in the distance, and she stops, looking left then right. And I realize she's really afraid. I've been so caught up in my own problems that I haven't thought about how she is handling all this.

"How have you been holding up here?" I ask, drawing her attention away from the sound in the woods but only seeming to direct it toward a touchy subject. She fidgets with the hem of her sleeve. I don't blame her for not wanting to open up to me. I'm not so sure I really want her to. To know her will only make killing her on Noonsnight that much harder. Deciding to take that risk, she takes a deep breath.

"I'm surviving, obviously, but this place makes me want to crawl out of my skin. Your Fae aren't exactly the most welcoming kind."

The word *your* makes me cringe a bit. I shouldn't feel shame about it. Our people were clearly wrong about the Fae. They aren't deformed monsters lurking about, waiting to devour our children or take over our island. They were merely seeking a temporary safe haven in the midst of this war. Our island is nothing compared to the far-reaching lands here. Yet, the merest part of me feels wrong about belonging here, feels uneasy trusting them with my life. For that, I can relate to her.

Spotting a piece of orange fruit overhead, the same kind that Liri gathers for us to eat, I swipe it off its branch and toss it to Hera. Never caught off guard, she snatches it midair. Damn, she's good. With a smug look, she bites into it. Seeing she is more content with the snack, I change the subject.

"You and Feliks seem to be hitting it off. When's the

wedding?" I tease, knowing full well she isn't one to settle down. Not that I can say I'm any different. Must be a common trait between Stone Holders.

"Laugh all you want, but he's quite skilled—in many ways," she boasts behind a mouthful of the juicy fruit. Swallowing the last of it, she tosses the remnants into the thicket and points her finger toward me. "The better question is why haven't you given Aero or Shade a trial run of their own?"

Refusing to answer, I roll my eyes. I should have known bringing up Feliks would only lead to this. She can't possibly understand. It's different for me. No one cares what she and Feliks do. They hardly have an audience.

Not willing to let it go, she reaches over and shoves me.

"Come on, I answered you. Now, it's your turn. From the rumors I've heard back in Meraki, you've never minded taking home a bar hand or two. Why not one of them? They certainly have more to offer than the likes of The Salty Stone."

"It's not the same, Hera. For you and Feliks, there is nothing tying you together when you choose to go your separate ways. If I don't bond with Aero or Shade, we all *die*. It's not exactly a fling."

My words sinking in, she narrows her eyes and slowly turns to face me. "Who said Feliks is just a fling?"

I don't think I've ever hurt Hera Terzi's feelings before, but in this moment, it's clear I've hit a nerve. Her hard stare is full of disdain. Enough that I move a little farther away, not sure she won't take a swing at me. I guess she truly does care for Feliks. With a pang of guilt, my face softens.

"I'm sorry. I didn't know. I shouldn't have assumed he meant nothing."

Without a response, she looks away and continues hiking. Something is seriously wrong with me. I see the way they look at one another. I should have known. Maybe I did know, but it's easier to feel like someone else is just as lost as I am. But maybe she isn't. Maybe she knows what she wants. I'm the only one who can't see who I'm made for. The one who fate has decided will make this crucial bond.

Fate is a dull-witted twit.

***

"Evanthe!" Diaspor calls out from the front of the group, calling me forward. I am grateful for the distraction. Something to pull me out of my head.

"The forest is only going to get thicker. Stay up here with me and help clear the way."

I follow his lead, pressing my magic into the bush and creating an easier path for those behind us. Diaspor peers back, appearing to check on Bel, who hasn't spoken a word all day. His head down, the water Fae doesn't acknowledge my mentor. Looking back to me, Diaspor sighs.

"Is he afraid that he's lost family? Because of the attacks at the Court of Ember?" I ask, whispering—not that I think Bel would object from his stoic state if he did hear me. Actually, I might be relieved if he did. With a swipe, Diaspor clears another line of shrubs from the path. "His betrothed lived in the Court of Ember."

"He had to leave them behind?" I ask.

"Well, the arrangement had just been made before we were called to bring the princess to a safe place."

A safe place. He means Meraki. At least they knew there was a safe haven in the human realm. My people only know Meraki, and to flee would mean they are weak. I'm sure, given the knowledge of such a safe place, most would still stay and die. All but Athena. She would run. That woman has only ever looked out for herself. Even though she knew how her relationship with my father would hurt my mother, her closest friend at the time, she still pursued him. He may have been just as much at fault, if not more for betraying his wife and his family, but she broke my mother's heart in a much different way. I know from the dark circles that surrounded her sad eyes. From the way it pained her to get out of bed each day. Athena took their friendship, their sacred bond, and threw it away for what she thought would be her own gain.

My mother always told me that the greatest leaders are prepared to sacrifice everything for the better of their people, but Athena Rokos only takes.

I feel Diaspor's gaze searching me for some bit of understanding that I don't have. I've never felt that strongly for a partner. I've never let myself. I contort my face into a way I hope will be seen as empathy. "I can't imagine leaving someone I loved so much behind."

Tilting his head to the side, he explains further. "They had never met before. Some of the marriages in our realm are arranged. In fact, it's quite common."

Hera's brow crinkles up in confusion. "An arranged marriage? I thought those were a myth, old stories about the days prior to Skira overtaking the throne."

Diaspor rolls his eyes, drawing in an exhausting breath as if it takes everything in him to explain another truth to us ignorant humans. "Yes, they're real. Not just in our realm. They exist in yours too. Just not on your islands."

Hera's mouth falls open, dumbfounded by the concept. I, too, haven't considered all the customs that the Fae might share with other parts of our world. Meraki is our everything. It's easy to forget how small we are in the grand scheme of things. Feliks, following along closely, overhears our conversation and nudges Aero. "Just like your arranged marriage with the drachma changer's daughter, Aero."

The who? I can't believe my burning ears. My hands drop, anger welling up in my chest, and I turn on a dime.

"Just like *your* marriage?" I ask.

Aero growls at his brother and turns to face me, his hands lifted with sworn innocence. Feliks panics.

"I'm sorry, Aero. I didn't think. You know my mouth moves faster than my mind—"

His gaze still held on me, Aero slaps the back of his brother's head.

"It was before I knew you, Eva. She means nothing. It means nothing. And it will be nothing as soon as I can make it so."

The pleading sound of his voice only rouses the fury inside me further. I've stopped dead in my tracks, and I can feel all their eyes on me. Every time I start to let my walls down for him, something else is revealed. Did he think *I* would be one of his *many* wives? A second wife? That I would gladly submit myself to such an arrangement? I may be caught between him and Shade, but that isn't the same. It's not my doing. I can't change the prophecy, and I would never expect anyone to share me with another.

I try to suppress the chaos of my rage, but it will not be stifled. My hands ball up into fists, and I beat on his chest, nearly punching him to the ground. I keep going. Throwing them into him. Striking his stupid, stupid body. Until I can't feel my arms anymore, and my rage simmers to something colder. Something far calmer yet far more dangerous. Keeping my gaze pinned on Aero, I point to Shade.

"And all this time, all your hatred for him while laying claim to me? And you are betrothed to another woman?"

Before he can spew another lie, I turn away. I'm screaming inside. I slash at the forest on a rampage, every branch, shrub, and blade of grass falling at my command. I can hear him calling out to me, his rough, broken voice begging for my ear.

Hera runs to catch up with me, side-shuffling along my warpath as she tries to talk me down from the mountain of fury I've scaled. "Why do you let him get to you like this? He's just a man. Who cares if he had some backwoods betrothal back in Meraki? He's clearly enamored with you now. Look how frustrated he is. No one gets so worked up over someone they feel nothing for."

If only she knew who he really is—the scheming, snake-faced version. But I've kept it from her. Protected him. Any sane person would have turned him in, especially a Stone Holder. I should be protecting my people, not him. At most, Hera would have used his sailing competency to get to Gallanberg and left him in the Stillstar prison to rot.

I should tell her the traitor that he really is. I should tell her that the same blood of the men who oppressed our women for centuries courses through his veins, but I can't now. Because that isn't true. Even if his allegiance is to them, technically he is only his mother's son and the son of Triton, god of the sea. And possibly a very important piece of the Fae prophecy. Either way, I can't win. And he knows it.

8

EVANTHE

I can't tell if the sun is falling from the turquoise sky or if night is upon us as we move deeper into the Repenlow Wood. The sounds are no longer of predatory feathered things flying overhead, but a mix of chirps, screams, and growls that only the kind of creatures moving along the forest floor and into the lower canopy make. My head snaps left and right with each new noise, my body unwilling to trust after the day's events.

I should take some deep breaths, try to calm myself, but I don't want to. At this point, I would rather let my instincts guide me. Clearly, my mind isn't doing so well with that task.

Liri stops and presses her finger to her mouth, gesturing to keep quiet. In the distance, a smattering of soft glowing orbs are flickering between the thickly lined path. Maybe it's only one of their many luminescent critters. Or maybe it's an ambush. My stomach clenches, and my palms start to sweat. I don't know if I can handle another beating today, but a part of me wouldn't mind taking out my frustration on one of King Murrick's soldiers.

The potential threat spotted, Aero moves through the group to stand closer to me. I shuffle away, putting Diaspor between us. The earth Fae looks at me from the corner of his eye. "Don't put me in the middle of this."

"You're *my* mentor, *not* his," I mutter.

Liri points toward the lights, drawing our attention away from the spat. "Look at the color. Do you see how it is more red than yellow or orange?"

I squint, trying my best to get a better look. I think I can see it, but my eyes are not as keen as theirs. I nod, as if I, too, find them more red, and the princess goes on whispering, "Survivors from the Court of Ember would only use red flames like those to light their camp. They are not as bright, so they are more difficult to detect from a distance and through the canopy above.

"What if it is only King Murrick's soldiers using the red flames to draw us in?" Aero asks.

Liri pauses, her mouth drawn into a thin, thoughtful line. In the past, I've hated taking her orders, only because I want to be the one leading, but right now, I don't envy her. This is her land. And from the solemn look on her face, there is no certain answer. We go and find friendly

Fae from her court, or we go and fight for our lives after a tiring day of travel.

There may have been a day when King Murrick was considered an honorable ruler, but those days are nothing but memories for the Fae who knew him before he fell under the Mortia's spell. The darkness has consumed him, snuffing out what little light remained inside him.

Hera starts to pace, the realization having struck her as well. She latches onto Feliks, pulling him aside. "Do you really think we can trust them? If we go in there and find the enemy, they won't give two shits about our well-being."

Diaspor sighs with defeat, the only Fae in the group who seems to care what the humans think of him at the moment. Hera may as well have said it in front of everyone, because even I could hear her. But she makes a valid point. They are only here as an extra set of hands—human hands that don't amount to much when battling against Fae magic. Liri folds her arms together and lifts her chin in a display of dominance.

"If we find Nuala, it will be much easier to move through the realm. She can rift us from place to place once the bloom starts to direct Evanthe. Hiking through these woods the entire time would be foolish, especially for you humans. The only way we find her is to find others and ask if they know where she might be. She could be right here." Shifting her weight from one foot to the other, she points back toward the red orbs. Nuala was her dearest friend before the war tore them apart. I can only imagine what I would do to see Sorrow, before Despina turned her into a vampyr, once more. I would run through Hades and back.

Still brooding behind Diaspor, Aero looks at the lights, then back to me. "What's it going to be? I'll go where you go. I trust you."

Of course he trusts me. I'm the one who can't trust him.

"I hate you," I spit, turning away and marching toward the death flames.

My heart hammers behind my chest wall, vibrating up my throat and making my teeth chatter as we pass through the glowing path. I clench my fingernails into my fists. The crystal bloom warms at the side of my thigh, urging me on.

This is the only way. *Let the sky fall. I will not tremble. I am the stone...*I repeat to myself, picturing Sorrow next to me, and my lip trembles. We move past one crimson orb at a time until a voice echoes off the forest floor, stopping me dead in my tracks. We all scurry behind a tree the size of my aunts' home and peer out from behind.

A tall, thin male Fae with wispy, ash-brown hair is standing at the base of a giant tree, pounding at what must be a door. Cirrus steps out into the open.

"Hagen?" The blood reader gasps as if he can't believe his eyes. I don't think I've seen him this astonished since the day he tasted Aero's and my blood.

The thin male lowers his fist from the tree door, his face breaking into a thousand lines around a smile. "Cirrus, my good friend."

The two run toward each other and meet in an embrace, Liri and Phira not far behind. The rest of us cautiously hang back. Well, those of us with human blood wait cautiously. Shade, in his usual state of indifference, simply isn't in a hurry to greet this Hagen, and I assume Diaspor doesn't know the male, as he is from another court.

At the sight of Liri, Hagen drops to his knees and bows his head. "My princess, I knew this day would come. That you would return to us."

Liri shakes her head modestly.

"No need for such theatrics, Hagen. Please, stand. There are others you must meet."

She looks back at the lot of us still peering out from behind our safe haven, waving a hand to draw us out. Swallowing the lump in my throat, I make my way toward them. Just as Liri did when I first met her, the male seems unimpressed with me. A glimmer in her eye, the princess places her hand upon my shoulder. "Hagen, meet the Final Guardian of the Fae Realm, Evanthe Sideris."

His jaw drops, the dull boredom in his gaze turning bright with a newfound interest. But not in the same way the others reacted back in Stillstar. This is more consuming. More intrusive. Feeling a bit like a book to easily be read, I break the stare, looking back to Liri. Seeming to pick up on my discomfort, she holds her arm out to address the entire group.

"This is Hagen Elleth, a counselor to my family and long-standing friend. He has a very unique gift. One that will give us a great advantage. The ability to sense anyone's greatest fear. We can trust him."

Apparently threatened, Shade narrows his eyes. "Anyone, huh? How exactly does that work?"

"It can't be called upon like our elemental gifts. This is more of an art. But when it happens, it's clear as day. It rolls off the air around them, allowing me to taste it. It's funny how fear can taste different from one Fae to another. One human to another. Some taste acidic, like a not quite ripe piece of goosebarb fruit. Others are more brackish, like the saltiest sea you can fathom." He draws in a deep, sentimental breath. "One female's fear tasted just like the buttery batter of a brew biscuit. Each one quite unique, the flavor of it brings a vision of the one thing that terrifies them the most."

The lanky Fear Reader nods at Shade and smiles. "But yours is quite potent. Like a tangy rhubarb blended with a bitter serving of poisonous nightshade."

Shade's gaze darkens, and a growl rumbles from beneath his breathe. Hagen laughs and folds his hands together.

"Oh, don't worry. Your secret's safe with me."

I suppress a shiver. It's one thing for Shade to sway me into another drink or sparking a tingle in between my thighs, but the power this male holds gives me worry. The rest of the group, seeming to battle the same dread, remains quiet. We follow him past more of the red flames lighting our path, past homes made in the hollows of the trees so inconspicuous you would have to be right in front of them to detect such a dwelling. Not a single window. Only the slightest notch in the side of the door, I assume to be used as a handle when needed.

"It's quieter than usual right now. Murrick's soldiers like to raid at night, so we have done well keeping the noise and light to a minimum." He glances back at Phira, who clearly has started sniffing the air to test how discreet they've been. "No one is allowed to cook food in the evenings either. All meat and fish must be smoked beneath ground far from our shelters. No excessive use of lavender or eucalyptus may be used to launder our garments. And we dress to blend in with the Repenlow Wood. No bright colors that would stand out amongst the earthly hues. We've been here since they took the court."

The words leave his mouth with a whisper of disbelief I recognize all too well. It took years for my mother's death to feel real. For the deep parts of me to accept it. From the dark circles beneath his eyes, I'm sure he lost more than just the court. Considering all they've been through, it's impressive that they've been able to gather the courage to build this safe haven. To hide in plain sight so well.

Up ahead, I spot a female slowing her stroll between the trees, a small Fae wrapped up in a brown blanket in her arms. I watch as she softly sways the baby between steps, occasionally glancing down to make sure its eyes are still closed. We get awfully close before she notices our presence, startling her and nearly waking up the young one. Throwing Hagen an angry glare, she latches onto the bundle tightly and backs away defensively.

"You're not supposed to let anyone else in. Why would you do this?" she asks in a panicked undertone.

Hagen lifts his hand toward Liri calmly as not to fluster the protective mother. "Our princess has returned."

Still clutching her child with one hand, the other lifts to her mouth as tears well up in her eyes and spill down her cheeks. "My princess." She bows so deeply her forehead touches the dirt beneath her. Her hushed cries and dramatic display draw the attention of others. One by one, they flock to us, from within the trees and shadows, seeming to appear out of nowhere, until it appears as if the entirety of the Court of Ember—or what's left of them —is gathered around us. A shocking number of them. Not as many that resided in Stillstar, but a good amount for sure. Enough to be considered a village.

The whispers hushing, Liri places her arm around me, and my heart quickens. I may have competed in front of large crowds in the Skira Games, but I didn't have to face them like this while driving a spear across the field or hitting my marks with arrows. I don't like being the center of attention. In the center of this war. The princess turns to smile at me, and I know this is when she will tell them who I am. Fucking Hades.

"Fae of Ember, how I have missed you. How I have missed this place. Broken as it may be, it is still my home. I don't intend to give it up so easily, and now I won't have to. This"—she grips my shoulder—"is Evanthe Sideris, the last of the Court of Shield and Shadow. Our Final Guardian of the realm."

Joyous tears and gasps erupt in a whispered wave. Rows of ashen, disheartened faces lift into something more like the flames that took everything from them. More like a blaze of hope.

9
EVANTHE

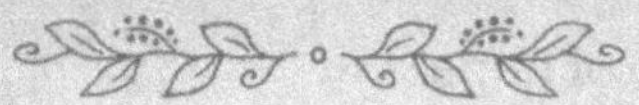

"Where've you been all day?" Aero asks the second my foot steps back out from my quarters. He's holding a knife and a stick, clearly pretending to be doing something productive. Who knows how long he has been waiting out here for me, hoping to win a chance to get back into my good graces. The thought of him sitting upon a throne, his bride to be from Baros attending to his every need assaults my mind. He can sit in front of my dirty stoop until he is old and wrinkled, and I still won't be making the same mistake of trusting him again.

Looking him up and down, I search his body for a flaw —something about him physically that will make me cringe the same way I do when I think of the deceitful prick he is. Deciding I can't settle on his scars, even in my enraged state, I won't use that against him. So, I go with his shoulders. They're too broad. He probably can't move through the forest well enough with them getting in the way.

"That's nothing to concern yourself with," I mutter, side-stepping around him, making sure my boot lands in the puddle of mud just so it splashes onto his trousers. I can practically hear the growl under his breath as I walk away. I think I've done him in, but then he calls out over his shoulder. "You can dig your heels in until you're blue in the face, Eva. You're only doing yourself harm."

He did not just say that. He's a walking, talking, swimming piece of dishonest shit. I've given him a chance. Maybe not directly, but he just keeps proving me right. And now he thinks I'm just throwing a stubborn tantrum? A ball of pure anger, I turn around to face him and slowly walk back until there is no more space between us. Leaning over, I point my finger in his face.

"If it means I don't have to spend the rest of my life with you, I'll dig in until my face is so dark blue it turns as purple as the bloom alongside my thigh." Slowly, I lift the hem of my skirt to show him, knowing exactly what it will do to him. His hooded, speckled eyes darken as they lower, and the ball in his throat bobs with a swallow. Having made my point, I abruptly throw the skirt back down over my legs and turn away, speaking over my shoulder.

"Even if I end up having to bond with you, you'll never *really* have me."

The village Fae mill about, quietly doing their work for the day—that is, until they see me coming. Great Divine, here we go again. A young male scurries over to me, a sad bouquet of green, spiked buds in his hand.

"I picked these for you," he says, his eyes full of aspiration to please me. It would be endearing if I didn't already experience a day full of such gestures. That's why I spent the afternoon hiding in my tree. But it's a nice reprieve from my altercation with Aero. I can feel the heat still stirring in my cheeks. I must look like a completely ungrateful asshat. Forcing a smile onto my face, I accept the ugly bunch of plants and jump at the voice beside me.

"They don't bring the bright-colored flowers from the meadow here for fear they will be seen by Murrick's soldiers," Cirrus says.

My heart still racing, I close my eyes to block him out. Today just isn't my day. I go from one shady male to the next. Taking a deep breath, I open my eyes, hoping to find he's left me in peace, but I'm not so lucky. The Blood Reader lifts a brow, insinuating that I'm being childish. Maybe I am. I shake my head at the thought. They were the ones who tricked me into coming here. Sure, I might have come of my own volition had I known the whole story. But how am I supposed to trust someone who felt the need to deceive me? Who thought I could possibly be made of the same thing Athryc was made of?

A dreadful twisting in my gut, I crouch down so as not to lose my balance. I feel like I might throw up. Cirrus's old bones crack and pop as he kneels down beside me. He rubs his palm in circles on my back, and the twisting subsides.

"The Fae of Ember have planned a little feast to the best of their ability for this evening. Why don't you try to enjoy yourself? I think it might do you some good."

I wrinkle my nose at the suggestion, but the elder Fae just nods knowingly. With King Murrick's soldiers hunting us, every night could be my last. It would be nice to let my braids down. To have a glass of whatever spirits they conjure in this forsaken place. I could use at least one glass, maybe two.

It takes a little more effort to convince Hera and Feliks to join me at the feast than I imagined it would. Oddly, I'm relieved that they are here. I certainly wasn't going to ask Aero. Even though I haven't seen him yet, I know he's here in the same way you can feel someone watching you from a distance.

Quietly, every Fae in the makeshift village finds their way to the long wooden tables on the far end, still wearing the colors of the forest but styled in a way for such an event. The garments of brown and green are fitted with sleek design and adorned with shiny gems that could easily be mistaken for the iridescent insects that glow in the night. The little bit of decor is disguised in the same way—clear, smooth stones in the shape of tear drops falling from the branches just as beads of dew would fall from them. Strings of budding vines hang overhead from a ceiling of woven branches that hover above the largest table in the center.

Diaspor and one of the other earth Fae who lives amongst the fire wielders used their magic to quickly assemble the communal area. With the swiping motion of his hand, he smoothes one of the corners and glares at me from across the way. He's clearly still upset that I denied his request earlier to help him and the other earth Fae prepare for the event. I may not be able to prove that he has betrayed me, but I don't need to. He's one of them. All it would take is one wrong move on my part. One *seemingly* wicked move, and they would deem me of Athryc's soul. I'd be thrown into a grave with no elemental ceremony. No legacy or glory to be known. They would probably give these woods another name in my dishonor and warn their young that the dark soul of Evanthe Sideris still lingers there, haunting all who pass. I look back at Diaspor and return the gesture, narrowing my eyes as I reach for a carafe of wine and fill my cup.

Hera joins me.

"Do you ever think that maybe this is all just a fucked-up dream, and we will wake up back in Parea like nothing happened?" she asks.

I fold my arms, taking it all in as I mull over her question. "Wouldn't that be nice? Then we could go back to hating one another," I chide.

"Who said I quit hating you?" she asks with a scoff, returning her gaze to all the busy Fae around us.

Although it doesn't have the same enchanting feeling that the gardens of the high tree did back in Stillstar, it's quite beautiful. The overgrown canopy looming over us gives the illusion of safe cover from what might be swarming above. I try not to look up or too far into the thick woods. It will only keep me from enjoying myself, and I need to let loose. Just one night without worrying about what might try to kill me. Finding it odd that Shade has yet to greet us with his presence, I peer from one end of the area to the other looking for any sign of him but come up empty. A hopeful flutter in my stomach fades. Maybe it wouldn't be such a disappointment if he didn't show, but a small part of me wants to know more about the wine deity. I can't tell if his all-knowing demeanor is merely his true nature or if it is intended to draw me in.

The sun fallen completely, two of the Fae of Ember quietly scatter into the forest around us, lighting the dimmest red orbs of flame, and the realm's most silent feast begins. Surprisingly, I notice Aero has found a seat at another table, still in eyeshot but not breathing down my neck as he usually would be. Two pretty females don't waste any time settling in next to him, scooting their chairs closer. He pays them no mind, but they don't give up so easily, batting their eyes and blushing at every word he says like a couple empty-headed hens. The one with the dark short hair reaches over, touching his arm, and gasps as if it is shockingly strong, making me choke on my salad.

"You alright? Do you need some water?" Hera asks, turning around to see what I'm looking at. "Ahhh, I see.

Looks like water god has some fans." She wiggles her eyebrows to insinuate such a thing were a challenge. I grab the roll from my plate and throw it at her. She snatches it from the air and swears, peering down at her own food.

"Although I'd love to smash this into your face, I'd only be doing you a service, distracting you from what's going on over there." She glances back at Aero again as one of the females is now reaching beneath the table and placing her hand on his leg. My chest tightens, and a flash of sick anger begins pounding inside me like a drumbeat. My eyes linger there where her hand sits on his thigh, and suddenly I feel nauseated. Colder. I shake my head, pulling my gaze up to find Aero is staring back at me, a glimmer of realization finding him. A knowing smirk tugs at the corner of his mouth. *Fucking asshole. Don't give him the satisfaction.* My fists clenching around my utensils, I force my gaze away and straight into Shade Addington, who is standing at the edge of the forest behind their table.

Dressed head to toe in black, he would completely blend into the dark forest if it weren't for his bright-blond hair and icy-blue stare. With a leisurely stroll, he makes his way over to our table and leans in next to me, his cheek touching mine and his breath on my ear. "Is this seat taken?" he asks.

The timbre in his voice makes me shudder. I shake my head, allowing the deity to sit down next to me. He reaches for the crystal carafe filled with what I can only guess is Fae wine, based on its shimmery, pink contents, and begins filling his cup. Noticing my goblet is already empty, he nods, offering to refill it with a glimmer in his eye. I recall Diaspor's spat with Phira for offering me the drink back in Stillstar the night of my elemental ceremony... *"That is Fae wine, not the wine you're accustomed to. One glass of that and she will be strewn out on the ground for the night."* But they all drank it that night, and no one seemed to be affected poorly.

I glance around the feast to find several cups full of the substance. Why should they be the only ones who get to have fun? I look up to see Aero burning holes through me with his glare, displeased with my new company. My stomach flutters with the opportunity to get under his skin. One of the females next to him lifts her hand and runs her slight fingers through his hair. Without another hesitation, I slide my goblet toward Shade.

"Yes, please," I say.

The seductive god smiles and gladly obliges, filling it to the brim. Aero seethes as the females around him continue their flirtation, their hands pawing at him but his eyes never leaving mine. I swear I catch a glimpse of hot steam pouring out of his face, the heat of it searing down to his heaving chest. *That's what you get. I'm done being good. I don't owe you anything.* Hera and Feliks watch with bated breath as I lift the goblet and tip it back, every last delicious, iridescent drop going down my throat.

Silently, they all wait for something to happen. For me to lose my mind. I pause with them, rubbing my chest as the sweet, fizzy drink settles. I don't know what I thought it would do to me, but this is certainly anticlimactic. I shrug. "What can I say? I can handle my spirits. Looks like your Fae wine is no match for a Stone Holder of Parea."

Hera lifts her glass to salute our status back in Meraki, but Shade just smirks, a knowing glimmer in his eye that makes me a bit uncomfortable.

10
EVANTHE

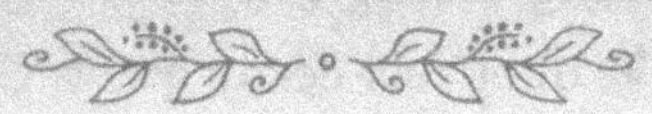

"This cheese, how does it taste like mallow fruit and freshly washed linen on a spring day all at the same time?" I ask in wonder, holding the Fae delicacy up toward Feliks's face. He takes a piece of it for himself and nibbles a corner. Seeming unimpressed, he puts the rest of it back on his plate.

"It's basic cheese. Maybe a little nuttier than the ones I've tried back in our realm, but no hint of fruit. No laundry of any sort or season. Are you sure that Fae wine isn't starting to take hold after all?" he asks.

"Noooo, I feel nothing out of the ordinary." I scoff a bit loudly. A female with straight blonde hair, taller than Hera, sitting next to Feliks, holds her finger up to her mouth to hush me. Not pleased with the gesture, but somehow not in the least bit angry, I do my best to pull my brows together in a glare. Shade chuckles under his breath.

"What good is a party if no one can speak freely?" I ask, now gazing out toward one of the glowing red lights in the distance, my words still echoing around me. I lift my fingertips to my mouth, wondering if they can steady the noise. Feliks, talking through muddled bites of mediocre cheese, agrees. "It does feel eerily quiet. Can it really be a feast without music? What I wouldn't give to strum my kithara for everyone."

Now his words are echoing too. Amazed, I reach across the table to put my fingers over his mouth.

"It helps quiet the ripples," I whisper. Pulling his lips into a straight line, he looks over at Hera, and they both bust into a reverberating laugh.

The tall, blonde female perks up, looking at Feliks. "You're a musician?"

"Well, I wouldn't say musician, but I've been known to conjure up a good tune or two when needed," Feliks says, his chest swelling with pride.

"He's actually quite good," Hera adds as if she is on a team with him. I giggle to myself. More points for the human squad. Not sure why that is so funny, but it tickles me.

The female doesn't waste any time placing her utensils down on her plate and pushing her chair from the table. She glances at the other Fae all preoccupied with their own hushed conversation. "Looks like we've all finished up here. What do you say we scamper off and I show you my talents?" she asks.

Hera narrows her eyes, looking to Feliks for an unspoken decision as they often do. Her brows are quite fluffy. I don't know how I haven't noticed it before. Like two dark, fuzzy caterpillars wiggling on her forehead. I reach out to touch one, but she slaps my hand. "Ouch!" Shade wraps his palm around my mouth, and the female whispers from across the table, "Quietly, remember? Let's sneak away before any of them notice."

Shade extends his hand to me. I look down at his soft, smooth skin and grab hold. Something tingles along my inner thigh, making me jump a little. It's so cold. I look down. Of course. The bloom. *Sorry, friend. Tonight, we play.* Hera and Feliks, unable to turn down a good time, slowly clear their plates and follow us into the shadows.

The night is dark and warm. A small, still pond sits beside us. The only light comes from a sliver of the moon peeking through the leaves above and the red orbs scattered in the trees around us. Apparently far enough from the others, the female musician lifts her arms, ushering us in closer.

"I'm going to cast the music to you. No one around you will be able to hear it. It only exists in your minds. We will all be listening to the same song. My very own creation. If you need to lower the volume, lock your thoughts onto it and imagine it quieting, just as you would build a magic barrier." She glances at Hera and Feliks. "Unfortunately, humans can't control it, but I will be sure to stop it when you are ready." She grins with glee, making my heart flutter, her excitement infectious. I can't stop myself from clasping my hands together and jumping. Hera, leaning into Feliks, snickers under her breath. "I like this version of her. Remind me to sneak some of that Fae wine into her canteen before we leave."

All of us agreeing to take part in her silent concert of sorts, the female closes her eyes and begins to concentrate. It's quiet at first, the dull beat of a drum and soft strum of some strings. But then it grows louder. And louder. Until we all can't help but move to the rhythm. Even the trees are swaying to the melody.

Wasting no time, Shade grabs my hand and sends me twirling in endless circles. His arm hovering over me, stationary, letting me spin under his gaze. I know he's watching me, because the air between us isn't black as the night. It's gray and sparkling, like a thousand miniature stars are lighting our way. I should worry that it's too obvious, a beacon for King Murrick's army, but something tells me it's a light only I can see, and I'm alright with that.

I pay no mind to the others, in my own little magical world. But then more faces seem to be popping up. More bodies. And we are surrounded by the other Fae of Ember, our musical conductor blessing them each with the captivating sounds. Apparently, it wasn't just me. This is what we all needed.

No longer twirling, but still moving to the music, I look back at Shade. He pauses, taking me in, the touch of his gaze searing along each curve of my body, sending a shiver down the nape of my neck. His jaw clenches as he places his hands upon my arms, letting them slide to my waist. He's pure perfection. Not just in the way that Fae are, but flawless. Not a single blemish or callous on his body. His eyes are crystal-clear blue. No speckles like Aero. So very different. So very intriguing.

"Are you using your gift on me?" I ask, swallowing a lump in my throat.

He leans in, pointing to his ear as a signal to lower the music. Ahh, that's right. He can't hear me. I close my eyes to focus, and the sound softens just enough to hear the song in my head and the world around me.

"Are you using your gift on me?" I ask again.

He lifts his chin, amused by my question. "Do you want me to?"

Do I want him to? Something warm and curious stirs in my core. Maybe I do. Just to remember what it feels like. So I know if he tries to do it again. So I know if it's him making me warm...or if it's just me.

"Just once. Just this time. Never again. Unless I ask you," I whisper.

His mouth parts, letting out a gasp, and one of his hands trails up from my waist. They graze the side of my breast, sending a pulsating beat lower, deeper. Stopping just above my collar bone, his fingers gently wrap around the back of my neck, pulling us closer. The space between us narrows. Thinner and thinner. Until nothing is left but his body and mine. He tilts his head, one small corner of his mouth curling before crashing into mine. My heart races as the world spins, the tiny silver stars all joining us, running tingles up and down the bits of my bare skin. It takes everything in me not to leap up from the ground and wrap my legs around his waist. I don't know how long we've been kissing, but it doesn't seem like I need to breathe. Like I could go on like this forever, yet something about it makes me uneasy deep down. The tiny part of me that hasn't been lured in by his power whispering a warning. Then, all at once, he pulls away. The stars plummet, the ground pulling me back, and it's clear that he's withdrawn his gift.

Still trying to catch my breath, something comes crashing into my hip, nearly sending me to the dirt. What the Hades? In a daze, I turn, looking for the culprit. Hera, still dancing with Feliks, snaps her fingers to get my attention. "What?" I whisper, lifting my hands in the only sign language I can think of. Her hands still in Feliks's, she nods toward the opposite direction, right to where Aero is standing.

Not moving to the music, he stands firm, his fists clenched at his sides. Even in my state and from this distance, I can see his eyes are narrow, something painful welling up inside them. I look away. Something clutches my gut, a pang of sickness taking hold. No. No, I won't let him do this. I've done nothing wrong. I am not his. The gut wrenching feeling remains. Pulling my attention back, Shade reaches out, tucking a strand of my hair behind my ear. "Hold still," he mouths.

He lifts his hands directly above me. I freeze, my body

stiff as a board, unsure what will happen to me if I move an inch. A warm hum starts flickering overhead. What is he doing? Before I can ask, he takes my hand and pulls me to the edge of the pond. Smiling, he points toward it. I look down at the glassy surface to see my reflection has a new addition. On top of my head sits a glowing, blue crown. I gasp, lifting my hand, but he grabs hold of my wrist.

"No, don't touch. It's hot. Very hot," he whispers, one of his brows arching.

I look back down, amazed with the way each licking flame softly peaks between each arch.

"Flames are usually red, orange, and yellow. Why blue?" I ask.

Turning me to face him, his gaze locks onto mine. "Blue flames are the hottest of them. They are superior. I would never place an ordinary crown upon your head."

A mix of fluttering anticipation and uncertainty, I return his smile and quickly return to the silent party. One by one, each of the gyrating Fae take notice of the glowing crest upon my head. One of them bursts into a grin, driving his fist into Shade's shoulder with approval, and suddenly, I'm not so sure this is sending the right message. Then Aero appears from the crowd, and I'm certain this is *not* the right message. Baring his teeth, he pushes up his sleeves and charges right at me. I flinch, my eyes pinching shut as drops of something wet pelt into my forehead.

Slowly opening my eyes, I look up to see a force of water dousing the blue crown until no flame remains, and the wake of it sitting on Shade's face, drops falling down his dark tunic. My jaw drops. The music stops, and every single Fae and human has stopped dancing. Aero is standing so close now that his heaving chest nearly touches my nose as it fills with anger. I can hear his teeth grinding together, his power vibrating through the air around us. The euphoric feeling from the Fae wine fades to nothing. Hera looks at me, her eyes wide, pleading. As if I could stop him now. I already feel the effects from the Fae wine having worn off, leaving me weaker in its absence. His nostrils flaring, he looks down at me. His speckled eyes swirl with disappointment. I've gone too far. I don't say a word. And his attention turns back to Shade.

Just when I think he will rip his head clean from his body or drown him in the pond, Feliks takes hold of his shoulders, pulling him away. "It's been a long night. Let's go, brother."

Holding my breath, I watch as he struggles to suppress the rage roaring inside him. I know Shade is powerful too, but I don't think he would survive this. I've never seen this kind of fury from Aero before. Not even the day he threw Liri's soldier off the cliff for taking a cheap shot at me.

Finally, drawing in a deep breath, Aero unclenches his fists and turns to leave with his brother. But not before throwing Shade a grimace.

An unspoken promise of what will come if he tries to claim me as his again.

11

AERO

Bel and Feliks don't say a word as they follow me into the depths of the Repenlow Wood. I didn't ask them to come, but I didn't tell them to stay behind either. I slap my shoulder, the blood of an enormous, winged bug sliding across my skin. If it doesn't try to kill you here, it will slowly drain you of whatever life source you have left. I glance back to find Feliks a bit more winded than usual. The air is thick with moisture today. Not something that will weigh Bel or myself down, but it's definitely taking its toll on my brother.

I pause, searching the low canopy for a spot worthy of perching on until a creature comes close enough to make a clean kill. I'm not really certain what can and cannot be consumed, but I need to be out here with a purpose. I need a place and a task to distract me from the way Shade's mouth pressed against hers last night. I grip one of my arrows tightly. The way her body melted into his. His hands running along her curves. His venomous flames hovering over her head, claiming her. My thumb presses harder, snapping the shaft in half and sending a splinter into the pad of my finger.

"Fucking Hades," I curse, chucking the broken arrow into the thicket.

"How about this one?" Feliks asks, slapping his palm onto the trunk of a large sapling.

Bel drops his satchel, rushes to Feliks and rips his hand away from the tree's bark. "Are you trying to lose a limb?" he asks, frantically. He gestures toward a thick, sticky substance slowly oozing down the trunk just above where Feliks' hand once laid.

My brother leans in closer to get a better look at the amber colored mess.

"Not so close," Bel warns.

"Is this the work of the Mortia?" Feliks asks, his voice lifting with curiosity. Bel shades his head. "No, this sap is common in this part of the Repenlow Wood."

Lovely. Just what we need, another way to die in the Fae Realm. He goes on. "It's toxic properties devour flesh upon contact. You can't go traipsing through these lands without a care in the world. There are too many dangers here to list. Just keep your eyes open and your hands to yourself."

Bel points toward a tree off the beaten path. "That one, right there. The thick branches hang low enough for us to easily climb to and from." He looks back at Feliks whose face is now beet red. "I think he could use a break."

One at a time, we climb up, settling on a nook of several branches growing out from the same spot. Feliks reaches into his satchel and pulls out his canteen and cloth to dampen. Leaning back, he places the cool material onto his forehead and takes a deep, ragged breath. It's days like this I wish he wasn't so concerned with my well-being. Then he would be back in the village, enjoying himself, instead of running himself ragged out here in this death thicket.

I place my bow and quiver against the tree and stare into the woods. It has been months in the making. Learning of the Omen. Sailing to Gallanberg and discovering who my real father is. Despising Evanthe to her becoming Eva. The Eva who is enchanting and beautiful beyond measure. My Eva who is frightening and cruel beyond belief. She knew exactly what she was doing with him. What it would do to me. She can't blame it on the Fae wine. Or on a betrothal to a woman I never intended to marry.

"Anything you need to get off your chest?" Bel asks, running the sharp edge of his knife across the length of a small stick.

"No," I mutter.

Bel's question seeming to bring him back to life—surely to jump at the chance to make me talk about my feelings—Feliks sits up. "It's alright to be frustrated, brother. Divine knows I would be if in the same predicament."

Bel nods, clearing his throat to chime in. "I can assure you, no one is judging you for dousing that crown off her head. In fact, I'd say at least half the Fae of Ember are betting on you."

Betting on me? Does he really think that makes me feel better? That I'm alright with Shade's tongue down her throat since half of them don't entirely hate me. "Is this some kind of game to you all? A fun gamble? Everyone get out your coin. Let's make a wager to see which deity gets our Final Guardian."

Feliks shifts over to where I'm sitting and folds his arms in tightly. Bel puts his knife down and lifts his hands. "It's not like that. I'm on your side here. And so are the half who want to see you bond with Evanthe. That's saying a lot, considering you are not Fae at all."

He speaks under his breath, but his voice is clear enough to hear the earnestness behind his words. Even so, it isn't much of a consolation. Shade makes that part easy enough for me. A Fae with his seductive nature isn't easily admired. Not truly anyways. I just can't imagine a world where he is the deity she's meant to bond with. The Great Divine couldn't be that cruel. He doesn't make any sense for her. He definitely doesn't have her best intensions at heart. Worst of all, she seems blind to his efforts. The way he slides into any opportunity to sway her to his side. What's in it for him? They say the bond is fated. He's a fucking snake. There has to be a way to get her to see. A way to catch him in his lies. If he wins her over, does that even impact the likelihood of her bonding with him? I turn my gaze back to Bel.

"If each of you want it badly enough, can that make a difference?" I ask.

He furrows his brow, trying to make sense of the question. "I'm not sure what you're asking exactly. Make a difference to whom?"

"Is the bond more likely? If you both want it to happen?" I clarify as I picture Shade spinning Eva around in circles, every calculating move to her liking. I don't understand how he does it. I can barely get her to say my name without it sounding like there's gravel in her mouth. Bel puckers his lips in deep thought.

"There's no way to really prove it one way or the other, but I've heard stories of others who weren't very fond of each other bonding. Mostly to avoid the misery of a life that would surely follow if they tried to make it work with anyone else. I'm not sure if their fondness ever grew, but one could hope. I, myself, have never bonded, so I can't speak from experience." He looks down at the ground below, a pained look upon his face. I'm not sure what struck a nerve, but I place my hand on his shoulder in my best effort to be sympathetic.

"I'm sure you'll find your fated mate one day soon," I mutter.

He opens his eyes wide, trying to keep the tears welling up from falling on his face. "I doubt that. She lived in the Court of Ember. No one has seen her since the attack. Either King Murrick's soldiers took her, or..." He can't force himself to say the words, and Feliks, changing the subject, doesn't let him.

"I brought a loaf of bread. Why don't we share it while we wait for some poor creature to come traipsing through these woods for Aero to murder." I narrow my eyes at my brother. As if he hasn't enjoyed many of my kills on his plate over the years. Bel dries his eyes, rips a piece off, and hands the loaf to me. But before I can break the bread, something in the distance catches my eye. I squint, trying to make it out, but it is so far away I can't see the details clearly. I lift one finger to my mouth and point at the movement with another. Bel tenses as the sight registers, his Fae ability to see long distances taking hold.

"There are at least four of them. King Murrick's soldiers," he says, his voice thick with worry.

Feliks, holding onto my shoulder for dear life, closes his eyes and starts humming. I slap my hand over his mouth, and Bel glares back at him. Pulling his knees into his chest in a strange rocking motion, Feliks nods rapidly to let me know he understands, and I slowly remove my hand.

Quietly, I watch the little specks of soldiers move through the thicket until they've hiked out of view entirely.

"Should we go after them?" I ask Bel.

"No. They're moving in the opposite direction of the village. We'll inform the others when we return and pray to the Great Divine they don't turn back our way."

It's dark by the time my fist slams into Shade's door. He answers, carrying a pipe in one hand and wearing nothing more than a patterned, silk robe of sorts.

"What the fuck are you wearing?" I ask, hopefully showing the disgust I feel upon my face.

"I don't come to your quarters and ask about your filthy wardrobe," he sneers, reaching for the door, no doubt to close it in my face. I kick out my boot, blocking him from shutting it.

"We can keep at this all night, or you can answer my questions," I say.

Amused with my persistence, he chuckles and opens the door wide. "By all means, come on in. I was just about to smoke some nilaroot." He holds up the pipe. "Care to partake?" The thought makes me sick.

"I'd prefer not to place my lips anywhere that yours have been. That's actually why I'm here. Why do you pursue Eva?"

Rolling his eyes, the male flings a spark from his finger to the bowl of his pipe and inhales. Locking onto my gaze, he blows the smoke out, directly into my face.

"Who says I'm pursuing her? Have you ever considered it might be the other way around? She was definitely enjoying herself last night."

Every inch of me coils up, sick with anger at the thought of his hands wrapped around her. Refusing to let him get the better of me, I tamp down the frustration.

"Only at my expense. I think we both know the most she feels for you is the slightest bit of curiosity. No different than the way a child feels about a shiny red button their yia-yia told them not to touch. The novelty will wear off, and she will discover who you really are. It's time to come clean," I growl.

He smiles, waving a hand through a swirl of smoke over his head. Keeping a straight face, I swallow the swell of rage rising once again. He places the pipe down on a marble table next to him and clears his throat. "You've known of this prophecy for all of a couple months. It is a great honor, but with such great things comes the great burden. If you are the one, you have no choice. Maybe if she were just a common Fae, you could go on avoiding the bond. But she isn't, and you can't change your mind if you get cold feet."

"My feet are perfectly warm. Get to the point," I interrupt.

"I've known all my life of this prophecy. It is a part of me. When the day comes—and it is coming so very soon —I won't hesitate. I won't fear the power of the bond, and I certainly won't push her away for my own simple devices."

"I would never push Eva away," I growl.

"Is that so? You will gladly stand by her side even when she chooses to lay with another Fae, god, or even man? You do realize that love has nothing to do with the bond. The bond is not a vow of monogamy. Even if you are the one, you may be the only bonded, but that doesn't mean you'll be the only one she's with."

The anger of a thousand Hades is rolling through my veins. I should lock the door shut and fill this cavern with a raging sea until he can no longer hold his breath, and I can watch the flame leave his cold eyes. But even more, I want to watch him swallow his words when that day comes. I want to see the devastation on his sad face when it's announced. That not only am I her fate, but she wants me and *only* me. Placing both my hands on the rounded arms of his chair, I lean in close.

"Mark my words, the day that we bond, there will never be another. And anyone that ever was before? They won't even be a memory. It will be as if they never existed. As if time has stopped, and it's only her and me."

12

EVANTHE

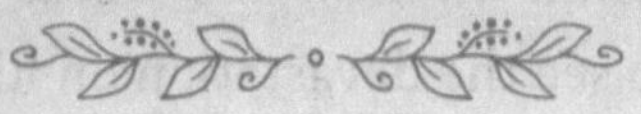

I try not to make eye contact with them as I make my way to Liri's quarters, but it's hard to ignore all the whispering.

Did you see her and Shade in the forest after the feast?

Of course I did. It's all anyone is talking about.

He placed a blue-flamed crown upon her head. Surely, he must be her fated.

No chance. She'll definitely bond with the sea god.

For her sake, I hope not. She doesn't seem very fond of him.

My stomach clenches, and I shake my head, trying to rattle their voices out of my mind. They remind me of the people of Parea. How they would talk about me beneath their breath when they didn't think I could hear them. The Fae and humans may be quite different creatures, but they certainly gossip the same. Pulling my hood over my head, I pick up the pace.

I haven't spoken to Aero since the night of the feast, and each time I step out into the open, the dread of running into him makes my legs a bit wobbly. But being holed up in that tree only seems to make matters worse. Left to my own devices, I sit there, staring at the bloom, waiting for her to send me a message, for her to find a voice and give me precise instruction. Clear guidance, not the swinging cold-to-hot pendulum she's been so far.

Liri is waiting for me at the entrance when I arrive. She welcomes me in, closing the door behind us, and my heart becomes a bit uneasy. Her hollow home smells like her—spicy cinnamon and vanilla. The scent fills my mind with the fond memories we have. I want things to be the way they were between us back in Stillstar. They may not have been perfect, but I didn't fear being alone in her presence. What if she's determined I'm unfit? All it would take is one blazing swipe of her hand and I would be gone. That's the thing between fire and earth Fae, the power isn't balanced. It would take a lot of dirt to extinguish that kind of rapid heat, and wood burns brightly. She knows it, and I know it. My only saving grace is the bloom. I'm the only one who can carry it. Without me, all hope would be lost.

Offering me a chair, she lifts a small kettle and pours the hot contents into a cup. There are three jars of herbs lined up on the other side.

"Are mint and honey alright?" she asks, her face immediately falling as she turns to me. My uncertainty is quite apparent. "I would never poison you, Evanthe." She steps aside. "By all means, assemble your own tea if you're concerned."

I shake my head. "I'm fine, thank you for the offer."

Disappointed, she takes a seat next to me. "That is actually why I asked you here. It's quite obvious that you don't trust us. That you don't trust me. I can't blame you for feeling so, but keeping this distance will only make it worse. Not far from here is a place called Hatquet Springs. It is known for its healing abilities. The waters can give you visions."

"Visions of what?" I ask.

The princess lifts her cup of tea and blows into it before taking a sip. "Visions of your life before. Sometimes a fond memory. Other times, a memory you may have forgotten. Either way, the waters will show you what you need to see. I would like to go with a small group, only us females from Stillstar. Hera may come as well. She is here with you, and I want her to feel welcome. Let it be a chance for us to bond so we might be able to better trust one another. Even Phira has agreed to go along."

I imagine all memories I've forgotten were done so on purpose. But I've always wondered why so much of my childhood is missing, so many years gone, as if they never happened. It might be nice to get some of them back—or figure out why they became lost in the first place. I swallow a lump in my throat. If anyone hates being vulnerable in front of others, it's me, but Phira is a close second. I suppose if she could muster the courage to do this, so could I. It would be nice to get away from the village for a day. Maybe the shock of my moment with Shade will have worn off by then, and I'll be able to walk through the village without drawing so much attention.

"When do we leave?" I ask.

Liri looks up from her tea, her eyes wide with hope. "After dinner, tomorrow."

Sheets of steam wave off the pools of hot water and rise into the thick forest air around us. They smell of earthy mushrooms and the slightest hint of sour vinegar. Not exactly a pleasant scent, but the Fae females don't waste any time removing their garments and stepping into the springs. I try to look away, but curiosity gets the better of me. I've never seen a full Fae naked before. But aside from their slightly pointed ears, they look like any other human woman. More beautiful than most, but all the parts appear to be the same. Seeming pleasantly surprised by their lack of modesty, Hera strips off her blouse and trousers and joins them.

I've never been one for vanity, but I'm not that brazen. Turning around to face the other direction, I remove my boots and step out of my dress, cupping my breasts with my hands. Hera, not missing the chance to throw a jab my way, hoots and hollers until I finally dip my toe into the water. Yikes. It's truly hot. I step in farther, my toes sliding in the slippery mud below, as a wave of pins and needles spreads across my skin.

"Doesn't your skin feel like it's on fire?" I ask, astonished that they all look so relaxed.

"Yeah, it's hot as Hades. But I'm not a little whiney bitch like you," Hera cackles.

"Very funny," I reply sarcastically, splashing her in the face.

Liri smiles, somehow finding humor in our constant bickering. Not as amused, Phira slides in lower and lays her head back on the ground behind her. My body must be getting used to the heat, because my muscles have relaxed, and my skin is no longer screaming. Liri looks off into the distance, and I wonder who she is thinking about. What memory she hopes to relive or remember. Maybe it's the friend she's told us of. I would be pleased if I could recall a lost memory with Sorrow.

"When will we get to meet this rifting friend of yours, Liri?" I ask.

The smile fades from her face. "Her name is Nuala Hilliard. She was my closest friend. We did everything together. But we were not on good terms when the war started closing in on us. Nuala believed that my father's closest advisor, and the female who had practically raised me, had fallen under King Murrick and the Mortia's influence. She claimed that she betrayed my family and the Ember Court. It seemed unthinkable at the time. This female was there when I took my first steps, when I accepted my gift—through it all, really. Nuala was right.

But it was too late. I had to leave. The last time I spoke to her was with anger. I had hoped we would find her with the rest of the Fae of Ember, but now she could be anywhere."

Or she could be dead. But I don't dare say that out loud. I know what it feels like to lose someone too soon, before you can take back the cold things you said, or before you could say all the things you should have long ago. Still, I hope this Nuala is alive. If she can rift us as she says, it would make returning to the veil a lot quicker if something went wrong. We've moved so deep into the Fae Realm I'm not sure I could navigate my way back alone if I needed to. The thought makes me sick with dread.

"The vapors will start to take effect soon. It would be good to think of who or what time from your past you would like to see. What visions you hope for. They can be quite powerful. Don't push them away. Embrace them, just as you did your elemental gifts. Hera, you just do your best." She winks at the human warrior as if she knows she will be just fine, but something behind her gaze tells me she isn't so sure about me.

13

EVANTHE

The Repenlow Wood tastes different. I close my eyes and stick my tongue out to try and detect the particular flavor. Not sour like the air around the springs, nor sweet like the mallow fruit back in Stillstar. It's something tart and floral. A blend of lavender and lemon, just like my mother smelled. Opening my eyes, the forest fades to a blur of green, and from within its shadow steps out a dark-haired girl no more than seven years of age. What would a child be doing out here alone? Wearing only a sheer white nightgown, she walks slowly with her head to the ground.

"Are you alright, little one?" I ask, but she doesn't reply. She doesn't even look up.

I ball my fists up and rub my eyes, hoping when I open them again she won't be there. That this isn't real. But still, she appears, moving toward me. A shiver runs across my skin. I need to help her. She won't survive the night out here with King Murrick's soldiers combing through these woods. I run to her. She stops and looks up at me, and I gasp, realizing she's looking right through me. I reach out to brush my finger across the dusting of dark freckles upon her cheeks and nose. But she doesn't feel my touch. Every detail of her is a mirror image of my younger self. As if these woods can reverse time. The way her brown eyes are lighter in the middle, bursting like a star into the deep outer rim within her thick black lashes. And more familiar is the sadness behind them. My sadness. Tears begin to spill from her eyes, and she cries out for help.

"Hello? Is anyone there?"

Her sorrow and fear ripple through me, coiling in my chest as I look for someone, anyone to help. I need to help her, but she can't see me. I'm nothing more than a ghost. Just like Skira. There is no one else. Where is your mother? *Where was my mother?*

"Why is no one here to care for you?" I scream into the faded nothingness surrounding me.

I turn in circles, tightly gripping my hair with my fingers, trying to think of a solution, but the chaotic frenzy inside clouds my mind. My chest tightens fiercely as I fall to the ground, gasping for air. *Let the sky fall. I will not tremble.* The mantra calming me, I reel in a deep, controlled breath. But when my eyes finally flutter open, the little girl is gone, replaced by my mother.

She stands firmly, a displeased expression upon her face, the same vexing fire within her eyes, and I know I've disappointed her. That she thinks I am weak. To have taken such a desperate leap into those Dyre Waters. I should have maintained my stone on my own. She peers down at me, seeming to know I recognize the ways I've failed her, and she steps closer. I gasp, extending my shaky fingers toward her. To touch her once more. Maybe she can forgive me. What I wouldn't give to feel her lift me into the air and chant my name, claiming me as her own once more. But just as I knew it would, my hand slides right through her.

She shakes her head and reaches out to wipe the tear from my face. My heart lifts with hope as she nears, knowing this single gesture will pull me from my shame. But the touch is not hers. The fingers are rough and cold, grating against my cheek, making me shudder. And suddenly, her face is another. A gaunt, pale face framed with raven-black hair. Hale Mortia.

I back up, stumbling to the ground, scrambling to get away. But he falls forward, his tall frame hovering over me, his spindly fingers winding into the earth around me, and I freeze in place. Fully aware of the control he holds, his lips curl into the slightest bit of amusement. "Why have you come here, my sad, half-blooded girl?"

"You know why I am here," I reply between gritted teeth.

He lowers his face toward mine, so close the biting cold temperature of his skin gives me a shiver. Locking my shoulders square into the dirt, I do my best to hide my fear. He leans an ear toward my chest. "You can't hide from me. You and I are the same. I can hear your dark, little heart racing."

I spit in his face. "I'm *nothing* like you."

His eyes narrow, and his mouth widens to the size of his dark, damp den beneath the Dyre Waters. And I'm swallowed whole. The water rushes in, filling my lungs until no air is left. But I cannot move. I close my eyes tightly. *You are not his. You are not Athryc's. You belong to no one.* I scream into the deep waters with all my might until my lungs are empty, until the sinister pool is no longer, until it seems I've banished the entire realm of all its seas, and I am left curled up in a ball upon a meadow, shaking.

My arms and legs tingle with a dull numbness. I pull them into my body tighter as if it will make it all go back to normal. Back to a time when I wasn't so lost. It feels as if the trembling will never stop, but then I hear his voice. "You're right where you're meant to be, Eva."

"Aero?" I ask, my head circling for him. But he is nowhere in sight.

"Close your eyes. You don't have to worry anymore. I'm here with you." The deep timbre of his voice runs through my veins, calming my shaky soul, and finally the trembling stops. I still cannot see him, yet the sensation of his warm skin runs over my cold arms. I move toward the comforting touch. His scent of salt and sage luring me to sleep, I let my eyes fall and drift away to somewhere else.

"Evanthe, wake up. It's time to go. Time to get up."

Liri's voice pulls me from my deep slumber, and I slowly pry myself off the mossy forest floor only to find that I'm completely naked, save the crystal bloom strapped within the garter around my thigh. Scrambling, I pull myself into a ball. The princess drapes a cloak around me. Memories of my mother, the Mortia, the meadow, and...Aero flit through my mind. Resting my head in my hands, I try to make sense of the strange dreams. They felt more real than any dreams I've ever dreamt. Liri crouches beside me and hands me her canteen of water.

"You were deep in it longer than we expected. We tried to help you, but you ran away every time. I was worried you would never come back to us," she mutters apologetically.

"What is that supposed to mean?" I ask, suddenly quite aware of my lack of awareness.

Phira steps forward. "The springs have their own magic. For us, it's simply a relaxing way to uncover the things we may have buried deep within ourselves. A healing process. We didn't realize that those with human blood don't metabolize the fumes at the same rate."

Aghast, my gaze turns to Hera. Although displeased, she isn't raising Hades like I expect to her to. I throw my hands into the air. "You're all right with this?"

Hera props her hands onto her hips and lets out a deep breath. "I'm not thrilled, but it wasn't really a bad experience for me, so…" She looks off into the distance as one does when they are exiting a disagreement. Great. Just wonderful. The one time I would gladly welcome her foul-tempered mouth and she leaves me to fend for myself. I know she told us that the vapors may bring visions, but what I went through was so much worse.

I turn back to Liri. "You, of all Fae, should have considered the toll this might take on us." The princess bites her lip and glances back at Hera, who merely shrugs. I slap the sloppy moss beside me. "Alright, you should have considered the toll it might take on *me*."

"I'm truly sorry, Evanthe. I thought it would be helpful. I've always found that the fumes brought me clarity when I couldn't find it elsewhere. No Fae I've known has had such an intense reaction to them. I feel horrible. You were panicking, frantically looking for something called your *gaia*. I've never seen you so scared."

She searches my face for some understanding, but I don't know what this *gaia* is. I shake my head. "Gaia isn't a possession. It is the Greek name for the Goddess of Earth. My mind was clearly not in its rightful place. There's no point in trying to make sense of what we saw last night."

Phira, unusually sympathetic, places a hand upon my shoulder. "I think your mind was right where it needed to be."

"And suddenly you're the expert of such things?" I scoff.

Right back to her true nature, the fiery Fae balls up her fists and throws me a sharp glare. Hera, although not perturbed by their magical springs as I am, is quick to step between the female and myself. Liri pulls the cloak around me tighter and looks into my eyes. "I might be wrong, but I believe your soul may be fractured, Evanthe. All this time I've been worried about how strong your magic is, of what might reside in you, but maybe I should have been asking what was missing."

I narrow my eyes in disbelief. "A soul is not an object. It cannot be broken. It just is. No?"

"Sadly, our realm has seen far too many broken souls. Watching you scream and cry for this thing, this *gaia*, last night... I just can't shake this feeling that it is a piece of you. As if it's calling out for you to find it. There is a Fae called Rennin Neriro. He mends souls with his gift. He lives back in the village with the remaining Fae of Ember. Maybe I am wrong. Maybe there is nothing missing. But what could trying hurt?"

This can't be. I look down at my dirty, bare feet sticking out from the hem of the cloak. They may be filthy, but all ten toes are there. Both legs are in place. Every part of me that can be seen is all in the right place. If a part of my body were injured, I wouldn't take offense to such an opinion. But she has the nerve to speak so boldly about something that can't even be seen or touched. No one in the human realm would question such a thing. Yet the bloom warms so greatly it nearly singes the side of my thigh. *All right, all right.* I swallow my pride and silently surrender to the relic.

"I'll see your soul mender, but I don't want a show of

it. Members of our group only, and if it doesn't work, I don't want to hear about it again. No more talk of my soul, broken or otherwise. That includes any of the Brackens having anything to do with it as well."

The princess nods, agreeing with my list of demands and hands me my dress. I pull the rumpled linen material over my head and shake the dirt from my hair. I'm sure my soul is fine as it is, but if some piece is missing this is my chance to find it. I'll need every part of me to defeat the Mortia.

14
EVANTHE

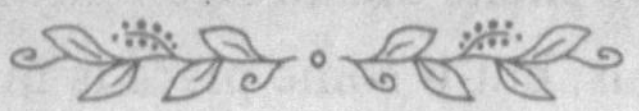

Without question, I volunteer to weave baskets with some of the Fae of Ember who intend to head into the Repenlow Wood and gather food for the village later today. The shoots of flexible vegetation wind around each other, forming braids upon braids with the slightest lift of my finger. I keep my eyes on their intricate patterns—a welcome distraction from Aero who is restringing bows alongside Diaspor and Feliks only a few steps away. Although I am able to focus my sight on the basket forming before me, it doesn't stop my mind from wandering. It has only been hours since we returned from the springs. I tried to rest and regain my strength, but each time I closed my eyes, I would see my mother's face morphing into Hale Mortia.

Now, it seems I'm moving in slow motion, my head floating in a sleepless haze and scattered thoughts.

Another basket complete, I place it next to the others and find my gaze straying toward Aero. He looks up from his bow to find me watching him. I should look away, but my reflexes are not their sharpest at the moment, and I don't have the strength to deny my curiosity. Holding my gaze, he pulls at the flaxen cord in his hands, stretching it from one tip of the bow to the other. He doesn't smile. He doesn't glare. But behind his eyes lingers something I recognize. A sadness that can only come from the pain betrayal brings. The sadness I felt when I learned of his betrothal to another woman. I wish I hadn't welcomed Shade's advances so openly. Or at all. But he has to understand there's always a chance that he and I won't bond. That I'm fated for Shade Addington. My body betrays me, a wave of nausea rolling through my body. Seeming aware of the tension between Aero and me, Diaspor shakes his head. I shoot him a glare. *Mind your business.* The earth Fae chuckles, making his chest shake the slightest bit.

I swallow the brackish taste forming in my mouth. I should be thanking the stars Shade showed up, not gagging at the thought. Otherwise, I would certainly find myself bound to that stubborn ox, Aero. His gaze still pierces mine, holding me in contempt. *Stop it. Just come over here and yell at me like you want to.* As if he can feel my wish and would never abide, he breaks eye contact and returns to his task. Infuriating ass.

Not finding the interaction amusing, Feliks throws his

bow and twine to the ground in a fit of frustration. For a moment, I think he will fall to the ground, kicking and screaming like a foul-tempered child, but surprisingly, he stomps in my direction and points a finger at my chest. "Why are you doing this to him?"

The question stuns me. I'm not doing anything to him. If anything, the question should be turned the other way around. I could go on all day about the things he has kept from me—the other woman he intends to marry being the least of them. I'm more concerned with the scheming he and his father have done. Their plans for Meraki. For my home. And he has the nerve to tell me I'm just like Skira. I smack Feliks's finger away. "The apple doesn't fall far from its tree." I say it loud enough with hopes that Aero can hear.

"I cannot begin to tell you all the ways that my brother is a better man than that king who he thought was his father. Even now, knowing he's a fucking god and owes nothing to the people of Baros or Meraki, he still fights for them." He steps closer. "He fights for you, Evanthe. Even though you've done nothing to earn it."

I search his eyes for a hint of dishonesty, knowing I won't find one. Feliks is many things, but a liar isn't one of them. He looks back at his brother, who still looks away, focused on his bow. "I know you've been consumed by the war at hand, but you can't deny what we all see."

"What?" I ask, afraid of his answer.

"The way he loves you."

I stand there dumbfounded as one of the gatherers

approaches alongside Liri and reaches across the table to thank me for my help with the baskets. I nod slowly, but my mind is somewhere else. Memories of Aero in the courtyard at the wedding celebration. The way he looked at me on my elemental eve. The fear in his eyes when he thought I had drowned upon entering this realm. And worse, the pain all over his face when he saw me dancing with Shade in the forest. A heartbreak that can only exist alongside the greatest fondness.

Feliks walks away as the gatherer whisks the baskets up, leaving me alone with the princess, and a dreadful sensation creeps up my throat. She's already made arrangements. I just know it. I haven't even gotten a chance to tell the others. Diaspor, Bel...Aero. *You agreed to this. This is on your terms.* So, I say it before she can. "You're taking me to your soul mender now."

She tilts her head. "Not right this moment, no. I thought it would be best if we were more inconspicuous. Not because the Fae of Ember would think less of you, but out of respect for your privacy. That is why I arranged for you to meet this evening, after dark, when the rest have retired for the night."

My shoulders soften a bit, her considerate words making me more at ease. At least this will only stay between our group. I'm still embarrassed that the females found me frantically running through the woods naked back at the springs. I don't need the entire village laying witness to anything similar. I would be mortified. I'm not even sure I'm comfortable with our small group being there.

"Will I lose my mind like I did back at the springs?" I ask, my voice shakier than I'd like.

Liri raises a reassuring hand to my arm. "No. This won't be anything like that. A soul mending is sacred. Rennin will be with your soul through it all, and we will be with your body, keeping it safe. But there is one caveat," she admits, gritting her teeth in anticipation of my distaste of such things.

"What?" I blurt out with all the gravel my voice can manage.

"It's obvious you have some unanswered questions about the bonding process that I can't answer, and Nerriro informed me that it is best to go into your soul mending with as clear a mind as possible—so there are no distractions." She glances back at Aero. Point taken. "I think some clarification around that topic would be very beneficial, so I sent Phira to your quarters. She can speak from experience and is willing to tell you anything you need to know."

You have got to be kidding. Phira hates me. Why her? Isn't there anyone else? Taking a deep breath, I bite back the rising anger. "Are you certain that Phira, of all Fae, would want me to know such personal things?"

The princess nods. "She specifically said, '*Anything to get this bond made and end the Mortia already.*'"

Well, that sounds more like her. Nothing about this sounds safe, but I made a promise to trust her, and I honor my word. With the nod of my head, I place my hand upon her shoulder.

"Alright, I'm putting my body and soul in your hands, Princess."

She smiles from ear to pointy ear, and I make my way back to my quarters to find Phira slouched between the two arms of my chair, tossing a large butternut into the air, singeing it with a small flame, and catching it in her mouth.

"Finally. I thought I might be waiting here all day," she says between bites.

I find a seat on the other side of the hollowed tree and prop my arms up on my knees.

"What do you want to know?" she asks impatiently.

My mind goes blank for a moment. Why is it when I'm left to my own thoughts, all I hear are questions, but when someone has all the answers, they disappear? There is so much I need to know. What if I forget to ask something important? She has bonded. *She can help you.* Knowledge is power. Let's start at the beginning. The simplest of questions. I clear my throat.

"Did you know who you would bond with before it happened?"

She swallows a lump in her throat. "Not at first. I didn't always know my fated mate. His name was Aimon. We met when I was only eighteen years old." She smiles fondly. "I know that's not so young to you humans, but relative to the many more years us Fae live, it's so very young. He wasn't from my court. He wielded the earth, like you. His family moved to the Court of Ember for sake of diversity as many of the earth Fae had passed or moved on. I was running along through the woods that day. I liked to do that. Still do. It helps clear my head. My mother and I had gotten in a fight, and I couldn't stand to be near her. She wanted me to train so I could become a fire hand for Liri's mother, our queen at the time, as she was. But I didn't want to sit in the castle day after day, waiting for a chance to be made useful. A fire hand was only there as a backup in case her soldiers were defeated and there was no one standing between her and her enemy. I wanted to wield my magic every day. My run had calmed my nerves by the time I saw Aimon, but something about him got under my skin. The way he taunted me as if I were more amusing than one to be taken seriously. I desperately wanted to be taken seriously."

"So when did you know?" I ask.

"Over time, I found we continued to run into each other, like many who are fated do. It was as if the realm was pushing us together. Some kind of force that couldn't be seen. Eventually, that same feeling that got under my skin started to feel different. I wanted to feel him next to me, and I didn't like it when he didn't pay attention to me. Then he started appearing in my dreams. Most dreams I recalled were more like nightmares. Something from the Underrealm chasing me. But he was never the villain. He always saved me. He brought me out of the darkness. I tried to deny it for quite some time, but eventually it just seemed foolish. It was so obvious that I could no longer resist."

I try to think of a time when Aero has been the villain in my dreams. A small part of me still hopes to come up with at least one time, but there are none. He has always been the hero. Damnit. And I don't think I've ever dreamt of Shade. Not that I can remember.

"What was it like? Making the bond?"

"You know how a tea kettle upon flames will bubble and boil until the steam builds and comes screaming out? It's a lot like that—the storm trapped in a tea kettle let loose. Like all those feelings coursing under your skin each time you touch are amplified to an intensity you can't imagine. And somehow, you just know that you would kill anyone that dared threaten them, that you would sacrifice your life for his if it ever came down to that." The female's face falls as she looks down at her hands in her lap, and it's clear that this story doesn't have a happy ending. I'm no stranger to such sad stories. Still looking down, she goes on.

"It felt like I had left my body and watched it all happen. The day King Murick's soldiers first attacked. The Fae don't take such a sacrifice lightly—giving our lives for another. We are taught from the youngest age that our lives are long and valuable. Letting go of that doesn't come easily, and it never comes for some—those who are not meant to bond with another. It is rare, but some are fated for none. Every bond that does exist serves a purpose for the realm. Once it is done, you might start to feel the things he is feeling as if they are your own. His joy, confusion, pain... It's like no other pain you've ever experienced, losing your fated mate. Losing a mother, father, brother, sister doesn't even come close to the grief you will feel when losing your bonded. It's like losing a part of yourself, and every time you remember them, the wound is reopened as if it was just inflicted. Most don't live long after their bonded dies. There are stories of one passing and the other's heart stopping right alongside them." She blinks away the tears welling up in her eyes. "Most days, I wish mine had stopped with his, but I'm here now, and I have to accept my fate."

It all makes sense. Why she's always been so angry. Listening to me complain about making a bond when she would give anything to have hers back. A heated shame crawls up, flushing my cheeks, and I take a deep breath.

"I'm sure it doesn't ease your pain, but I'm glad you're here. I will do everything I can to ensure you avenge his death."

She nods once, a truce between us. Both bound by vengeance.

15
AERO

It's peaceful here beside the stream. Far enough from the village that I can't hear what they're all chattering on about, but close enough that I can be there quickly if anything happens. I can't shake the feeling that those soldiers milling about the woods the other day haven't entirely moved on. Their faces were stern. Driven. They were after something. Someone. *Eva.* No soldier moves with such conviction if their path isn't premeditated. But I can't easily watch for them from within the village. I need to linger about the perimeter, where they would be hiding, watching us from afar. Through the foliage, something rustles, and I snap my head in its direction. Feliks and Hera come bursting through the bush, laughing.

"Just when I think I've found a quiet hiding spot, you

two come traipsing through the woods like a couple blithering rabbits frolicking about."

Hera scoops a handful of water from the stream and throws it at me. "Don't be so pissy."

"You might want to think twice about who you're splashing," I warn.

The warrior rolls her eyes and falls back into Feliks's embrace while he runs a tickling finger down her arm. A heaviness fills my chest, and I curse myself for feeling anything but overjoyed for my brother. He, if anyone here, deserves to be happy. Yet watching him and Hera grow closer with each day only reminds me of the distance between Eva and myself. The distance that we bridge only for it to be torn down over and over. Each step forward is followed with several steps back. I hurt her. She hurts me. It's a miserable, never-ending cycle. Feliks, seeming to recognize my struggle, removes his arm from Hera. "You know, I don't think Shade means anything to her. In fact, I'm quite certain of it."

"Good Divine, has it really come to this? I don't need your pity, and I'm not out here hiding from her," I grumble.

Drying her hands on her trousers, Hera chimes in. "No one would blame you if you were. She's miserable company." She laughs at her own joke. "That said, he's right. Back at the springs, I heard her calling out your name. She was pretty inebriated by those fumes, but the Fae say they only bring out the truth, and truth be told, she wanted you there with her. Not Shade Addington."

The thought both pleases and worries me. The fact that she was afraid and needed me there when I wasn't. But she called for me.

"That stays between us. If she found out I told you, she'd slit my throat in my sleep for sure," she adds.

Finding the humor, I smile and get up to dust off my pants and make my way back into the village, but a sound reverberates off the forest floor. Not the rustling of those frolicking. It's a much louder sound. A slashing. All of us on alert, we search the surrounding wood to find the mob of King Murrick's soldiers, but this time, there are more of them. At least two dozen. Without hesitation, I grab Feliks by the shoulders. "Back to town as fast as we can. You find Princess Liri. I'll warn Eva and the others."

I run like my feet could lift from the earth and soar into the sky like an air Fae. The village Fae notice the alarm plastered across our faces and immediately start clearing the tables in the center. I pound on Eva's tree door and rip it open, giving her no time to answer. "King Murrick's soldiers are on their way. We don't have much time. Come."

The scowl on her face quickly turns to wide-eyed fear, and she follows me toward Liri's quarters. Upon our arrival, the princess pushes Diaspor toward us and gives him an order. "Take all of them now." She points toward us, Feliks, Hera, and Shade. "Listen to Diaspor, and keep that bloom with you."

She turns away to warn the others, and we run with Diaspor to the other end of the village, behind the row of tree homes that line the entrance to a larger tree deeper in the wood.

"What is this?" Eva frightfully asks.

Finding the hidden nook in the bark, he opens a small doorway I fear I may not fit through. "Get inside and go deep. Princess Liri, Phira, and I will be hiding nearby. Don't come out until we tell you to."

"We're just going to hide?" I ask in disbelief.

The Earth Commander stands up on the tips of his toes to get in my face. "Would you rather we put idiotic, brave faces on and watch them slaughter the entire village with magic we can't anticipate, rip the bloom from Evanthe's hands, and bring her back to King Murrick, where he can torture her for the rest of her miserable life while you watch? Because that is what will happen."

I unclench my fists and reply between gritted teeth. "No."

"Then get in the fucking tree."

The dirt crunches beneath my boots as I pace the short length of the dark hollow. On the other side, a warm light glows from Shade's finger as he pulls a small candle out from his pocket and sets the wick on fire with a smirk. Grimacing, I find a nook as far away from him as possible and sit down. It's bad enough that King Murrick's soldiers are right outside, roaming through these woods on the hunt for Eva, and all I can do is hide in here like a coward.

But what's worse is being trapped in here with him. *Shade Addington.* I refuse to look in his direction and give him the satisfaction of thinking he could ever have what is mine. And I've seen enough of Feliks and Hera today, so I look at Eva. She doesn't notice at first, and I take in the way she picks at the hem of her shirt when she doesn't think anyone is looking. The way she chews on the inside of her cheek when she's nervous. Great Divine, she's perfect.

Reaching back for her cloak, she notices me watching her. I don't look away, and even in this dark, damp hole, the flush it brings to her face is visible. The sound of Shade clearing his throat draws her attention away, and I sneer at the wine deity. He doesn't flinch, and I can feel the amusement oozing from him. Having tied her cloak, Eva gets up and sits down beside me.

"You're not jealous, are you?" she chides in a whisper.

Unwilling to dignify her question with an answer, I narrow my eyes.

"Not that it's any of your business, but nothing really happened between Shade and me that night. It was just a dance. A meaningless kiss."

Her voice sounds hopeful, apologetic even, but my jaw clenches upon instinct at the mention of his name, the gut-wrenching thought of his lips touching hers. It takes everything in me not to fill every corner his lungs and watch him slowly drown.

"Glad to hear you're making wise decisions," I reply through gritted teeth.

The air thick with tension, she looks about the small

space to find a way around this subject. In the silence, I recall Hera's words earlier: *"Back at the springs, I heard her calling out your name."* I glance down to find Eva fidgeting with her tunic again, and I don't know if I've ever seen her so nervous. I can't stay mad at her.

"Tell me about the springs. I hear those fumes are no laughing matter," I say, giving her an out. She looks up through those thick lashes, a gratitude swirling inside her amber eyes.

"It was terrifying. I've never felt so out of control. You would have hated it." I laugh, knowing she's right. I can barely stand being locked inside this tree to save our lives. I place my hand on her knee, and she smiles at the way it wraps around her perfectly.

"Tell me more."

She draws in a deep breath and looks off into the distance. "I saw myself as a child. Then my mother appeared, but she turned into Hale Mortia."

She winds her fingers together, gripping them tightly, and I know she doesn't want to go on. But I need to know. I need to hear it from her. "Then what?"

"You showed up, but I couldn't see you. I could only feel you. Hear you," she says, her voice shaking. A shallow sigh escapes my mouth as relief washes over me. I was there for her—even if she couldn't see me. Regaining her composure, she shimmies on her haunches to sit up a little taller, and it makes me smile. Such a proud, willful woman.

"Does this mean you dream about me?" I ask, nudging her with my elbow.

She scoffs. "Don't get excited. It was more of a hallucination. One that has tied me to another dreadful journey I do not look forward to, I'm afraid."

"What are you talking about?" I ask, searching her ashen face.

"Some of the things I was saying led Liri to believe a part of me is missing. That my soul is fractured. They have a male here in the village who is known as a soul mender. I agreed to meet with him tonight after dark."

"You're not going off to meet with some soul mage late at night by yourself," I blurt a little too loudly. We all become mute with horror, frozen in silence to hear if any of Murrick's soldiers heard me. A moment passes and nothing. I let out the breath I had been holding and wrap my arm around Eva. "I'm sorry. I just don't think this is necessary. Nothing is wrong with you."

"It's not that anything is wrong with me. It's to ensure all of me is present. I don't know if she's right or if this will help, but I would be lying if I said I've always felt complete. There are a lot of memories missing, Aero. And it doesn't make sense. Maybe this will show me what I need to see so I can move forward and put an end to the Mortia."

I can see in her eyes that she wants this to be the answer. That even if nothing happens, she will be better for doing it, and I'll be the last one to stand in her way.

"Can I at least come with you?"

She smiles. "Yes, I want you there." My heart leaps in my chest. She glances over at Feliks and Hera, who somehow have fallen asleep despite the grave danger we are all in. "Them, too, I suppose," she adds, her nose wrinkling up with a hushed giggle, and I nod, pulling her in tighter.

16

EVANTHE

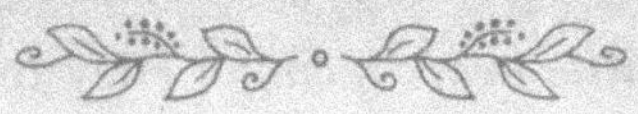

It doesn't take long for King Murrick's soldiers to pass through our hidden village. Part of me hoped it would take longer so I could put off this soul mending to another night, but no such luck is mine. Stepping out from the hollow tree, I'm amazed with how quickly the others removed any signs of the village. It appears to be a forest like any other.

The tables and chairs are all gone, not even a mark left from their legs in the dirt. The sun about to set, they decide it best to leave everything hidden in case his soldiers circle back while we are all asleep. Princess Liri instructs everyone to keep as quiet as possible as they return to their homes for the night. I watch as the Fae follow her orders, their eyes cast down, their bodies limp from the nerve-wracking afternoon. And I wonder if they would have gone through all this if we weren't here. If I wasn't here.

I saw what King Murrick did to their court before we arrived, but I can't help but feel like his soldiers had already took what they wanted from them. Maybe the Mortia know I'm here. I can hear Hale's voice back at the springs. *"You can't hide from me. You and I are the same. I can hear your dark, little heart racing."* They must know. Now, they're just looking for me, and all these innocent Fae are at risk.

Liri helps the last family to their quarters and looks up at the darkening horizon. "It's almost time. Meet back here once the sun has completely fallen, and I will take you to the soul mender."

I try to rest, but it's no use. My legs are crawling with creeps, and my mind won't stop wandering. My soul is about to leave my body and travel with someone I've never met before. I don't even like the idea of leaving my satchel with a stranger, let alone my soul. What if we can't find our way back? Is my entire soul lost forever? My body left lying on the ground, empty? My stomach clenches, and my hands grow cold and clammy. I need to think about something else. Anything. I close my eyes, but all I can see is my lifeless body lying in the dirt. A soft knocking sounds at the door, and Hera peers her head inside. "It's pretty dark out here. You ready to get this over with?"

Thank Divine. I don't think I could sit in here much longer. "Yes, let's go."

The others are waiting in the spot Liri mentioned. Feliks wraps his hands around my face. "You've got this."

"Thanks, Feliks," I reply through smashed cheeks. I'm surprised to see Shade standing with them, as I didn't ask him to attend, but I don't make anything of it. He came here with us, so he might as well join in. Aero makes a point to stand at my side as we follow the princess through the dark woods. He leans in and whispers into my ear, "If anything doesn't feel right and you need to get out of there, just say the word." Grateful for the support, I try to smile, but my face is too frozen with fear.

We stop at the opening of a dark cave not far from the stream just outside the village. A hooded silhouette approaches, reaching out and grabbing both my hands. The slightest bit of moonlight shines into his cloak to reveal the weather-worn face of an older male with curly silver hair. He smiles, and all the lines of his face curl up with it. "It is a pleasure to meet you, my guardian. I'm sorry it took me so long. I'm not much for the bustle of a village and much prefer the quiet of this place." He lifts a hand to welcome me in. We follow him down the dark corridor until a small group of flickering orbs greets us.

"Please sit." He gestures to join him next to the glowing lights. Liri whispers something to Shade and Diaspor, and the males make their way back to the cave entrance.

"They are going to be on guard," she respectfully explains to the older Fae.

He nods with understanding and brings his attention

back to me. "My name is Rennin Neriro. I understand Princess Liri has told you what I can do with my gifts?" he says, more of a statement than a question.

I nod, and he continues. "It is a dangerous journey. We must travel through the Underrealm, the kingdom of the Mortia and those they torture. If part of your soul is truly missing, it will likely be guarded by terrifying creatures. Things even your worst nightmares can't imagine." He pauses, holding me in his piercing gaze, and I fear I might throw up. "In order to find this missing part of you, our souls must leave our bodies. I will be with you the whole time, but there is one very important rule you must follow. You must hold onto me, and under no circumstance should you let go. Do you understand?"

"Yes, I understand," I reply reluctantly, and the old Fae takes my hands in his. "Alright, I need you to close your eyes and lower any shield you may have unintentionally put up. It's quite common going into a quest like this. Just do your best to relax and let me in."

Drawing a deep breath in through my nose and out through my mouth, I do my best to let down my guard and welcome the soul mender. At first, I feel nothing, then much warmer all at once. Like I'm full to the brim with hot, gooey honey, and it's sticking to all of me. It's a soothing sensation, but then it starts pulling harder and harder until I cannot hold on any longer, and with a rushing thump, I'm yanked from my body. It's as if my bones have melted into jelly, but I don't let go of Rennin's arm as we move through a haze that can only be described as a blurry painting of the Fae Realm. The distorted work of art whizzes past us as we travel at the speed of light, then we dive down. Deeper into the layers of the realm that go unseen. Right through the plush flora, the soft dirt, past the hard rock, and everything grows darker, colder. My form, once warm honey, is now nothing more than a frigid fog latched onto that of Rennin. Then we slow down, and the walls of black rock around us clearly come into view until we completely stop.

I try to find my feet as I normally would, but they don't seem to work in the same way. Nothing is pulling me to the ground, and yet I'm not moving through the space as the air Fae would. Noticing my confusion, Rennin places his finger to his lips to ensure I remember to keep quiet, and he whispers, "Just think of where you want to move to, and you will, but only with me. Follow my lead."

I tighten my grip around his arm, a part of me relieved to just hang on for the ride. Something about this place makes me feel disoriented, as if it is familiar yet all wrong. Like I've put my clothes on, but I put them on backward and inside out and can't figure out how to turn them out right. I can barely see right in front of me, but things start to come into view the farther we go down the dark cavern. The lines and cracks in the black rock surrounding us seem to have patterns, some of them forming faces and bodies that appear to be Fae. "Who drew these?" I quietly ask.

"They are *not* drawings," the soul mender replies with a warning gaze. With a shudder, I pull myself in closer to him, letting his movement tow me along through the daunting maze. This better be worth it. As if in response, a blood-curdling cry echoes through the hollow gallery ahead, and I can feel nothing but blind terror.

We move forward for quite some time, Rennin on alert but aware of this place, and I am clinging to my one thread of courage remaining. It seems like it has been days. But then I see something laying on the cavern floor that is truly familiar—the worn cream fabric sewn together with green yarn. And it all comes rushing back to me. My gaia. My small, dirty hands clinging to the comforting blanket. The way it smells of crisp lemon blossom and the fruit of loquat trees. I hold it up to my nose, the scent calming me. My mother storming about the room, ranting and raving. *"You are four years of age, Evanthe. You shouldn't need a sewn-up scrap of linen to sleep. You are a Sideris. Not lowly chicken heart."* She rips the treasured object from my hands and throws it into the fireplace. I run after it, nearly throwing myself into the flames to save it, but my father catches me mid-air, letting me kick and scream until my lungs could bear no more, the painful loss leaving me breathless and broken. And there it is. My gaia. Down here. Maybe this is what I needed to find. The bloom still tied against my thigh back in the Fae Realm must still be able to come through, because my thigh is stinging cold where it would be touching. But it's not enough to draw my attention away from the blanket.

Still holding onto Rennin's arm, I move toward it, reaching out to grab it from the ground. But he pulls me back, a frightening look in his eyes. "What are you doing?

You don't touch anything here. Do you understand?" he asks with an urgently hushed voice, his head on a swivel. But I can't stop from feeling its pull. I'm meant to have it. "I think it's what I came here for," I whisper, reaching out toward it once more.

He slaps my hand, and I'm stunned that I can feel the sting from such a misty form. He points back to where I was reaching. "There is nothing there. This place will make you see things that do not exist. If we find your soul, we will both be able to see it. From now on, touch nothing and keep quiet."

It pains me to move on without it, but I do as he says. The air grows thinner, if that is possible, as we go deeper into the cold cavern. Another eerie bellow assaults our ears, making the hair on my neck stand at attention. I so badly want to turn around. Every part of me screams to go back. Yet the bloom does nothing. Some magical relic it's turned out to be so far. It's dark, but I can feel the walls around us turning, and around the corner, a faint humming glow emanates in the distance.

The soul mender stops and waits. For what, I'm not sure, but something darker seems to be moving about the smoldering gleam, as if shadows were dancing around it with a jerking motion. A screeching pierces the air, and I nearly let out a scream, but Rennin has placed his other hand over my mouth. Crouching down, he whispers so quietly I'm not sure if I heard him speak or just read his mind. "You see that glow?"

I nod rapidly.

"They're inside it. Can you see those fine lines? The details within?"

I don't see anything but a glow at first, but narrowing my eyes, I start to see what he speaks of. "It's a girl?" I ask quietly. He gets right beside me and points so my eyes line up with his finger. It falls directly where her hand would be hanging at her side, and there, in her grasp, I see it. The gaia.

"It's me," I gasp.

The soul mender nods, relieved that I understand. "Those shadows moving around you are called shadred. They are some of the oldest souls held captive by the Mortia."

"How did they end up here?" I ask.

"They were born to the Fae Realm like any other. Most made bargains with the Mortia and could not uphold their end of the deal. Now their souls are bound as guards of the Underrealm. They no longer wield their elemental magic, but if you look closely, you can still see hints of the lost gifts." He points to one of them. "See the way that one twirls in a flurry around the glowing light?" I watch as the shadow spins in a bluster as he says, "Air Fae." The soul mender points to another. "And that one, look at his fingertips." My eyes widen with wonder at the way they shift from black as coal to the heated red of a molten metal. Fire Fae. All of them once belonged to a court above. My stomach turns. All of them were once desperate enough to make a deal with the Mortia—just as I did. This could be me. I can hear the stories of my legend now. *She was once the last guardian of the Fae Realm. Now she spends eternity tortured by her failure, guarding the gates of the Underrealm.*

One of the shadred leaves his post and creeps away down another dark corridor. Rennin pulls me closer. "Where's that one going?" I ask.

"Probably called away to do another task for the Mortia. There are only two of them now. This is our chance before another shows up to replace him." He looks down at a pile of jagged rocks near the wall and then toward another dark tunnel leading in another direction. "I'm going to throw one of these down that cavity. The shadred are very sensitive to sound, and capturing an intruder would earn them a great reward. They won't be able to resist it. If they both take the bait, we won't have much time. Hang onto me. As soon as we get there, you must go straight into her. Straight into the missing piece of your soul. Do you understand?"

I swallow the massive lump in my throat. "Alright, you better throw it far."

Without hesitation, the soul mender picks up the largest rock and launches it so far I'm afraid I won't be able to hear it when it lands. But the cracking impact comes through, and the dancing shadows pause for the briefest second before bolting toward the sound. Rennin launches toward my younger self. My nails dig into the sides of his arms as I hang on for dear life. Terrified, she stares at me through the glowing hum until there is no more time, and my sheer skin touches hers. The light is blinding for a moment. The cold, damp air comes alive, and I swear a wave of tiny metal needles are prickling my skin across every inch of my body. All the missing memories of my past come to life in my mind like flitting through a catalog of Chronicles at record speed. My chest is heaving, but I've never felt more at ease. I could stay in this moment forever, but I'm literally yanked from euphoria as Rennin rips me back down the cavern from which we came.

My eyes flutter open to see the two shadred chomping at my heels as the soul mender pulls me in tighter, every detail of their ravenous, gaunt faces in view. Their teeth gnash together as they run on all fours more like an animal than Fae. I contort my body as far away from them as possible as Rennin hastens forward. Looking back, I see the darkness fading.

The shadred, still salivating, come to a stop as we launch up higher and higher.

Back through the blurry painting.

And return to the warm, gooey honey.

17
EVANTHE

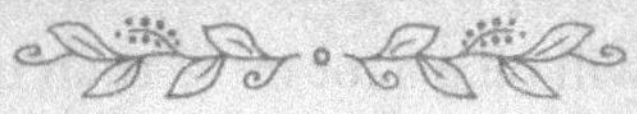

The concern in Aero's eyes is alarming.

"Are you injured?" he asks.

Still reeling from the whirlwind of a journey, I take a moment to feel for anything out of place. The prince impatiently crouches down, searching my body for any wounds. I've never seen him so panicked. But it's all for nothing. I've never felt better. Even despite the revelations of years gone missing, something inside me that once felt empty and longing is now bursting at the seams. A force of luster I never imagined could come from within me. In an effort to calm him, I place my hand on the side of his face. He freezes in place, shocked by the tender gesture I'm sure, but more than that, the spark it sends from my skin touching his, a magic all its own. Surely, he feels it too.

"I'm perfectly fine, Aero. In fact, I'm better than fine. I feel fantastic."

His body warms at my words, yet he lifts a finger to move a strand of unruly hair from my face and continues searching me for signs of something awry. I know that look. The look that comes right before that horrible, inevitable thing happens. Just when all seems well, the worst comes. It will take a lot more than my word for him to accept such pleasant news. Even in my enlightened state, he's infuriating.

His fingers run along the length of my limbs, making my skin pebble with each touch. All the times in my life I've said I was fine, it was always a lie. But not tonight. Tonight, for the first time, I know that it's true. All the time that went missing didn't come back to me in pieces. It came all at once—and fast. The knowledge not overwhelming but empowering. The illness of my mother that my aunts spoke of was real. It's so clear now. I can see how my soul broke. It broke to protect me. I wasn't ready to face that truth. My younger self was always left feeling rejected, a disappointment. The fear of the shame my magic would bring to my family haunted me. But it wasn't me. It was never about me. My mother wasn't like everyone else, and now the shadows that had hid her flaws are gone, exposing her for who she really was. But not just the dark parts. The good ones too. The nights she would come in well after I had gone to bed, tears running down her face. She didn't think I was awake, but out the corner of my eye, I could see her standing there. And I could hear the pain behind her voice. I didn't understand it as a child, but I do now. She didn't know how to love me right, or in a conventional way, but it wasn't because she didn't want to. And that's all that matters.

I leap up from the cold, damp ground, plant a kiss on Rennin's forehead, and look up at Princess Liri. "Thank you for this. For looking past what might linger in my soul and helping me find the piece that was missing." Astonished and relieved, Liri smiles and pulls me into her embrace.

"I should have never doubted your strength," she whispers in my ear.

The soul mender nods knowingly, and I take off past the others, out the mouth of the cavern and into the dark woods. The sun will be up soon, and my body may be exhausted, but my soul is too awake to sleep, so I explore the forest with what's left of the night. The others retire to their beds. All but Aero. Although not right at my side, I can feel him lingering behind me, hear the slight crunch of dead leaves beneath his boots as he watches me, waiting for the inevitable.

"I'm not going to burst into wicked flames and devour you if that's what you're waiting for," I call out over my shoulder.

The crunching abruptly stops. I quickly turn around to find him right in front of me now, my chest rising and falling right along with his, the sight and smell of him so close weakening my knees. I shut my eyes in an effort to bring them back to life, but they buckle beneath me. His hands catch me before I fall, and my eyes snap open.

"I won't let you fall, let alone devour all of the Fae Realm," he says, his breath tickling my lips.

Something quivers low in my core. Still holding me above the forest floor, his gaze pierces mine with promise. A promise that goes far beyond his words. "Well, thank my lucky stars. I don't know what I'd do without you," I say with all the sarcasm I can muster while in his arms.

The side of his mouth draws into a grin, but the promise in his eyes remains as he pulls me in tighter until our noses touch, and his lips brush against mine the slightest bit, making my stomach flip. Closing my eyes, my mouth opens for him. But just as quickly as I have literally fallen backward for him, he teasingly pulls me up and places me on my feet. My jaw snaps shut and a rushing, hot embarrassment fills my cheeks. Without a second thought, I reach back and send my palm into the side of his face. The slap is loud, echoing off the forest around us, so I know it stung, but he merely laughs and begins hiking back toward the village.

Hera tosses me another arrow. "You've landed nearly every shot today."

I look at the targets we've set up in the distance, and

sure enough, she's right. I recall all the days of training back in Parea, hiding my greatest strengths from her and her cronies. It seems a lifetime ago. I watch as the warrior looks down at the bow in her hands and wonder if she is having the same thought, the same question running through her mind. Will I be able to kill her the day Noonsnight comes? Could I watch one of these arrows shoot through her heart and watch the life fade from her eyes?

"Must be my lucky day," I say, hopefully awaiting a smart-mouthed response to lighten the mood.

But she only leaves me with a scoff and glances back to the outskirts of the village, where Shade is lounging with a jug of wine. His lazy gaze unabashedly follows Aero's every move as he spars with Diaspor in the distance.

"You see the way he watches him, don't you? Like a slithering snake waiting to strike?" she asks.

If I'm being honest with myself, I've been more intrigued by the way his power might make me feel than the way he looks at Aero, but I know full well what she speaks of. I observe the way Aero's bare upper body moves with his sword, each muscle flexing and pausing in a seemingly effortless dance. I can see why Shade would envy him. Even as a fellow god, he can't move that way. His gifts are far different. I pry my gaze away to find the god of seduction wearing a menacing glare now as he remains fixated on Aero. "Does he do it often? Stare at him like that?" I ask, an unsettling feeling in my stomach.

"All. The. Time," she says, looking away with a shiver.

Shaking off the eerie feeling, I move to follow her toward the targets to gather the other arrows, but a scorching heat radiates up the inside of my thigh, stopping me in my tracks.

"What's wrong?" she asks.

I reach into my garter and pull out the crystal bloom. Beneath it, my skin is left pink and tender to the touch. I breathe through the pain. "It's been much more vocal since my journey into the Underrealm." I draw a hand over my brow to shade the sun as I try to look past the trees in the direction we were heading.

"Care to elaborate?" she asks impatiently.

I don't quite know how to explain it, the bloom's hot and cold demeanor, but I do my best. "Each time it's been warmer, it seems to point me in the right direction—or the direction it wants me to go. I'm pretty certain that its coldness is more of a warning—its way of telling me that I'm going the wrong way."

"So just now, were you moving the wrong way or the right way?" she asks.

I look back toward the vast, unknown forest beyond our targets and swallow the lump in my throat. "It's telling me I was moving the right way."

She chucks her arrows into her quiver. "Then what are we waiting for?"

I hate to admit it, but she's right. I've been putting this off. It's been days since the soul mending, and the bloom has practically been shouting at me to move farther into the Repenlow Wood. I have felt the strength inside me building. My magic hums louder than ever before, as if it were desperately clawing to escape, and I wonder if this is the way it would have always felt had all of my soul been in place from the beginning. Despite the struggles this place has brought, I've actually grown quite fond of this little village. The place of my mending. But if I want to save it from the Mortia, it's time to move on.

"Follow me," I say.

"To where?" she asks, scrambling to keep up with me as I race back into the village.

"To Liri's quarters. Some of the Fae saved the belongings of the Earth warriors that didn't survive King Murrick's attack. It's about time someone put them to use again."

The princess gladly welcomes us into her tree and props open the trunk sitting beside her bed. Inside it lays piles of formal wear and trinkets. All relics from the earth Fae that once resided in her court. She pushes the delicate things aside until reaching the bottom where a neatly folded set of leathers sit, waiting for me. She unfolds them and raises them up to compare their size to mine. "These should fit you perfectly. Try them on."

I take them from her and pause, realizing there is nowhere to change discreetly in the open room. Hera diverts her eyes in another direction to give me privacy, but Liri doesn't seem to catch the hint. I suppose it doesn't really matter as they all saw me running around naked and hallucinating by the hot springs not long ago, so I strip down to my undergarments and pull the well-crafted armor over my head. The cool, soft leather hugs the curve of my bodice and the small of my back as if it were tailored just for my body. I turn to face the small mirror hanging on the curved wall beside me, admiring the shimmering green and gold stitching. Princess Liri's and Hera's reflections appear behind me. With a little shimmy, I strap the bloom to my thigh and place my hands on my hips to pose for them.

"Someone's feeling quite right in their own skin," Hera laughs.

"As she should," Liri says in all seriousness.

They're not wrong. I am feeling good about myself for the first time in a long time. Despite the many mistakes I've made, that is no longer all I see when I look in the mirror. Now, I can see the parts that led me to those mistakes *and* the parts that carried me this far. I'm not the monster anymore.

Despina Petrini, who has taken my father and my closest friend.

Athena Rokos, who destroyed my family and took my mother.

King Murrick, who is taking the Fae Realm.

And the head of the monster...

The Mortia, who seeks to devour us all.

They are the monsters lurking in the shadows. The ones who have had the upper hand. But I've traveled their dark roads, seen their dark hearts, and felt their dark pains.

I will be the one to end them all. To watch the life drain from their eyes. To finally let my mother rest in peace. To fulfill the prophecy as the Final Guardian of the Fae Realm. No matter the cost, *these* are my stars.

18

EVANTHE

When the group is finished gathering their belongings, they make their way to the village center to say their goodbyes. I am not surprised by the wet cheeks and parting gifts bestowed upon us as the Fae that remain from the Ember Court have grown quite fond of us, and us of them.

Cirrus, not much of a fighter, opts to stay behind. Liri thanks him for all his service with a cloak that once belonged to her father. He tries to deny such a gracious gift, but she insists, bringing tears to his eyes. I hand him a small, square cloth to dry his nose with and he smiles. "You go on and listen to what that bloom tells you."

"You know, if it wasn't for you, I would never have known what I'm made for," I say.

"I may not have known you years ago, but I think you've always known that you were made for more, Evanthe."

"I will miss you," I say, blinking my eyes to keep the tears from falling.

Cirrus tucks the square cloth in his pocket and lifts his chin. "Make us all proud." I nod a silent agreement and draw the string of my satchel tight. As the blood reader turns away, I notice a young female approaching Aero from behind. He is completely unaware of her presence, as he is in the middle of helping Bel pack up the rest of his things. She shifts her weight from one foot to the other and fidgets with a small package in her hands until summoning up the courage to speak with his brother, Feliks. She places the little package in his hands. "Will you give this to your brother?"

Grinning ear to ear, he does his best to reassure the little one. "Of course, may I ask what it is?" He leans in close so she may whisper, but I hear her loud and clear.

"It's my lucky stone. So he may become the one bonded to the Guardian." Her tiny nose wrinkles up mischievously as she points toward me. Once she has returned to her parents, I nudge Feliks with my elbow. "Looks like Aero has a little admirer."

"Children always seem to see people for who they truly are. I'm surprised she wants my brother to end up with the likes of you," he replies snidely, keeping a cheerful shine to his expression for those surrounding us. A bit shocked by the insult, my jaw drops.

"I know you're not the fondest of me these days, but surely you can understand my hesitation," I whisper while shaking the hands of those we are leaving. I try to keep a pleasant face, like Feliks does, but I am not as good an actor. Quickly, he shifts his gaze to me, narrowing his eyes.

"I'm quite certain the question you should be asking yourself is if *you* are worthy of him. Not the other way around."

Leaving me no room to retort, he flings his satchel over his shoulder and stomps away. Stunned, I lag behind the others, letting him have the last word as we venture into the Repenlow Wood. What a ridiculous thing to question. If I am worthy of him? He's a smug, deceitful beast. Unable to help myself, I glance over at him, taking in the way he clenches his stubble-peppered jaw as he focuses on the unbeaten path ahead. I fight the urge to move closer to him, cursing myself for wanting to take in the salty scent that swirls around him. As if he can hear me thinking of his adversary, Shade moves in beside me.

"Looks as though you're feeling even more at home here in our realm. It becomes you," he says.

I think about his words, debating the validity, but something doesn't sit right. There is nothing wrong with the Fae Realm. I've grown to be more comfortable here than I was the day we arrived, but it's not my home. If anything, I'm more at home in my own body. It doesn't take long for Aero to notice Shade's efforts. Even so, he doesn't seem to let it stir his temper. He catches me glancing over at him as the seductor pays me another compliment. The corner of his mouth curls with amuse-ment, making me choke on a laugh. I pass it off as though I need to clear my throat in an effort to keep our little inter-action secret. It seems to suffice this time, but I don't know how much longer I can go on pretending he doesn't have a hold on me. I hate that I live for these moments when he shows me a new side of him. This time, a glimpse of his sense of humor. Even rarer, the times I see him soften at my touch. Yet, I don't know if I can imagine being bonded to him without wanting to kill him at the same time, if there would be anything left if I didn't hate him. Or if my fondness for him would grow too strong, rendering me weak.

On the other hand, Shade is still very much a mystery. He is intriguing, never boring. But he's not Aero. I would be lying to myself if I said I felt anything as strongly for Shade as I feel for Aero. Could we be content as a bonded pair? Allowing for other partners maybe. Oddly enough, I don't think I would mind if Shade chose to be with someone else. I actually think that kind of lifestyle suits him. But the thought of Aero taking another woman to be his wife makes me sick to my stomach. It makes my blood boil, and I can't help but hate him for it. Life before him was simple. To feel nothing would be so much easier, but at some point, I need to take the leap. I need to make a choice and find out if it is the right one.

The woods seem more alive than ever tonight. I lie perched upon a branch, my legs softly swinging beneath me to the rhythm of the creatures chirping about, until a roar ripples through the night air, sending a tremor through my body. The others spring from their resting states and grip their weapons tightly as we collectively try to determine which direction the threat is coming from.

"No one leave their perch. It's best to stay above ground for now," Diaspor instructs.

Disobeying the order, Aero pulls himself up onto my branch, making the commander spit profanities. One after another, the booming roars repeat, and it's clear there is more than one of whatever it is. Then they come crashing through the forest floor, latching onto our tree in a mad dash. The glow emanating from the chirping creatures around us provides just enough light for me to see how agile the giant, angry beasts are. They are covered in fur, head to tail, and much resemble a bear, but they are twice the size, and a horn with the slight curve of a goat's but sharper extends from each of their shoulders, providing them with armor as they bust through the wood. One of the beasts slashes for Hera below. With the flash of my hand, a thick branch rams into it, throwing its balance off. Hera looks up, stunned by my intervention. "Go!" I yell at her.

Our cover clearly blown, Diaspor cries out, "Move! Now! As fast as you can!"

Leaping from one tree branch to the next, my bones seem to turn to water, allowing me to contort my body in any way I need to so as not to be eaten by one of these furry savages. I glance back to find Aero at my back, moving like the god he is through each limb and shoot until we reach a small opening, and it becomes clear we won't have the thick cover to protect us for a stretch. He looks ahead where the thicket starts back up. "When we hit that ground, you're going to run straight into the forest and don't look back. You hear me?" he says, more a command than a question.

I open my mouth to deny his demands, but nothing comes out. I remain frozen with hesitation, staring back at him until he snaps, "For once in your life, just do what I tell you." He fires his finger toward the thicket in the distance. "That's your battle ground. That's your weapon. Go to it." The thundering timbre of his voice rolls over me like a wave that demands respect. And just this time, I decide to follow his order. My feet move like they are running across hot coals over the patch of barren ground, and I am back in the thicket before I know it. But I don't keep going as he instructed. I climb as high as I can go. High enough that I can see most of the battle ensuing beneath me. With all the magic I can muster, I pull roots and branches to protect the others. They slow the giant beasts but only for a short while as their massive horned shoulders bust through the wood and flora as if it were merely thin strands of string.

The fire Fae work together, flames bursting from their hands, to bring one of them to its knees long enough for Hera and Feliks to bring their swords down upon its back over and over until it falls limp upon the dirt. Diaspor manipulates the earth beneath them as best he can, while Bel and Aero shower one of them with blinding torrents of all the water they can muster. But the beasts are strong and relentless, pushing them farther out into the open space. I can see that Diaspor's magic is fading too quickly, the flora around him responding slower and less aggressively to his command, and I wish I hadn't listened to Aero. I thought they would have defeated them by now. I should be in there with them. Bel struggles to fight one of them off when a curly haired, blonde female I've never seen before swings from a branch, knocking the monster down with a forceful kick. Before it can regain its footing, she blasts it with a scorching flame to the back as Bel drowns it with a powerful swell of water. Who is she?

Not far behind them, I spot Aero again. With one swipe of its paw, one of the beasts knocks Aero's feet out from under him, sending his sword across the ground and out of his reach. Bel looks back, but he is already in the middle of another battle, as are the others. There has to be at least eight or nine of the massive horned bears. I pull from the forest behind, launching a strand of roots to Aero's aid, but it's too far. They don't reach, and if I crack the ground beneath them, Aero might fall through. Saliva flies out of its maw as the beast roars over him and reaches back its paw to make a final blow. Unable to hold back any longer, I draw my sword and leap from the thicket. I charge toward the beast, sending every lick of wood and vine I can in its path. As I get closer, I can see its white milky eyes staring off into the distance as its foul roar sounds again, the cloudy stare sending a jolt of adrenaline through my veins. Just when I think I'm about to collide with it, Diaspor tosses Aero his sword, and the god rears back, lodging it deeply into the giant bear's chest, then into its gut, and finally, slashing its throat. The beast falls in a heap, and Aero's sword drops, his eyes rolling back in his head as he, too, falls to the ground.

19
EVANTHE

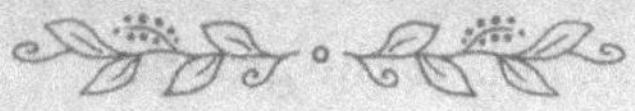

"You should get some rest. Eat something," Diaspor says.

The moon has come, gone, and nearly arrived again, but Aero still lies here in this strange home—Nuala Hilliard's home in the middle of nowhere. She was the female that came to our aid amidst the attack back in the woods. It just so happened that the home she's been living in wasn't far from that part of the forest.

When the dust had settled, she and Liri both burst into tears. Bittersweet tears as Aero's grim condition was storming down on their reunion. What were the odds of finding Liri's long-lost friend at the same time Aero nearly lost his life? This place doesn't play fair. For each win, there is loss. This can't be a loss. Not him. I watch intently as his chest barely rises and falls. Each time his eyes move beneath their lids, hope flutters in my chest, but they never open. I don't want to leave his side. What if he wakes, but only for a moment, and the last thing I said to him was laced with so much scorn. I'd slapped him. Right across the face. His stupid, perfect face. And for what reason? He had teased me. He made me think that he was going to kiss me, then pulled away. I was only angry because he was right to think it would infuriate me. Because no matter how hard I try to deny it, a part of me wants to feel his lips pressed to mine.

I lift his tunic to see if the salve placed on his wounds is healing him yet. The gashes are thick and long across the side of his abdomen. The sight makes my stomach turn. I can only imagine how painful the blow had been. It's a miracle he's still alive.

"It's only been minutes since you last checked it. Give the salve time to work," Diaspor says, his voice pleading.

Before I can reply, Feliks walks through the door with Liri and hands me a fresh pile of linens. He looks down at his brother, his brows furrow, and he clenches his fists. The unspoken worry is written all over him. The same fears I've been replaying in my mind since he fell to the ground. *Is this it? Is his heart still beating? Tell me he won't die here. How long can he go on like this before his body gives up? What can I do? How can I save him?*

"He will be alright. He's a god. He will heal fast," he says through shaky lips.

"What were they? Those beasts?" I ask Diaspor.

"They are called faloths. It's been said that they were

extinct. Back when we were here before the war started, so much time had passed since a single Fae had seen one. I don't know if that much has changed or if it is the doing of the Mortia. It seems impossible to be attacked by so many of them."

He looks to Liri to gauge her reaction. She shakes her head, seeming just as bewildered as he is. Feliks crouches down next to Aero. "The irony of all this is that they looked so much like bears. When he was younger, our father put him in a cage with a bear. His way of making Aero prove he was a man. He was only ten years old."

My heart drops.

"That's what all the scars are from?" I ask.

Nodding slowly he shudders.

"Most of them. The others are from our father and our brother, Iason. He faced his greatest fear and defeated it. The Great Divine can't let him die like this. What kind of reward would that be?"

Choking back the tears, he lets his head fall into his lap. Liri reaches over to place a hand on his back when her eyes light up with revelation, then fall with horror. "No, it can't be," she utters quietly.

"What can't be? What do you know?" I ask demandingly.

"I don't know anything. Not yet. I can't be sure, but did any of you see him speaking with Hagen Elleth back at the village?"

We all rack our minds for any recollection. "He was around. It was fairly close quarters. I suppose he must have at some point, even if no one actually noticed. Why? What would he have to do with this?" I ask. She chews on her bottom lip with hesitation.

"Feliks said that facing a bear would be Aero's greatest fear..."

The realization dawns on us. That fucking wretch. He must have found a way to get close to him. To taste his greatest fear and use it against him. But why? Has he been working against us the whole time? One of King Murrick's spies? I begin pacing the room.

"I thought he was one of your family's closest counselors? Your friend? Do you have any friends that don't betray you?" I shout just as Nuala walks through the doorway. She's unable to hide the wince from her face and turns back around, Liri chasing after her, calling out, "She didn't mean you, Nuala!"

Feliks narrows his eyes with disappointment. "Nice," he spits.

Diaspor sighs, and they both leave me to think about my sharp tongue. Liri and Nuala had such a joyous reunion back in the woods despite Aero's condition. They seemed to pick up right where they had left off. The closest of friends. A friendship like I had with Sorrow. The sight of them embracing made me homesick for the friendship I lost. I had always pictured Sorrow and myself living in the high tower together once I had defeated Athena and the others. I never would have allowed myself a spouse, but our friendship seemed invincible. I could always count on that. But it's gone now.

I didn't think before I spoke. I didn't know Nuala would still feel hurt after so much time. Surely, Liri recognizes that she was wrong, that Nuala had been right about the advisor betraying her family. I foolishly assumed Liri had apologized for not believing her, but clearly they haven't had a chance to talk about it yet. I gaze down at Aero. "How is it that I wield a sword so well but always manage to hurt those around me with my words?" The pain builds inside me and bursts from my mouth every time. When will I learn? I rest my hand on his lifeless chest.

"I'm not going anywhere, so you can wake up now," I whisper.

Nothing. Stubborn ox.

"I take it all back. I really don't know what I'd do without you." I search him for any signs of life. Sliding off my chair and onto my knees, I beg the Great Divine to heal him. Pleading. "Let him live, and I'll change. I'll do better. I'll...I'll even make the bond."

A creaking sound shakes me from the deep slumber I had fallen into despite my best efforts to stay alert in case Aero wakes up. My eyes flutter open, and I realize I'm still rooted in the same spot at Aero's side, but we're not alone anymore. The sleep emptying from my eyes as I blink them awake, Shade's silhouette above becomes clear. How long have I been asleep? Confusion sets in when I see the wine deity's hands wrapping around Aero's throat. At first, it looks as though he's merely inspecting him, maybe to gage the progress of his healing, but then his icy eyes become filled with malicious intent as he starts to apply more pressure. What is happening? He can't be doing this. Something primal inside me unleashes as I leap from the floor, screaming and clawing at his face until the others come bursting into the room and pry me from him.

He lifts his hands in the air as if he is innocent. As if he wasn't just trying to choke the life out of Aero while he isn't able to defend himself. My limbs continue flying at him as Diaspor attempts to hold me down. I'm shaking with the need to pull his insides out and strangle him with them.

"I'll kill you! I'll kill you with my bare hands! You stay the fuck away from him!" I scream, my eyes wild with molten fury.

"What is going on here?" Liri asks, pushing her way between us.

"That deceitful prick was trying to strangle Aero," I spit with all the venom of a thousand horned vipers.

I'm blown away as his jaw drops with utter shock and offense. He folds his arms defensively. "I would *never*. His quilt was falling down. I was merely pulling it up to keep him comfortable."

"No! Not even close. Your fingers were laced around his neck," I shout pleadingly toward Liri. "Do something about this. You have to. If he's willing to do that to Aero, he's a danger to us all."

Keeping a stoic face, the princess looks to Diaspor and then to Shade. Folding her hands and taking a deep breath, she addresses the group. "It's not that simple. Although, I am the highest royalty amongst us, this is not my home, and Shade has never broken my trust in all the years I've known him."

"There's *nothing* complicated about it. I saw it with my own eyes. He's not a full-blooded Fae like you. He *can* tell a lie," I urge.

Liri cautiously steps closer. "Unfortunately, you too are able to tell a lie. It wouldn't be right for me to take your word over his without proof, Evanthe. There's still a chance Shade is meant to be your bonded. If he is, and we end his life, the Fae Realm and the human realm won't stand a chance against the Mortia. We must abide by the prophecy." I shake my head at her. How can she let him get away with this? Of all of us, she knows I despise him the most. She knows I'm telling the truth. She must know.

She gently places her hand upon my shoulder. "You have to understand, this isn't about my allegiance to you. It's about the oath I took as princess to act for the greater good of our realm. To break it in such a way would strip me of my power and damn you all to the Underrealm."

Also displeased with such news, Feliks steps between us. "Then what do we do with him? Just let him run amuck? Who knows how many of us will turn up dead by tomorrow morning if he's allowed to go free."

"What kind of justice would that be?" I ask.

Liri looks back at her newly found friend. "I wish there

was a better solution right now, but this is Nuala's home. By Fae Accord, she is obliged to keep her guests from any harm while staying here. If any of you happen to act in a way of violence against another guest, it is up to her to decide your punishment. That said, I will advise her to keep the previous issue of his potential bonding status in mind."

My mouth fills with bile as I recall his lips touching mine, imagining a bond forming between us, and I recall Phira's words. *"You know how a tea kettle upon flames bubbles and boils until the steam builds and comes screaming out? It's a lot like that—the storm trapped in a tea kettle let loose. Like all those feelings coursing under your skin each time you touch are amplified to an intensity you can't imagine. And somehow, you just know that you would kill anyone that dared threaten them, that you would sacrifice your life for his if it ever came down to that."* I so desperately wish I had leapt from the thicket sooner, before the faloth took him down. Even so, I'm certain I would have fought Shade to the death had the others not pried me from him.

I don't understand it. Why I was ever curious about what being with Shade would be like. Why I ever thought about how nice it would be to let loose with someone like him. To be free of the pain that would come with true intimacy. And maybe he could offer me such a life, but I don't want it anymore. I want to go back to the time before I used Shade to get under Aero's skin. A time when Aero wasn't lying on his death bed.

Flashes of Shade's fingers wrapped around Aero's

throat assault my mind, leaving me breathless with anger. The way I would have ripped Shade apart in that moment...the way I still want to rip him apart...What's come over me?

I swallow the lump in my throat. Nuala nods repeatedly, wrapping her blonde braid around one of her fingers as she deliberates the best way to handle this, and I know what I need to do. I have to try. It's time. I turn to face Shade so I can see the look on his face when he hears my words.

"When Aero wakes up and becomes strong enough, I will bond with him. No more waiting. No more wondering. Until then, tie this one up."

His face doesn't betray him, but beyond the charade, past the sheepish act, I see the festering alarm hiding in his gaze, and I wonder if his greatest fear tastes like the salt and sage of the sea god that he has wronged.

Just wait until he wakes up, Shade. Just you wait.

20
EVANTHE

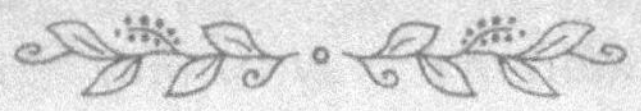

The walls of Nuala's home are barren. Not a single painting or drape to be found. The rich scent of Diaspor's stew simmering in the kitchen has started to waft around us, but I'm still not hungry.

I am staring off into space, but I can feel Feliks's eyes on me as we sit at Aero's bedside. My discomfort with such attention brings me back to life, and I tilt my head his way. His hair is greasy and matted upon his head. Dark circles rim his eyes, and his slumped posture accurately portrays the weariness that has also settled deep into my bones, both of us wearing our exhaustion like a tattered garment that's been run over the washboard one too many times. We stare at each other half-heartedly until Phira and Hera walk into the room, each carrying a fistful of trinkets. Hera pulls the round, wooden table from the corner between our chairs and tosses a small stone upon it. Right behind her, Phira pours her handful of tiny bones upon its surface and lifts her hand toward the offering.

"Someone told me that you like to play a game called knucklebones back on your island. I thought this might help pass the time."

"She couldn't find any teeth, but I guess the bones would be the traditional way to play," Hera says with a hopeful voice.

I look down at the pieces and lift the stone to see how the shiny parts reflect in the candlelight. It's nice of them to go out of their way like this. The least I could do is show a little enthusiasm, but I just don't have it in me. Feliks sighs, also seeming to struggle with the idea of fun during such a time. I know Aero wouldn't want his brother fading away like this. Phira is right. A little distraction might do us good. I reach across the table and place the stone in his hand. "Alright, but only if we all play," I say.

Feliks places the stone on the table, letting his hand slump back into his lap. I hold his sad gaze in a moment of silent understanding. It takes everything in me to keep the tears from spilling down my cheeks. I can't cry. People cry when they lose someone. We are not losing him. Hera sits down beside Feliks and runs her fingers through his greasy hair. "Come on. He wouldn't want you sulking like this." She tosses the stone and swipes two bones from the table. "Your turn," she says, passing him the stone, and the most sullen game of knucklebones continues to move around the table.

After my turn, I look back at Aero, hoping to see his eyes open. Hera seems to notice and places a finger to her chin in deep thought. "I still don't know why he did it. The bond can only happen with the one you're meant to bond with, right? Him killing Aero gets him no closer to being the prophesied god."

She raises a valid question—one that has been running through my mind all day. The only thing that gives me relief is knowing that Shade has been rendered unconscious and tied up in the attic. I pick up the stone and toss it. "Maybe it's not about bonding with me. Maybe he only wanted the glory, and if he couldn't have it, then he didn't want anyone to have it."

The bloom instantly warms at my thigh. That's it. It was about power. As if she can read my mind, Phira points toward the crystal bloom. "Liri mentioned that the bloom can bring out the worst in some humans. Did she say if a deity could fall under the same sort of spell?"

I recall my conversation with Liri back in Stillstar. "*You needn't worry about the Fae, but you may need to guard it closely around humans. It's entirely dependent upon how much darkness already festers inside them and how long they have been in its presence. Some are weaker than others.*"

"*What about deities?*"

"*It's unlikely.*"

"She said it isn't likely, but she didn't know for sure." I look at Hera and Feliks. "Have either of you felt yourselves growing easily agitated?" Hera, displeased with me for even asking the question, narrows her eyes.

"No, I have not. I think we both know that if I had been growing angry, you and I would have had a physical altercation by now," she says.

That much is true.

Feliks rolls his eyes and shakes his head. "Other than the agitating desire for you to end the Mortia, put Shade's head on a spike, and get us out of this war-torn death realm, I've felt wonderful."

Not missing the sarcasm in his voice, I lift my hands in surrender. "Alright, clearly you two are not spinning into power-hungry fiends."

"But that doesn't help us determine if Shade isn't," Phira says, raising her brow with suspicion.

"No, I guess not," I reply.

Hera tosses her bones onto the table. "Then I guess it's settled. If the bond happens with Aero, he gets to dismember Shade and shove it down his throat."

Phira snorts. "I wouldn't mind a front row seat to that."

I wouldn't mind either. But I can't ignore the pressure building around this bond. I might spend the rest of my life regretting it. We'll probably kill each other eventually. What a story for the Chronicles that would make. *The pair bonded for all eternity and, most likely to be thwarted by a spiteful star, finally couldn't stand one another any longer. Some say you can still hear them bickering in the Elysian Fields if you listen closely on a quiet night.* The thought brings the slightest smile to my face.

Having lost interest in the game, I place the bones in

Phira's hand and they clear the table. Hera convinces Feliks to get some sleep in their room, and I look back at Aero. I need this to work. I need him to wake up.

Sensing my distress, Phira pours me a glass of water. "Don't worry. He'll wake up. Knowing him, he's probably just waiting until you leave the room for more than a few minutes. Come with me to gather more water. It would be good to get some fresh air."

Reluctantly, I pull myself from the rickety wooden chair, and we make our way out into the dark meadow that surrounds Nuala's home. The air is cool and still but refreshing in comparison to the stale room I've spent the last two days in. I take a mental note to open a window in there when I return.

"It's good that you've decided it's time to make the bond," Phira says.

"I hope so," I say, lowering myself to the ground and looking up at the stars in the night sky. "I know we've been over this, but tell me again. If the bond works, how will I know for sure?"

She draws in a deep breath, letting the memories of her bonded come back to her. "You'll feel him in a way you never have before. When you're apart, you'll know he's alive because you'll feel his heart beating in tune with yours. And when you're near each other, like you will be during the bonding ceremony...let's just say, it's like nothing you've ever known before, but you will know without a doubt."

She speaks with a warm, reassuring voice, and I'm

grateful for it. "Thank you for reliving it all for my sake. I'm sure it isn't easy to think of your bonded," I say.

She lets out a sigh.

"It's not just for you. We all benefit from this bond. I've waited a long time to figure out why I'm still here."

She doesn't elaborate, but she doesn't have to. I know she's referring to the fact that most don't live long after their bonded passes away, and she's still here for a reason. This is her reason. To guide me through my bonding.

"I'm sorry for stirring things up between Liri and Nuala earlier. I wasn't thinking clearly. I should have held my tongue."

She sits down beside me and crosses her legs. "Liri and Nuala will be alright. They just have a lot of history to unpack. But you probably should share that apology with Liri. It may not seem like it, but she's quite hard on herself. The burden she bears for our realm is great. One that I don't think I could carry. She may know that you were only speaking out of pain, but that doesn't mean she didn't take it to heart."

On the other side of the meadow, I spot a bush blooming with blue and yellow flowers. I brace myself to get up and gather some into a bouquet for the princess when Hera's voice calls out from the cottage.

"Evanthe! He's awake!"

My heart leaps.

Without pause, I sprint through the dark meadow and up the cottage steps. Of course he would wake up the one time I'm not right by his side. Even in a sleeping state, he finds a way to get under my skin. I burst through the door, out of breath, to find him sitting upright, his gray-speckled eyes glistening back at me, and my heart nearly breaks with joy. Feliks is leaning over, kissing him on the face. I scurry around the bed and push him out of the way to get closer. We sit there for a moment, staring at each other.

"What took you so long to wake up?" I ask, propping my hand upon my hip.

The side of his mouth draws into a smile. He reaches up to tuck a strand of my hair around my ear and clears his throat. "Even on my deathbed, you're a handful."

We both burst into laughter, but it causes him to wince in pain. I pull up his tunic to make sure he hadn't injured himself further. "You took quite the blow back there," I say, pulling the garment back in place. "We should probably get you some more salve and clean bandages." I shift to get up and gather them, but he grabs my arm, keeping me at his level.

"Why didn't you keep running like I told you to?" he asks, his voice gruff, a stern look upon his face.

Because I couldn't leave you there to die. I pull my arm free.

"When have I ever taken orders from you?" I ask, wiping a tear from my face.

Not pleased with my response, but too exhausted, he rolls his eyes and lays his head back on the pillow behind him. I know he was only directing me to run away from the faloths because it was the responsible thing to do.

Because I'm the Final Guardian. The one that must carry the bloom. Without me, the Mortia could destroy this realm and ours, but the prophecy says I will only end the Mortia if I'm bonded to a god. He needs to understand that he might be just as important. He has to be.

His eyes close again, and it's clear that he needs more rest to gain his strength back. I pull his quilt up further to keep him from catching cold and ask Feliks to follow me out into the hall.

"I was starting to think he was never going to wake up," he says in a hushed, excited voice.

"We both know he's too stubborn to go out like that."

He smiles and lets out a deep breath. "When are we going to tell him?"

"About what?" I ask, knowing damn well so much happened while he was asleep.

Feliks throws his hands up in the air. "Well, we could start with Shade's attempt to end him while he was unconscious, Hagen tapping into his greatest fear to ambush us with giant horned bears, or maybe the part where you finally decided to try and make the bond with him. All things he might need to be privy to, don't you think?"

I place my finger to my lips and shush him. "Keep it down. He just woke up from his worst nightmare, and he has the biggest gashes I've ever seen across his torso. He couldn't even stay awake long enough to eat something. Let's give him some time to gain his strength back. Once he's healed, we can tell him everything."

He turns to walk away but calls out over his shoulder. "Fine, but three moons max. I doubt he'll even need that much time. He is a deity after all."

That much is true. A deity who can certainly heal faster than most. Who can command the sea like no other. Whose power truly intimidates me. And if the bond is made, he will be able to feel all the ways he affects me. The way my core melts at the sound of his voice. The way my stomach flips at his touch. How truly astonished I am with the way he wields his gift. But bonded or not, I can't get lost in its pull. I have to maintain some control. There is still so much to do. I just need a little more time to tell him. Diaspor was able to gather more primith thistle. That should be enough to keep Shade detained for several more moons.

21

AERO

The nights here have grown colder, making it easier to sleep, but I've grown tired of sitting in this bed. It's been two moons since I first woke, and everyone is coddling me like a child. Especially Eva. If she brings me another bowl of broth or tries to offer me a game of knucklebones, I'm going to lose my mind. My wounds are healing rapidly. There will certainly be some scarring, but the tissue has nearly mended completely back together. I don't care what they say. I gather up my trousers and a fresh tunic. It's time I joined the world outside this room again.

I march through the small hallway outside my room and head straight out the front door before any of them can stop me. Eva, Nuala, and Liri come chasing after me, but I've already made it this far, and I'm not going back in anytime soon.

"Get back inside. You're not healed yet," Eva barks.

I ignore her, shutting my eyes and lifting my chin to the night sky. I let the fresh air fill my lungs. Its cool sensation energizes my body and refreshes my mind. I feel alive again. Really alive.

"No chance. I'm done healing," I say, lifting my tunic to show her the closed wounds.

Her brow furrows with worry. "It's too soon."

Liri takes a closer look and purses her lips in mild approval. "It is looking good. If he feels ready, I say let him be."

Not hearing what she wanted, Eva folds her arms and scoffs. What's her problem? She should be overjoyed that we can pack up and get back to following the bloom. I'm sure it's driving her crazy by now. The others come out to see what all the commotion is about—everyone but Shade. Come to think of it, I haven't seen him since the faloths attacked. Feliks pats me on the back. "I'll gather some kindling. It will be nice to take some time to catch up around a fire. And Evanthe just gathered some auxolot fruit today. Apparently, it's divine cooked over an open flame." He winks at Eva. She glares at him. What the fuck is going on?

Either they were right and the charred auxolot is delicious, or my ravenous appetite will trick my mind into eating anything right now. Eva hasn't said a word since we sat down. On any other occasion, I would be goading her about it, but the pale color of her face tells me she isn't doing so well. I lift the last piece of fruit in her direction. "Aren't you going to try any?" I ask.

She shakes her head. Something definitely isn't right. "What's wrong, Eva?"

Her fearful gaze slowly shifts toward Feliks. He folds his arms and raises his brows, challenging her. "Go on. Tell him. Or I will."

"Is it Shade? Did one of the faloths get to him?" I ask.

After taking a deep breath, she clears her throat. "No, Shade wasn't harmed by the faloths. However, he is currently locked in Nuala's attic."

Locked in her attic? I glance up at the peak of her cottage.

"Can't say I'm mad about that, but do tell me why."

"W-why don't we talk about the faloths first. Liri wanted to know if you had spent any time with Hagen," Eva says.

That's an odd deviation, but it would be good to know how to avoid the faloths in the future. "The only time I spent near him was the night we arrived—when Liri introduced us. Why would she need to know that?"

"Feliks told us about the bear in the cage when you were a boy. How they are your greatest fear. And it seems that faloths were all but extinct when Liri and the others were here all those years ago. It just seems odd that we would randomly be attacked by so many."

My stomach turns with the mention of my time in that cage as a youngling.

Liri leans forward. "Did you tell anyone else about them? Anyone could have passed the message along to him." She sadly lowers her head. "I'm not sure who we can trust anymore."

I recall the young male from the village who had been pestering me one of the days I went to get water from the stream. "There was a young Fae who begged me to tell him about my most frightful battle. I thought nothing of it. He seemed truly intrigued. There's no way he was spying for Hagen."

Liri sighs. "Anything is possible. Under the Mortia's influence, I'm sure King Murrick would gladly breed those creatures to do his bidding."

All that time, Hagen had been lurking in the shadows, eating it up like a starved rat. "I should have been more careful," I mutter.

"None of us saw it coming, Aero. It's not your fault," Liri says.

I draw my attention back to Eva. Her knee is bobbing up and down at a rapid pace, and she can't seem to stop fidgeting with the hem of her skirt. I'm not the most observant when it comes to women, but this one I know, and she is definitely nervous about something. "Tell me why you have Shade locked up in the attic," I say.

Her weary gaze shifts my way, blinking rapidly. "When you were still unconscious, I woke to find him trying to strangle you."

Her words are quiet, as if saying them out loud will prompt my head to erupt, and I'm afraid it might. I've always had my reasons for despising the wine deity, but this is on a whole new level. Growling, I look to Feliks. "Please explain."

"As they were the only two in the room, and he is a deity with bonding potential, Liri and Nuala have drugged him with primith thistle until we can come up with a better solution." He glares at Eva. "Why don't *you* tell him about that, Evanthe."

"I think we should try to bond," she blurts out.

Her chest rises and falls with her rapid breaths, and her pupils are dilated to the size of drachmas. I can hardly believe what I'm hearing. Did she just say what I think she said? Or am I hearing things? Maybe I'm not feeling very well yet.

"What did you say?" I ask with disbelief.

"You heard me. I'm done doing this. I'm done traipsing through all the Fae Realm with both of you, wondering which one I'm going to end up with. Let's just get it over with."

Her voice is thick with resentment. It's quite possibly the least appealing proposal of sorts I've ever heard, but I can't help the grin from spreading across my face.

"And you want to try bonding with me first?"

"Don't ask foolish questions," she spits. But it's worth the glare she throws my way. I much prefer her this way to the coddling woman she's been while I've been holed up in that room.

It takes more self-restraint than I thought possible to refrain from climbing up into that attic and ripping Shade from limb to limb, but I made a promise to Eva that we would complete the bonding ceremony first.

Phira joined me this morning to gather water and tell me everything she knows about bonding. Learning what Eva already knows, I can see why she might have been anxious to tell me. It's a lot to ask of someone. To allow them to feel what you feel. They say it's not against the Accord to marry another when bonded with someone else. Phira said, given the conditions of the bond, it rarely happens, and I can see why. Not that I want to marry another. And I'm not afraid to know what goes on inside Eva, but I can't deny the dread of her having such a grip on me. For her to know the vulnerable things I hide. It's more than unnerving.

"I can't help but feel like we are preparing for your wedding," Feliks says, tossing me a leather hide and a knot of rope as we pack up supplies for the group to use in setting up the ceremony. They've agreed the best place would be where the Sunderline Woods meet Twiltrie Lake. Apparently, when two Fae of different elemental families bond, it takes place where their elements would best meet —so, in our case, a shoreline. I made sure to mention I'm not a Fae, but of course they felt it was still important to follow tradition, and I am staying far away from any arguments about such things.

The only real challenge is how far away Twiltrie Lake is. It would take two moons to hike there as a group, but

Nuala has reassured us she can rift us there—just not all of us at once. The largest group she's ever rifted consisted of five Fae other than herself, so this afternoon, she and the others will rift there to set up. She will need to regain her strength through the night and return in the morning for Eva and me.

Feliks ties the last satchel shut. "Will tonight be the first night you spend alone with Evanthe?" he asks, the realization just dawning on him.

"We won't really be alone," I reply, pointing up to where the attic is located.

He brushes off the retort. "He's hardly there. Have you seen the effect that thistle has on him?"

"I haven't paid him a visit."

I make it sound as if I don't pay the snake any mind, but truthfully, I don't think I could restrain myself from killing him if I did go up there. Tonight will be the first night I'm alone with Eva, though. I don't know what to expect. So much has been left unsaid between us, and I prefer it that way. There are so many other ways I'd like to show her just how right she was in choosing me.

"Well, try your best not to flood the place and enjoy your last night as a free man," he snickers, heading toward Nuala and the others.

"I'll still be a free man!" I shout after him.

I'll still be a free man.

They might believe this is only about saving the realms.

But it's so much more than that.

22

EVANTHE

The cottage is so empty and quiet I could hear a pin drop.

The others left a while ago, and Shade is so thistled out of his mind I don't know if he's capable of making a peep. Aero sits across from me, reading one of the old leatherbound Fae tales Nuala keeps on her shelves. The warm candlelight and flames from the fireplace dance along the dark, wooden walls around us. I take in the way the muscles of his forearm flex as he turns the page, how intently his eyes follow the words, as if they are in a race to the end of the story. I never would have imagined a man like him would have such an interest in reading. The men banished to Baros have always been described as ruthless brutes with more brawn than brains. He certainly has the brawn, but I can't say he lives up to the mindless legends I've read of.

If the bond links us the way Phira told me it will, this will be the last night we spend together as two entirely separate individuals. Once it ties us, he will be able to sit across from me and know exactly how I'm feeling. He will know how frustrated he makes me without me saying a word, but worst...he will know what the sound of his voice, the hint of his scent, or even the slightest brush of his finger across my hand does to me.

"Losing interest in that story already?" he asks, peering up from his book, a glimmer in his eye.

I quickly open it up and flip back to the beginning. "No, I've already finished reading it."

I've actually read through it several times now since we left Parea. I should have taken more books from my aunts' library, but I never thought the journey would stretch this far.

"Would you like to pick out something new?" he says, raising a hand toward the several books perched on the shelves right behind him, an offering that isn't really about the book at all. Cautiously, I remove the knitted quilt from my lap. I don't look, but I can feel his eyes trailing my body as I stand from my seat and slowly make my way toward the bookshelves. Taking another dangerous step, I remind myself to breathe until I am standing right in front of the shelves and right beside him. I try to focus on the titles scribed along the spines, but an unstoppable force pulsates through the air, making it impossible. Unable to deny it, I feel myself being pulled closer toward him. Without a word, his warm hand glides around the small of my waist and pulls me into him. I fall onto his lap, and his lips find the soft spot behind my ear, the hairs of his stubble sending a shiver down my spine.

"No, we can't do this," I say, my mouth betraying my body.

Unrelenting, his full mouth moves along my neck, grazing my jaw and stopping just long enough to reply, "Give me one good reason why we shouldn't."

"We're enemies by blood." I gasp.

He wraps his fingers around the nape of my neck and runs the pad of his thumb across my lower lip. "Enemies who are about to be bonded for an eternity. Look me in the eye and tell me you don't want this. Tell me you wouldn't wonder what it would have been like for all of eternity if we don't."

"I won't wonder. I don't want this," I lie, my eyes still pinched shut.

"Open your eyes, Eva," he growls.

My heart races as they flutter open.

"Look me in the eye and tell me," he repeats.

My mouth opens, but nothing comes out. Under his gaze, I can't force myself to say the words, and he knows it.

"Stand up," he says.

I hesitate, my desire to feel his touch grappling with the anger I still hold for him. But my feet find the floor once more, and his fingers trail down the bare skin of my arm, leaving a trail of goosebumps in his wake. He grabs the hem of my shirt, sliding it over the top of my head, letting my breasts fall. Never looking away, he tosses it behind himself and reaches for the string of my skirt. I feel the leather strand pull taut when he unlaces it all the way. His hot breath skims my stomach as he shimmies it down my thighs along with my undergarment, letting it pool on the floorboards beneath me. Then he spreads my legs so he can pull them around him as he places me onto his lap. My cheeks burn with the slickness between my thighs leaving a mark upon his trousers, and I curse myself for letting him have this effect on me. It doesn't slip his attention. He cocks an arrogant brow. I reach back to impale him, but he catches my wrist and holds it firmly in place.

"Say it. I won't go any further until I hear the words," he says, pressing the hard length of him against me, and I can't help but squeeze my thighs around his hips.

"Fuck you," I whisper.

"You can. All you have to do is say the words," he growls before capturing my nipple with his mouth, letting his teeth graze the peak as the warm and cold sensation sends my heart racing until I can't take it anymore.

"I want you," I blurt out between gritted teeth.

Without hesitation, he lifts me from his lap and gently lays me onto the fur pelt in front of the fire. Only for the sake of torturing me more, he takes his time removing his tunic and trousers. The soft light flickers across every hard line of his body. My fists ball up, clenching the fur between my fingers to refrain from reaching out and touching him.

He lowers to his knees and places his mouth on my thighs, running soft kisses up my hips and then my stomach. Humming as his lips find mine, one hand caresses my left breast, the other pressing between my thighs, skillfully driving inside me, touching a place that's almost too intense and somehow finding it repeatedly. I can't believe this is actually happening. My back bows off the fur pelt as tremors roll through my body, climbing higher and higher. I'm about to fall over the edge when he slides his hands beneath me and pulls me on top of him so I'm straddling him.

Darker than usual, his gray-speckled eyes devour me.

"Fuck, you're perfect, Eva."

His hands wrap around my hips, guiding himself to my entrance, and he drives inside me. I cry out, my fingers digging into his chest as he remains still, letting my body adjust to the fullness of him.

"Quiet, Eva. I won't have him hearing you. Those sounds are only for me. Do you understand?" he asks.

Unable to speak, I nod rapidly.

As if Shade knows what's happening beneath him, a groan sounds from above, making me shudder. It's just the old wooden floors. I clench my jaw, trying to keep the pleasure from escaping when Aero withdraws. Tightening his grip on my hips, he thrusts inside me again, filling me more perfectly than I ever could have imagined, and I know in this moment that it will never be the same with anyone else. That I am in *so* much trouble.

I begin to rotate my hips, rocking back and forth as he,

too, picks up the pace. Seeming to grow even harder, he reaches a place inside me that makes me see stars. My body tightens and shakes uncontrollably until my eyes roll back, and my mouth falls open in a scream that I could never silence.

He drives into me once more, following me into the constellations, his groan rippling through me.

"Fuck, Eva," my name rumbles from his mouth so deeply it shakes me to my core.

"Wake up, Evanthe. It's time to rift."

Hovering above me, Nuala smiles far too enthusiastically for this hour of the morning. I sit up, rubbing my eyes as she hands me a cup of mushroom water. The strong, earthy scent assaults my nose, but I take a sip to appease her. I glance around the room, letting out a sigh of relief as Aero is nowhere in sight. I know we are about to try bonding in front of everyone, but Nuala walking in on us in bed together is just too much too soon. I can barely wrap my head around what happened last night. Finding it apparent that I'm still a bit sore, I let out a groan as I find my feet.

"Have you seen the satchel I left? Aero was supposed to make sure it's ready," Nuala asks, looking around the room frantically. Just as she turns, he is standing in the doorway with the bag she's been eating the world for dangling from his finger.

"Speaking of Hades..." I grumble.

The sentiment not lost on Aero, he flashes a roguish grin, sending goosebumps down my arms and making my nipples stand at attention through my nightgown. Scrambling to cover up, I reach for my cloak. I hate him. He will forever hold this power over me. It's only a matter of time before my strength wanes and I give in to him. I can see myself teetering on the edge of a cliff, staring down at the raging water below. He is that stormy sea, luring me closer. If I don't keep my balance, I will fall right into his swell. I have to hang on just a bit longer. Long enough to ensure my people are safe from the Mortia and from his men back in Baros. I can't let them take back Meraki.

"As soon as you're dressed, we will be ready to go," Nuala says, glancing up at the ceiling. "But I'll need to make sure the primith thistle hasn't worn off first."

"Do you need any help?" I ask, hoping the answer will be no, as I'd rather not see his face until the bonding ceremony is over. If it doesn't work and I'm forced to bond with him...I don't know what I'll do. Nuala shakes her head. "No, I've got it. It will only take a moment." I don't need to ask any questions as Liri explained how the process works. All it takes is the smoke from a small burning bundle of the plant, and his fire magic comes crashing to a halt for quite some time.

Nuala makes her way up into the crawl space, and I wave my hands to shoo Aero away so I can change in the privacy of my room. I expect him to make note of how much of my body he is familiar with now, but he only nods respectfully and waits for me outside the cottage.

Seeming pleased with herself, Nuala closes the front door and leads us to the meadow in the distance. I've had plenty of time to prepare for this, but somehow, I've completely neglected to ask her how being rifted will feel. She throws her satchel over her shoulder and reaches her hands out for ours, gesturing for us to lock hands as well. Aero's hand engulfs mine, pulsing his grip ever so lightly to reassure me.

"How does this work exactly?" I ask, my voice shaking a bit.

"We all stay connected, and you have nothing to worry about," she says.

It all sounds so simple, but I know magic is more complicated than that. For every push there is a pull. If this realm has taught me anything, it's that there are always limits. There are always rules.

"How does your gift work? Can you rift us anywhere?" I ask, hopeful I'm not prying too much.

"Uh," she says, pausing to determine the best way to explain it. "I can rift a small group anywhere that at least one of us has been. However, it works best when I have been there myself. See, I need to be able to picture this place. To know the way it smells and sounds. If one has a vivid memory of that place, I can pull it from them and feel it for myself. But today we are rifting to a place I know very well. In fact, it's one of my favorite places."

Her eyes widen as if to let us know we are in for a treat,

and in this moment, I am glad Aero and I are not bonded, because that would mean he would be able to feel how terrified I am to let her rift me. I recall all the girls growing up back in Meraki, tumbling over backward across the fields like it was nothing, their feet flying over their heads, bodies bending with ease as they roared with laughter. I tried my best but could never seem to gather the courage to go all the way. It always seemed so unnatural to me. Each time my feet would almost reach that place, I would tuck in, bringing them back down in a hurry, cursing profanities beneath my breath. Letting go of that control has never been a strong suit of mine, and I'm well aware. Trusting Nuala like this feels eerily similar, but I grab hold of her and Aero's hands tightly, shut my eyes, and before I can tuck away, we are off.

23
EVANTHE

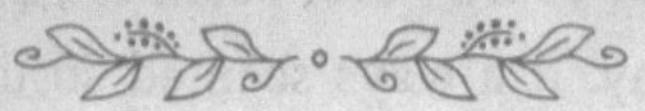

My heart leaps into my throat, and I fear my stomach is going to follow behind and fall right out of my mouth. My tongue fills with the flavors of tangy drachma and bitter citrus. I thought this would feel more like flying, more like tumbling, but it's nothing like that. It's a sharp snap of breaking away from one place and catapulting at the speed of light toward another so fast it feels like I might shatter into a thousand pieces, all of them scattering across the Fae Realm for eternity.

When we come to a halt, the worst ache fills my head, as if my mind hasn't quite caught up with the rest of me. I hunch over, bracing myself through the pain, as does Aero.

"You could have warned us about this part," he murmurs.

"Sorry, probably should have mentioned that. It takes some getting used to, that's for sure," she replies, patting him on the back as if that will lessen the pain.

Once the throbbing stops and I'm able to catch my breath, I take a look around, expecting to see the others, but they're nowhere in sight. "Are you sure you rifted us to the right place? Because I don't think I can take another ride like that today," I mutter.

Securing her satchel, Nuala points in the distance. "Yeah, I didn't rift us to the exact location. I'm pretty accurate, but I don't quite trust myself well enough to land right beside a lake, and I don't think you would have enjoyed arriving in the middle of it. Especially with it being your first time rifting."

Well, she is right about that. I would not have found that pleasant, but it definitely doesn't give me more confidence in her abilities. Let's hope none of our future destinations involve water. Aero draws in a deep, displeased breath, and it's clear he isn't impressed either. "Exactly how far away are we?" he asks.

"Oh, not far. Just through those trees up ahead. No more than half a day's hike," she replies, her voice full of cheery enthusiasm.

"*Half* a *day's* hike?" I grumble with disbelief.

She winces and shrugs her shoulders. "Maybe I was a bit over-cautious."

"Yeah, I'd say so," Aero says, marching ahead.

It's late in the day when we stop to rest and eat something. Nuala pulls out one pouch filled with berries, another with nuts, and we devour them like ravenous animals. She watches us with wide eyes and wonder. "You two have quite the appetites. Do all humans and deities eat like this?" she asks.

Aero wipes his mouth and glances at me out of the corner of his eye, and I know what he's thinking. We definitely worked up an appetite after last night's activities.

"It's been a long week," I reply, not missing the corner of his mouth curling with amusement.

Full and hydrated, we move on, taking in the beauty of this part of the realm. The trees are just as tall, but their leaves and blooms are brighter. And the sounds of the forest are different. Less croaking and buzzing, and more humming and churring.

"What's this forest called?" I ask Nuala.

"Sunderline Thicket," she replies with a nostalgic smile. "I've been coming here since I was a girl. Liri wasn't able to join me often as she had more royal responsibilities."

"It's very different from the Repenlow Wood," I say, observing the way the breeze tickles the leaves above us.

"That it is. Just wait until you see Twiltrie Lake. I know magic is held by beings like us— Fae, deity, even some humans. But I've always thought Twiltrie Lake had magic of its own. I told my mother if I ever bonded with another, I wanted the ceremony to be here."

Her head falls a bit, and it's clear that her mother is no longer alive. She may have fallen prey to King Murrick, but I don't ask. No one likes to relive times like those.

"It's still possible that you may bond with someone one day, no?" I ask, giving my best impression of a hopeful person.

Swallowing her grief, she reaches into the bushes and pulls them aside, revealing the most serene landscape I've seen. "I present to you...Twiltrie Lake," she says, a cheerful lilt back in her voice.

I stand in awe, stunned by its beauty. I think I even hear Aero's breath catch, but he doesn't let his face show it. Feliks and Hera spot us and come running, their faces lit up like two children on an adventure.

"You're finally here," Hera gasps.

"Just in time for a quick smoke before the ceremony," Feliks says, holding up his pipe and dragging Aero off for some sort of male bonding ritual. Hera and Nuala walk me down to the edge of the lake where Liri and Diaspor are driving long wooden sticks topped with kindling into the dirt. Liri brushes the dirt from her hands and wraps me in her embrace. Letting me go, she stretches her arms out toward the scene before us. "What do you think? Isn't it gorgeous?" she asks, her eyes wide with wonder.

I take it all in, the rising and falling landscape hugging the curve of the lake's deep, dark waters. I look down to find my reflection crystal clear upon the smooth, still surface, and my heart lurches for a moment. The pool reminds me of a different place, a different time, not all that long ago, only a short distance from my home in the thicket outside Parea—the Dyre Waters. The darkness swallowing me, paralyzing me. The water shockingly warm and smooth, my skin slipping though it like a bar of soap in a bath as my body slowly sank deeper and deeper into its trance. Washing up onto that hard surface and wiping the blood away from my knees. The cavern's scent of mold and sulfur fill my nose as if I am truly there. A weighted dread twists in my gut, and a low beating sound drums in my ears until his voice rips through it all. *"You can't hide from me. You and I are the same. I can hear your dark, little heart racing."*

A heated fury rises up inside me, swallowing my fear. He doesn't want this to happen. "You are scared, Hale Mortia, and you should be," I whisper under my breath.

"What was that?" Diaspor asks.

"Nothing. Just agreeing with Liri. This is wonderful," I say, an effort to reassure myself more than them.

Finding me satisfied with the location, Hera whisks me away to help me get ready for the ceremony. Behind a row of trees tightly woven with gobs of ivy, she's procured a little nook with two chairs, surely built by Diaspor, and a blue gown made of the finest silk I've ever seen. "Where did you get this?" I ask, hesitating to touch it with my grimy hands.

"It's one of Liri's. She knew this day would come, so she's carried it with her all this time." Bouncing on the balls of her feet, Hera lifts it up, sizing it to my body. "I let out the hips a bit, and I think it's going to be just perfect. Try it on. The ivy grows so thick here I don't think a dragonfly could peak a glimpse through it."

I glance back at the wall of flora. She's right. The space is quite sheltered, but I still lift my finger to draw another layer of the vines for safe measure. The gown slides over my body, and I turn so Hera can run the laces down the back. She grunts a bit as she pulls them taut and turns me back around to assess her work.

"It's definitely a bit tighter than it was on the princess, but if I'm being honest, I think it suits you better. But don't tell her I said that. I don't need her frying my hair to a crisp in my sleep." She runs her fingers through the long black strands. "Aside from my arsenal of weapons back home, it's my only prized possession." She winks.

I have no mirror, no way to know if this is a flattering garment on me, but looking down at the dress, it seems to lay nicely, so I take her word for truth. "Sit down," she says, patting the back of one of the chairs. Pulling up the skirt of the gown, I do as she asks and try to make myself comfortable. She pulls the thread tied at the bottom of my braid and unlaces it with her fingers, working through the strands until they are less of a mangled mess.

"Are you nervous?" she asks, knowing full well what a loaded question that is.

"Of course I am," I mutter.

Dividing my hair into sections, she giggles. "Who would have thought the great Hera Terzi would be braiding Evanthe Sideris's hair on her wedding day," she says, cackling now.

"It's *not* a wedding," I snap.

"It may not be called that, but it might as well be. Two people, Fae or deity...whatever, agreeing to be tied to the other for the rest of their lives, no?" she asks, weaving a braid around the crown of my head.

I try to think of a good rebuttal, but there really isn't one. The thought makes me squirm in my seat. I'd like to see how well she'd be handling this right now. It's not like I had a choice. I'm not going to let them all burn in Mortia Underrealm flames. I clear my throat. "You know, what I'm doing is actually quite courageous. A bonding is much more than a spousal marriage. It goes much deeper. A responsibility *most* would find far too terrifying."

She pulls on my braid just enough to send a jolt of pain down my scalp, but I don't react.

"Don't tell me you're not hoping that this bond goes through, responsibility or not. I see the way you look at him. You can't fake that kind of attraction, and I don't blame you. If I were faced with such a responsibility, I would at least try to make the most of it too."

Damn her. How does she always find a way to throw dirt in my face and come out looking clean? She couldn't possibly know what this has been like for me. But oddly enough, I'm glad she's here. I would have liked for it to have been Sorrow and my mother, but I've grown fonder of Hera than I'd wished. Just as I should keep a watchful eye on Aero, the other should be on her. When the day comes that the moon swallows the sun, she won't think twice about ending my life. And I need to remind myself of that each day that we grow closer. She is still my competition. A Stone Holder like any other.

"How's our guardian doing?" Liri asks, peering her head through the ivy and stepping into our sanctuary.

"Looking good if you ask me," Hera replies.

Liri takes a seat on the chair across from me and crosses her legs. "The ceremony will require very little of you, but there is one small task you must perform in order for it to take full effect. When I say the words, 'Aero Vouvali, with you goes the earth,' you are going to coat your thumb with the offering I give you and wipe it across his forehead."

"That's it?" I ask, expecting there to be more.

"That's all. Simple." She leans over and kisses my cheek. "You look stunning. I will see you out there soon." And just like that, she's gone.

Circling around to the front of me, Hera carefully prods and pulls at the crests of the woven strands of hair until it seems she is pleased with her work. I lift my hands to feel the artful masterpiece, the way most of my hair is pulled up in scallops, but a few long strands fall freely around my face. I know without being able to see that it's better than I could have done, and all my rules that keep her at a distance fade away. "Thank you," I say.

"It's nothing," she says, brushing me off. But I reach out and take her hand before she can walk away. "No, really. You didn't have to come here, to this realm. You could have stayed back in Meraki, but you didn't, and I'm grateful."

She holds my sincere gaze for just a moment, then breaks away as she yells over her shoulder. "They'll be expecting you down by the water soon. Don't take too long."

24

EVANTHE

"**I**f you don't want to walk alone, I'll walk beside you," Diaspor says.

The voice of a loon, or some similar creature, sounds in the distance. Some find their call eerie, but I've always loved it. The soft hoot soothes my nerves. It's sweet of Diaspor to think of my comfort. Even if this event may benefit him as well, he didn't have to make such an effort. If I were getting married back in Parea, before Athena lodged that spear into my mother, it would have been her walking alongside me. Diaspor tilts from heel to toe, a bit unsure what he should be doing in this moment. It lifts my spirts. I guess it would be nice to have someone to hold onto, in case my knees buckle underneath me and I start to go down. But I want to do this on my own.

"I'll be alright to walk by myself, but thank you for the offer," I reply.

"Alright, when Feliks starts to play, that's your cue," he says.

My heart fluttering, I swallow the lump in my throat and nod. I can't believe this day has come.

Convinced that I'm not in need of anything else, he retreats to join the others. I watch as Phira lights the last torch lining the rim of the water from the cover of a fern leaf hedge. They've paved a path leading to a circle where Liri stands surrounded by what appears to be a moat of water adorned with blooms of every shape and color. A path that will lead me to Aero. The one I've called my enemy. Flashes of his hands wrapped around my hips last night ripple through my mind. My lover.

Then the music begins to sound. My feet start to move, and I don't dare take my eyes off of them. Reaching the path beside the torches, I look up to see him standing in the circle beside Liri.

Great Divine, he's handsome.

Not in a conventional way. In an unnatural way. No one should look like that. He doesn't wear the kind of traditional, formal garments a groom would wear back in Meraki, but a simple black tunic with a V-shaped collar adorned with the leather pattern a warrior might wear. A thick leather belt held by a dark-bronze metal buckle sits around his waist. His dark, shoulder-length hair is drawn back into a high braid on top of his head, and several other pieces are woven along the sides. I nearly stop to stare at him but somehow manage to keep my legs moving. My body is humming yet numb at the same time. It's only when I reach the circle that I am able to breathe again.

I can feel Aero's gaze burning across my skin, and I can't help but look up and meet it. It feels like all the blood in my head has fled my body, and I'm floating with the oddest feeling. It's like I've been here before. My mind is torn between how familiar this all is and knowing it's the first time in my life that I've been here. Fucking Hades. I close my eyes to gather myself and make sure to draw my attention to Liri when I open them. She smiles knowingly, as if she and I are kindred. And I guess, in some strange way, we are. She opens the book in her hands, and the ceremony begins.

"Tonight, we gather to witness the bonding of Aero Vouvali and Evanthe Sideris. As many of you already know, a bond is sacred above any other ties." She looks directly from Aero then to me. "It will draw your souls together and give your bonded access to your deepest desires, your greatest pain, and your most blissful joy. When apart, you will yearn to be closer, an ache that is impossible to ignore. But when returned to each other, you will find your strength. Together, two bonded are stronger than they ever could have been apart.

Once it takes hold, there will be no one who can question it. There will be no magic that can break it, and you will both be marked with a symbol of your undying bond."

Bel hands her a small glass bottle filled with water. She places it into Aero's hands. Diaspor crouches down and scoops a handful of mud from underneath the moat surrounding us and places it into Liri's hand. A glimmer in her eye, she gestures with her other hand for me to make a cup with mine. I do as she directs, and she places the cool substance into my palm.

"Aero Vouvali, with you will go the earth."

I place my thumb into the mud. His speckled eyes capture mine as I run my thumb across his forehead, leaving a tawny streak.

"Evanthe Sideris, with you will go the sea."

Without hesitation, he presses the opening of his bottle to his thumb and paints the warm water across my forehead. A small drop falls from my brow, but I don't dare wipe it away. The princess places our hands together, the bottle of water and pool of mud sitting together.

"May uyla waters bring zu treui den healing
May uyla earth bind den steady zu
From above may uyla cheppel tresdna bright den constant
Den below may uyla stone kekkel firm den patient
Za manei the Evanthe Sideris den the, Aero Vouvali bound
sewq eternity."

"May your waters bring you life and healing
May your earth bind and steady you
From above may your stars shine bright and constant
And below may your stone be firm and patient
I name the Evanthe Sideris and the Aero Vouvali bound for eternity."

A round of applause roars from the crowd, and I hold onto Aero's hands tightly, waiting for a rush of something.

Aero lets go of me, and I'm certain it didn't work. There are no sparks, no magic to be seen that would signify a change, but then an overwhelming sense of relief washes over me. I look up to see Aero staring at his forearm with awe. He lifts it to face me, and my jaw drops.

Trembling, I pull at the sleeve of my right arm but find nothing. My heart sinks into my stomach. Aero gestures for me to look at the other arm. I can feel all their eyes on me, waiting with bated breath. This is it. If nothing is there, that means I'm meant to bond with Shade. I cringe with fear and slowly pull the fabric away to reveal my fate and leap at the sight. The same marking upon Aero's arm is slowly appearing upon mine. I watch as the last few black lines of the mark scroll across the delicate skin of my underarm. The symbol of a nautical compass, bursts of blooms rushing around its center, and a crescent moon shining over all of it. Every black mark aligned with perfect realism. So evocative it's hard to believe each petal and prong aren't actually real. Once the last bloom is complete, I raise my arm to the others, coaxing them into a roaring cheer once more.

The perfect joining of our gifts, one for Aero's sea and one of my earth, but the moon is something else. I look down at the crescent symbol upon the hilt of my mother's sword sitting in my garter and smile, knowing she is here with me. She is here for this bonding.

A small feast is set up upon a table—curated by Diaspor, no doubt. Aero peers down to inspect the detailed design of the stools. The legs of half of them are carved into the shape of raging waves, the other half rows of climbing flora. Diaspor stands beside Liri and Bel, awaiting our reaction, a nervous look upon his face.

"How did you do all this in just one evening? You didn't have to go through so much trouble," I say, truly overcome with emotion.

"It was the least we could do. Most Fae bonding ceremonies take place after days of traditional celebration," he replies.

"But what happens if the pair doesn't bond? Isn't that a huge letdown for everyone involved?" Hera asks.

"That's honestly the best part. There are few things that shock or surprise a Fae after so many years. The anticipation is delicious."

"You're all absolutely devious," Hera replies.

Bel bursts into a Hades-bent laugh and pops a piece of cheese into his mouth. Aero lifts his chin suspiciously as he examines the table full of bread, fruit, and cheeses.

"Where did you get all this cheese from?" he asks.

Nuala takes a seat at the table next to Liri. "I have two civets behind my cottage," she replies, as if we will understand what that means. Liri, picking up on our confusion, explains. "They're like the goats of your realm."

"Evanthe, you have a goat back home, don't you?" Hera asks through a mouthful of bread.

I had nearly forgotten about Gusta—all the time I

spent milking her and carrying it into market for the drachma I needed to buy weapons. It seems like a lifetime ago. Feliks, already a few glasses of wine in, raises his goblet of wine in an effort to gather our attention.

"I'd like to make a toast. Never did I think this day would come. Well, to be fair, never did I know this was a thing up until recently, but nonetheless, I am stunned." An abrupt hiccup causes him to pause. "Like I was saying, my big brother has been swatting away the advances of women looking to tie him down since—"

Aero knocks the goblet of wine from his hands, and Feliks loses his balance, falling off his stool. Dusting himself off, his brother crawls back up on his stool, and a strange sensation jabs at me. Aero doesn't let it show, but a wave of concern wells up inside me that I'm certain isn't mine. Then I remember the bond. It's his worry that I'm feeling. And somehow, I know it's for my well-being. He doesn't want Feliks's drunken comment to make me jealous. Well, obviously I'm not. I pause, taking note of any lingering feelings inside that might suggest otherwise. I don't think I am. I'm not.

"What's wrong with you?" I ask, jabbing Aero with my elbow.

"Hmm," he replies with a low rumble.

I wait for him to explain. What the Hades is, '*Hmm*,' supposed to mean? Sometimes he does live up to the men of his lineage.

"I'd always wondered what that temper of yours felt like. Now, I know."

Liri waves at me, smiling from across the table like a proud mother on her daughter's wedding day.

"Well, get used to it," I say through gritted teeth, doing my best to smile back at her.

"It's going to be a long eternity," he grumbles.

25
EVANTHE

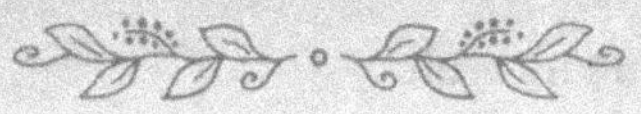

After filling up on bread and wine, we dance until our feet are aching and our eyes begin drooping. The last of the wine was drunk long ago, and there isn't a crumb left on the table. Hera and Feliks have already passed out between the roots of a tree when Bel takes our hands. "Follow me," he says.

"Aren't we sleeping here with everyone else?" I ask.

"On your bonding night? Absolutely not," he replies, shocked I'd ask.

A prodding irritation tells me even Aero seems a bit offended by my assumption. He drags us through another thick row of bushes to a clearing, where a canvas-covered shelter sits, its entrance lit up with candles of different heights and widths. It's like every young Parean girl's dream. Maybe a bit more rustic, but very close to what any of them would imagine for such a night.

It never crossed my mind that they would make special arrangements for us. All this time, I've been too busy reminding myself that this is no more than a necessity. A way for all of us to survive, but it's clearly so much more to them. And I'm afraid it's starting to become so much more for me as well.

Bel claps his hands together. "Well, if you don't need anything else, this is where I leave you. Try not to be too loud." And with a wink, he dashes back toward the others, leaving Aero and me alone—not for the first time ever, but for the first time as a bonded pair. We both stare at the welcoming tent. Even from a distance, I can see it's filled with plush fur pelts, much like the one we laid upon last night, and feather-filled pillows. But I'll be damned if I'm the first one to jump at the chance to lay with him again.

Seeming to sense my reluctance, Aero lifts a hand toward the opening of the shelter. "Ladies first. That is... unless you'd prefer I slept out here."

I roll my eyes. He knows exactly what he's doing. We both know I won't make myself out to be a cruel wretch and make him sleep out here in the thicket while I'm cozy inside there. Lifting my skirt, I climb inside and remove my boots. Not far behind me, he finds a place on the other side of the tent and makes himself comfortable with his book. Alright then. I guess I'll just make myself comfortable.

I pull the stockings and crystal bloom down from my

thighs and place them inside my satchel. I try not to be, but I can't help feeling offended that he would rather read that story over paying attention to me. He's enjoying this. Grabbing one of the quilts, I lie down and roll over so I'm not facing him. At least that way he won't be able to see my frustration. Then I hear a deep chuckle from across the tent. I'm such a fucking idiot. *The bond, Evanthe.* He can feel everything. And all I'm gathering from him is pure amusement. I'm going to kill him. We'll never make it an eternity.

I try my best to think of something else. Anything else. But the boning of this dress is digging into my ribs. I toss and turn, but it's no use. I need to get comfortable. Luckily, the shelter is tall enough that I can stand up to try and remove this gown. Reaching back, I do my best but can't quite reach the end of the laces. I struggle a moment more, knowing he's lapping this up. "A little help here?" I blurt.

With a sigh, he gets up from his comfortable spot. "Well, since you asked so nicely."

"I didn't know it was so much to ask," I snip.

His fingers untie the bow and fumble with the laces until they finally feel loose enough for me to let it drop to the ground, leaving me in nothing but my undergarments. I bend down to reach for a quilt to cover myself, but he stops me and growls in a deep voice. "Don't you dare."

He pulls me up, the front of him pressed to my back. His hand roams from the small of my waist and brushes across my breast, sending a shiver down my spine.

"I-I hate you," I manage to stutter, terrified of what comes next.

His fingers hook around the strap of my undergarment, the sheer fabric falling from my shoulder at his command. I reach up to stop him, my hand trembling. Knowing it's not what I really want, he swats it away. His free hand finds its way between my legs as his lips graze across my ear.

"Tell me just how much you hate me."

And I know, without a doubt, that he knows just how badly I want to give in and let him take control. It doesn't matter how hard I try to hide it or to think of something else. There is no hiding from him. But it goes both ways, and I know just how badly he is aching to oblige. So I let the venom fall from my lips.

"I hate...the way you tell me what to do. I hate your stupid, perfect smile and your big, dumb shoulders. I hate it when you're right and that somehow you know what I need even when I don't. But none of it amounts to the way I hate myself every single time I try to push you away."

Each word rips through the night air around us, and a tortured groan escapes him. In the blink of an eye, I'm off my feet and on my back. He frees himself from his trousers and pulls my hips down to meet him. I brace myself. But he pauses, pressing himself against my entrance and over the most sensitive parts of me, teasing me over and over.

When it feels like I can't take much more, he thrusts forward until he's fully inside me, and every star in the night sky flashes before my eyes. Rolling my hips along with his rhythm, a wave of pleasure rocks through my body.

"Great Divine," I gasp.

His fingers grab a fistful of my hair, pulling me into his dark gaze.

"Not yet, Eva. Not until I tell you."

His voice rumbles through me, making my legs shake. A coiling heat builds inside me, and I lift my chin, pressing my lips to his and bucking my hips, willing him to move, but he remains infuriatingly steady. An unnatural whimper escapes me, and I want to pass away with embarrassment.

"Do you want more?" he asks, searching my needy gaze, knowing exactly what I want.

"Yes," I breathe.

He pins my hands above my head and pulsates inside me. "Tell me you're mine."

"I'm yours. I'm fucking yours," I cry out.

"That's right. Now come for me."

Release shudders through my body, one earthquaking rumble at a time, as he thrusts into me, drawing out each aftershock until all that's left is the sound of my heart hammering in my chest and the bond that ties our souls together. It sweeps through me, latching onto him for dear life. There is no telling where I begin and he ends.

Aero crashes into me once more, and the night sky trembles, the seas roar, and despite the odds, he is mine, and I am his.

Another night fades to dawn, and this time, I wake before him. He lies beside me, one hand upon his chest, the other wrapped around my waist. The light slowly begins to shine through the canvas of our shelter, and I take in one last breath of salt and sage. I want to stay in this euphoric trance forever, but I know it isn't reality. *You can do this. One step at a time.* Quietly, I slide out from his grasp and bring a blanket with me to watch the sunrise from the shoreline.

The sky lifts from the still, dark waters, reminding me that the others will be arriving soon. It's been easy forgetting about all my responsibilities here with Aero—so easy it makes me question if I'll have the strength to leave this place and face the Mortia. But the bloom is persistent, refusing to let me ignore my duty. If it isn't prodding my thigh with its heat, it's nearly burning a hole through my satchel. I know I'm just prolonging the inevitable.

"You might as well just wake me," Aero says, startling me.

"Sorry, I forget," I reply, referring to the bond's tenacity. I, too, found it challenging to sleep when he would leave my side. "I hope it gets easier," I say, thinking of all the times we may need to be apart. I don't do well without enough sleep.

"Why? Plan on abandoning me already?" he asks, lifting a brow.

He knows the answer to that. Smug prick. I pick up my blanket and stretch. "I guess we should start packing up."

"Yeah, you should," Hera says, bursting through the trees behind us. "How've you been, love birds?"

I nearly throw up in my mouth. "I never want to hear you say those words again," I say.

"Aww, come on. It couldn't have been too bad if both of you stayed here the whole time," Feliks adds, looking to his brother for confirmation. In his true nature, Aero doesn't so much as nod.

The group lends a hand taking down the tent and gathering the remaining blankets and pelts. Phira rolls the last one up and ties it to her satchel. "Has the bloom had anything to say?" she asks, her voice lifting with a bit of hope.

I sigh. "Yes, it's been very loud." *And distracting.* "It's pointing this way," I say, pointing past the lake, straight west.

"Alright, then. Since Nuala just rifted our group here, we will hike back to the cottage today. Once we've delt with Shade, she can rift us farther west," Liri says.

Aero's jaw clenches as a dark cloud falls over him. "Is he still locked in the attic?" he asks, his voice thick with murder and his fury thrumming through our bond.

"Yes. Nuala and I have discussed the transgression, and considering the circumstances, we've decided his punishment will be death."

From the heaviness in her eyes it's clear the decision wasn't made easily.

"What kind of death?" Aero asks.

Liri glances toward Nuala. "Since the transgression was against Aero, it will be in his charge." The rifter folds her arms and huffs, clearly not in favor of their choice. How could she object? I saw him trying to choke the life from Aero. The thought of it going unpunished is inconceivable.

"Shade is guilty. Don't you believe me?" I ask.

"That doesn't matter. I'm fond of you and Aero, but this isn't the way things are done," Nuala says, stomping further ahead of us.

Diaspor, reading the confusion on my face and Aero's, leans toward us and whispers, "Never has a Fae been sentenced to death at the hands of another being that isn't also Fae. It's not something that we take lightly. Liri fought for this. For both of you. To show you that she trusts and respects you. We're putting our lives in your hands, so we are willing to protect yours."

Time moves painstakingly slow. We hiked straight through the day and night. My knees and feet ache to keep pace with the others through the Sunderline Forest. I can feel Aero growing impatient with each step bringing him closer to putting an end to Shade. I can't say I blame him. I certainly don't feel sorry for the wine god. He deserves what he has coming. Liri may have kept her fears for my soul a secret, but this is different. She deceived me for the good of all. It was her burden to bear, and I know how it ate her up inside. This...what Shade has done...is a true betrayal. It's the first time a Fae, beyond the Underrealm, has deceived me for their own gain, so I will gladly step aside and let Aero take vengeance for us both.

Just ahead of me, Liri watches Nuala with worry. I still can't believe the princess risked their friendship to prove her loyalty to me and Aero. I don't know if I would have done the same to Sorrow. I need to try and fix this.

Pushing forward, I move alongside Nuala. She doesn't acknowledge my presence.

"I want you to know that I don't take this lightly, what you're doing for us. I can't pretend to fully understand the gravity of it, but I won't forget it," I say.

"I'm not the one you should be thanking. If it were up to me, Shade may not even be sentenced to death, or at the very least, his executioner would have been one of us."

The words are a slap in the face. It's my word against his, and she would much rather take his.

"I know we've only just met, but I promise that you won't regret this. Until then, you're just going to have to trust me," I reply, less empathetic this time.

With a roll of her green eyes, she breaks away, pushing the thicket aside to reveal her cottage in the distance. Thank Zeus. I don't know if I could have gone on much longer. Aero, seeming to feel my relief, steps forward and stops the branches from slapping me in the face as the rifter abruptly lets them go.

"She seems nice," he says.

"The nicest," I reply, holding back laughter.

26

AERO

The second my satchel hits the floor of Nuala's cottage, I waste no time pulling the trap door to the attic open. Diaspor warned me that the primith thistle may have started to wear off by now, but his hands are still tied behind his back with steel chains. I take each step up slowly so he can hear his reaper coming for him.

When I reach the top, I find him sitting along the opposite wall, still detained as Diaspor said. The small space is dark and cramped like the dingy broom cupboard of a ship. He smells of too many days without bathing, and dark rings circle his eyes, but there is just enough life left inside them to feel every blow. How I have waited for this moment.

"They sent you?" he laughs mockingly.

And it's all I need to hear. I grip a handful of his greasy hair and drag him away from the wall. He opens his mouth to speak, but before he can say another word, I slam the blade of my sword down upon his wrists, cutting off his hands in one swipe. The horror that becomes his face is delicious. The realization that he just lost his only means to wield his fire.

"Are you going to seduce me out of this?" I ask, my voice thick with malice.

The pain taking effect, an unnatural sound escapes his mouth.

"That's good. Let's take you out for a little fresh air."

Grabbing the back of his collar, I drag him down the attic stairs, letting the weight of him fall with a thud down each one. I don't stop when we pass through the front door or when we reach the meadow where the others wait. Nuala and Bel gasp when they see the dismembered deity. I lock eyes with Eva. She nods with approval, and I drag his worthless form right to her feet.

"Apologize to my bonded," I command.

His eyes roll back in his head as he lifts his chin. "Never."

I slam my fist into his face. "I can do this all day."

He spits a mouthful of blood onto the grass below but still refuses to obey. I step closer, pressing the end of my sword to his piss-soaked groin. "It looks like you've had an accident."

He scowls, and I press harder.

"I'm sorry," he growls.

"That's a good lad. Now, let's go for a stroll."

I drag his body to the edge of the meadow and fill my hands with all the moisture I can gather from the air until there are two large, raging orbs hovering above both my palms. I give him a painful moment to take in the sight, then send them crashing down his throat, filling his lungs until his eyes are wide with horror. I picture his mouth pressed to Eva's, his hands placing a crown upon her head, claiming her for himself. He thought the only way he could defeat me was when I was lying unconscious on my death bed. But he was wrong. He could never defeat me. He thrashes and gasps for air until it seems he can't take any more, and I let off. He shudders and shakes, but it's not enough. It will never be enough.

"You knew it wasn't you. Not only that you were never going to be her bonded, but she didn't want you to be. You couldn't stand that, could you?"

He says nothing. I'm not sure he's capable of speaking anymore. I place my boot on his throat, making his icy eyes bulge from his head, and I raise my sword. This is for Eva. This is for our bond. I drive the blade down with such a force that it slams through his body and deep into the earth below, only leaving the hilt exposed from his chest.

I breathe in the fresh air, letting my legs move with the land, and they thank me with a burst of adrenaline. I stick close behind Eva but leave enough room for Hera to move up beside her.

"Do you think we're getting close?" she asks Eva quietly.

"I hope so," she replies, wishing she had a better answer for her. It has to be infuriating, taking orders from the bloom without any end in sight. "Sometimes I wonder if it's all in my head, but then it leaves a burn on my thigh," she says.

"Pretty fucked-up way of reassuring you," Hera replies.

"I'd say. But you never know. Maybe this will be the last stretch that leads us to the Mortia."

The second the words leave Eva's lips, my mouth goes dry. This really could be the last journey toward the place that will determine our fate. Her fear is loud, ringing through my head. She's afraid that she's not ready yet, but I know that she is. Her fury will be more than enough to defeat them.

I step closer to her. "It will be alright, Eva."

My words soothe her, but it's short lived.

"You can't possibly know that," she whispers.

Maybe so, but it has to be. I won't return to our realm to find it overtaken by the Omen. I didn't come this far to watch them devour the people of Baros and the people of Meraki. I reach out for her hand.

"I choose to believe that, and I refuse to let anything happen to you. That I *do* know."

With a reluctant nod, she lets go of my hand, and I take the hint to give her some space. I meant every word that I said, and she knows it. She feels it, but it's not enough to break her fear. I watch her moving ahead of me, sullenly leaping from one raised root to the next. Even bonded to her, she is an enigma.

My word might mean more than most, but she still sees me as her enemy. I could throw myself over her like a shield a thousand times to keep her from harm, but until she knows without a doubt that I'm not interested in taking the throne of Meraki—until she's able to clean up the mess we've left back there—it all means nothing.

I draw back to walk beside my brother. He breaks off a piece of bread from the small loaf in his hands and offers it to me.

"No thanks. I'm not hungry," I mutter.

"Is the honeymoon over already?" he asks.

One would think, after so many years, he would know when I'm not in a humorous mood. I let out a deep, exhausted breath. "I don't think we ever really had one."

"That bad, huh? Well, at least you have all this war to keep you busy," he chides.

"I'm afraid that's the problem. Have you thought about what will happen between you and Hera after all this war?" I ask, drawing the attention to his relationship.

His mouth draws into a straight line as he stares at the ground before him in deep thought. I don't think I've ever seen him so contemplative. Seeming to be at a loss, he shrugs. "I'd like to think we could return to Meraki, welcome our people of Baros, and start our lives together." His head drops. "But I doubt anything is that simple."

Turning a corner of bramble bushes, we find the others stopped ahead. I pat him on the back. "We have our work cut out for us with these women, little brother."

His eyes lock onto Hera sharpening her blade. "We most certainly do."

27
EVANTHE

Nightfall is upon us, and there's a dense fog settling over the forest floor, making it difficult to see more than two steps ahead. We didn't make it as far as Liri had hoped, but she and Diaspor agree it's best we stop and set up camp for the night.

"Phira, here's some dry wood. You go ahead and get the fire started," the commander calls out from the canopy above. She catches the narrow logs, places them together in a pile, and lights them ablaze with her magic.

I take a seat upon a large, mossy stone and watch Aero retreat into the forest with Bel to gather water. My chest tightens. Partially because this damn bond craves him by my side, but mostly because of the way we left things earlier. I should be happy. We're so much closer to defeating the Mortia. The bond has finally been made, and Shade is no longer lingering in the shadows, waiting for me to slip up, waiting for me to have a moment of weakness so he can slide into my good graces. It took me too long to see him for what he really was. He knew there was a chance that Aero and I were fated to bond, that the legacy that he had always believed was his for the taking may have belonged to another. And all along it was meant for Aero. But Shade didn't care that both the Fae and Human Realms were relying on that bond to survive the Mortia. He only cared about himself. How will I be able to trust my instincts when I'm faced with the king of deceit if I was fooled by Shade?

Hera sits down beside me and slaps me on the knee, breaking me from the daze of doom. "If you keep scowling like that, your face is going to stay that way."

She wrinkles up her face in the most pitiful, disgusting display.

"Like you're one to talk," I retort.

"Touché. How does it feel knowing Shade Addington is gone and dead?" she asks, raising her canteen to her lips with her pinky finger raised, as if it were a light conversation of gentle ladies.

"Like I'll be scrubbing my mouth out with soap for ever letting his lips touch mine for all of eternity."

She places the canteen back in her satchel and nods knowingly. "Been there, done that. You can't blame yourself, though. He *was* something to look at, and his primary power was seduction. I've fallen for far less."

The admission makes me smile. She may be rough around the edges, but she owns her missteps, and I like that about her. "I do recall hearing about you and the Ariti sculptor's son," I say, pretending to gag.

"Hey, that's a low blow coming from you. Who knows the Salty Stone lowlifes that have been thrown from your balcony in the thicket?"

I burst into tears, laughing. "I think I've struck them from my memory at this point."

"Good call. You know, I've been meaning to ask you something... When the faloths ambushed us back in the Repenlow Wood, why did you help me?"

All humor is stripped from her face, holding me to an honest answer. So, I only give her a partial truth.

"You're a part of this. If you die, we will have one less warrior to fight the Mortia. I was just doing my part, like everyone else."

Clenching the leather strap of her satchel, she purses her lips with disappointment. *You deserve more, but please don't prod further. I can't say more. Nothing I say will change the way things are. I won't give up my stone back in Meraki, and neither will you.*

"Well, it didn't go unnoticed, so thank you," she says, wrapping a cloak around her shoulders and turning to join the others setting up camp.

"It was the last thing she asked of me," I blurt out.

She stops in her tracks. "Who?"

"My mother. I made a vow to take the throne back from Athena."

Her brows raise. "Is it true that she was your mother's closest friend at one time?"

"Yes," I reply, my voice hoarse.

She nods, and a silent understanding passes between us. The only two Stone Holders in all the Fae Realm. Only she can understand what such a vow means. And now she knows why we could never be friends.

"Pack up. We need to get farther today," Liri says.

Her dreadful voice pulls me from the dream of dreams. Take me back in the bonding tent already. Aero rubs the sleep from his eyes and smiles down at me. "That must have been a good one."

My cheeks burn. "Who said it had anything to do with you?"

"It better have been, or you will pay for it later," he growls playfully.

I scoff and push him away. "You heard the Fae lady. Get your shit together."

Fresh-eyed from a good night's sleep, the group is in bright spirits. Even Nuala seems to have let her grudge go, and Bel hasn't complained at all yet. The two of them lead the group, letting Liri stick beside Diaspor to navigate. I do my simple part of telling them which direction the bloom would like us to go, and they do the rest. Far in the distance, the peaks of a mountain range come into view.

"Will we be going through the mountains ahead?" I ask.

A dreadful look upon his face, Diaspor sighs. "Yes, but not for some time. They're much farther than they appear. We may try to rift there tomorrow morning if Nuala has built up enough strength. It's a great distance to rift so many of us."

It doesn't take long until the trees of the thick, lush forest start to thin, piddling into a ghastly sight. Diaspor halts abruptly. Every tree, blade of grass…everything is burnt to a crisp, leaving a skeleton of what it once was before us. The commander crumbles to his knees, and I fear I might do the same, some primal need to grieve for the life loss taking hold of me like never before.

"What happened here?" Hera asks, her voice shaking.

Liri's face hardens. "King Murrick happened here. The Mortia happened here."

There has to be something we can do to bring them back. I look up at the remains of a Kenaf Ash and place my hand to its charred trunk. Closing my eyes, I feel something still humming inside it. "They're not all dead," I gasp. "We can bring them back to life."

Defeated, Diaspor bats the idea away with his hand. "It's no use, Evanthe. Let's move on."

"No, I'm not leaving yet. We have to try."

I place my other hand on the oak and let magic flow from the deepest part of me. "I can feel it healing!" I shout. When I open my eyes, I find the bark of the tree has brightened, but there are few leaves. Not as many as it should have. My heart sinks.

"Just forget it. It's no use," Diaspor says, turning away.

Aero stops him. "Just let her try." Then he draws an orb of water from the air around us and places his other hand onto the tree with me. Together, we pour our power into the plant, the force flowing through each of us in a cycle—Aero, the tree, and me. Again and again until I feel it overflowing and look up to see the tree in full bloom, fuller than any spring oak in the realm.

Liri leaps up and down, clapping her hands. "You brought it back from the dead. From an Underrealm flame. That's impossible."

Diaspor slowly walks to the tree, his eyes wide in wonder. Reaching out, he lays his hand on it and laughs. "It's amazing."

"This area isn't too big. Let's bring it all back, send a message to King Murrick's men," I say, looking back at Aero for his agreement. He scans the area for a moment.

"We can do it, but we're not going to use up all our power to do it," he says, smiling toward Diaspor and Bel.

Great Divine, he's a genius. Of course. If he and I can do it, they probably can too. How have they not thought of this before? Shaking his head, Bel points a finger at himself, then Diaspor. "Me and him?"

"I don't think so," Diaspor chimes in.

"Just try! What do you have to lose? Just one tree," I plead.

The two of them make their way over to another dead

oak and put their magic to work. We all watch, waiting in suspense. But nothing happens. The bark may have lightened the slightest bit, but nothing in comparison to what Aero and I had done.

"It's the bond. You're both very powerful on your own, but together, it's like nothing I've ever seen," Liri says, her eyes welling up with tears.

One tree after another, Aero and I bring the Sunderline Forest back to a thriving expanse. I know it has to be draining all my power, but I've never felt more exhilarated. And I know Aero feels the same, his rush of adrenaline growing with each rebirth. Had I known this is what our bond could accomplish, I would have done it so long ago. It damn near rivals the things I felt back in that tent.

Finding that we have done what we set out to do, we stop and sit down in the shade by each other to reflect on our masterpiece. The midday sun is beaming overhead, and I realize just how hot I've gotten. Wiping the sweat from my brow, I lift my canteen and take a drink of water. Nothing has ever tasted so crisp and refreshing. Phira hands me a slice of thorn pear, and I let the sweet fruit melt on my tongue. I stretch my arms letting the bouts of power still coursing through my veins run freely. Fuck you, King Murrick. I'm coming for you.

I fall into Aero, letting my head land on his chest and my eyes close. I'd say we earned a nap.

"What's that in the sky?" Bel asks.

Aero pushes himself up, pulling me with him. "Sit up, Eva. Sit up."

"It's too soon," Hera says.

I peer up at the darkening horizon and my heart begins hammering in my chest.

She falls to her knees, her eyes locking onto mine. It can't be. I pinch my eyes shut, recalling the day we arrived here, the haunting voice of Shade Addington echoing in my head. *"Our worlds may be quite different, but in many ways, they do mirror one another. This is just one of them. We have one sun, one moon, and they both rise and fall at the same time those of Meraki do."*

The day has come. I look up at Aero.

"It's Noonsnight."

Beneath a sky where darkness reigns,
Warriors stand on stones, unchained,
In shadows cast by an eclipse, profound,
A battle for the throne, on sacred ground.

As light emerges, and the eclipse departs,
The sound of victory fills her heart,
Upon the stone, a legend is born,
A warrior will rise, for the throne they'll adorn.

- An Ode to Noonsnight
The Monarch Chronicles

28

EVANTHE

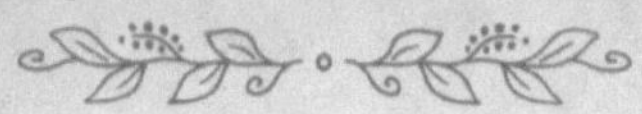

I've dreamt of this day so many times, my soul yearning for this moment. I would find the moon swallowing the sun from many places near Parea, but most of the time, I was milking Gusta when it would happen. I would leap from my stool, spilling the bucket of milk into the dirt, to gather my weapons. My body was on fire as I ran through the forest, running toward my destiny. It always felt like my mother was running beside me, but I never reached my stone. All those dreams, and not once did I face Athena. I would wake, my heart hammering in my chest, and immediately shut my eyes again, willing myself to fall back asleep.

Now, that moment is here. It isn't a dream, and I'm not a quick run away from my stone. I'm an entire realm away. An impossible distance if I didn't have Nuala. I lock eyes with the rifter. "You have to rift us back to Meraki. Hera and I have an obligation to our people. It can't wait," I say.

She scoffs. "You have an obligation to ending the Mortia. What could possibly be more important?"

"I made a vow. You're all constantly going on about how important oaths are to the Fae. Well, I made an oath to my people. I can't break it!" I shout.

Liri steps between us to address her friend. "The eclipse triggers a battle of sorts that will determine the next leader of their kingdom."

Nuala throws her hands in the air, backing away. "No. Absolutely not. You're not abandoning us so you can win a throne in the human realm."

I didn't plan for this. I thought the Mortia would already be defeated—and that my hatred for Hera would still be existent. Sensing my frustration, Aero places his hand on my shoulder.

"There isn't enough time to explain. They aren't listening," I whisper.

He pulls me closer. "Then make them understand."

His gaze is dark with intent, and I know what he's saying. The Fae are no strangers to war tactics. They've lived long enough to know everything comes at a cost. I'll make them hear me. With my hands upon my hips, I address the group.

"If you rift us back to our stones in Meraki, I'll return with the bloom and end the Mortia. If you don't...I'll let it all burn."

The rifter's green eyes narrow. She pushes me away and turns to Liri.

"Do you hear this? Your precious guardian...threatening us?"

Folding her arms, the princess holds her ground. "She won't do that. There has to be a solution."

She better not call my bluff. I'm not sure if I am bluffing, but I know if Nuala doesn't rift me back, I'm turning around and heading for that veil. Even if I can't make it on time, I'll be able to live with myself knowing I tried.

Diaspor steps forward. "Is there no other way for you to take this throne once you've defeated the Mortia? You're so much more powerful now. Can't you overthrow the one who sits upon it? Or maybe we can help you somehow?"

"We are not helping her with that," Nuala snaps.

I know his intentions are good, but there is no way around this. The people of Meraki are not going to throw hundreds of years of tradition away, and if I overthrow the monarch, they will all hate me. I would be despised by my own people forever. And it's not what I vowed to do. I must kill Athena, and it has to happen the way my mother would have wanted it. Just one opponent facing the other. No Fae magic. Sadly, I shake my head. "If there was another way, I'd gladly take it. But there isn't, and we need to return...now."

Phira steps toward me.

"All to sit upon a throne? The human blood does run thick in your veins, or maybe it is Athryc Bracken's. Greedy to the core," she sneers.

The painful words rip through me like the sharp point of a blade. But I suppose they are justified. They'll never understand this the way Hera and I do. Even with the bond, Aero can't fully know such things. If one of them had the ability to strip King Murrick of his power, they would do so in a heartbeat. This is my chance to take Athena down. She is Meraki's King Murrick. My soul is my own. Human, Fae, a guardian, or a Bracken...it's all a part of me, and I won't be made to feel badly about it.

"That's not true. I'm a Fae *and* human of my word. It was my mother's dying wish, Phira. The only thing I've been living for. If I don't fulfill this promise, none of this matters."

Nuala stomps her foot and points to Hera. "And what about her?"

Hera lifts her eyes to meet mine, a moment of sorrow passing between us. I clear my throat to say the unthinkable. "She, too, will fight to the death for that throne."

Nuala's jaw drops.

"This is what you do? You fight your own people?" She points at Liri. "I could never harm my princess, my friend. And you're willing to take Hera's life for this?" she questions, her scowl dripping with disrespect.

If she had asked me this months ago, I would have said yes. Without a doubt. But today, I don't know if I will be able to. That's what scares me the most. But we do what we have to, the women of Meraki. It's our way. If we don't, someone else will take control—like the men who ruled before us. I can't let that happen again. I know that's why

Hera trains to fight as well. Noonsnight ensures our people are left the strongest monarch. For years, we have toiled away in those fields and competed in the Skira Games to earn our place as Stone Holders. The heroines of our island. Without us, it all falls apart.

"I don't want to fight her. I have to," I say, my heart heavy.

Feliks throws his hands into the air. "Maybe they're right, Hera. You don't have to do this." Hera looks away, refusing to make eye contact with him.

"Evanthe's right. We have to follow through. It's our duty to Meraki," she says.

He grips her arms, forcing her to look at him. "I've seen the way you and Evanthe are together. She isn't your enemy anymore. You care for her. She is your friend."

"You wouldn't understand," she whispers.

The others turn their gazes on me, waiting for me to make this right. But there is no making it right. Hera has to make this decision herself.

"I don't want to fight her," I spit, furious with them for making me say the words out loud.

Hera's eyes begin to water, and my chest tightens. *Don't you dare cry.* The Hera I know that chased me to the edge of the Dyre Waters would fight, but maybe she isn't the same person. Maybe all this time away from the island has changed her. She doesn't have to die. I clench my fists at my side and clear my throat.

"Maybe you should stay back, Hera. Or come along.

But you don't have to fight. You've seen how strong I've grown. Please don't make me kill you."

The pleading sound in my voice sickens me, but worse is the scowl that becomes her face. Her ego shatters into a molten lava before my eyes. I should have chosen different words. Slowly, she steps closer.

"So high and mighty now that you've found your Fae magic. But I know you. I know all your strengths and all your weaknesses. You really shouldn't underestimate me."

"I didn't mean it like that. I know you're a strong warrior. I just want what's best for you," I say, trying to mend the fault between us, but everything I say just seems to make her more furious.

Feliks grabs Aero by the collar. "Make your bonded see what a fool she's being. You can't let her do this."

"Don't talk about Eva like that," Aero growls at his brother, the anger coiling up inside him.

Liri and Diaspor pull the rifter aside and talk amongst themselves. The sun grows darker, and I start to panic. There isn't enough time. Athena Rokos and Selene Kallis will be standing upon their stones soon—if they're not already. If I'm not on my stone when the horn sounds, I'll lose my place. Feliks, choosing the worst possible moment in time to start a fight, shoves Aero, and I'm afraid a death is going to occur before Hera or I make it back for Noonsnight.

Aero knocks him to the ground, Feliks landing with a thud. He quickly gets back up, but before all Hades breaks loose, Diaspor pulls them apart and makes way for Liri to speak. She walks past the others and stops directly in front of me.

"I struggle to believe that you are this short-sighted. I've clearly placed too much confidence in you," she says, her voice dripping with disappointment.

Her opinion of me matters more than I'd like to admit, but I do my best not to let it show. They can pin me down and make me stay here, but they can't make me follow the bloom. They can't make me fulfill my purpose as their Final Guardian unless they let me take care of this unfinished battle.

"I made a vow, Liri. A vow that carries more weight than you can imagine."

"And what happens if you don't make it?" she asks.

A new anger churns inside me. I will never let Athena or any Stone Holder get in the way of avenging my mother. How could she even entertain the thought?

"It's been made very clear to me that you all see humans as some kind of lower-level creature to the likes of you. But that half of me is just as vital to bringing down the Mortia. If you deny me this, you deny yourself freedom from this war. If you've trusted me to be your Final Guardian, why do you doubt me now?"

Liri's nostrils flare, her chest rising and falling with each frustrated breath, but I don't let her intimidate me. I won't back down. There's still time. I can feel it. With a huff, the princess turns on her heel, walking away from me, but she calls out over her shoulder.

"Go on and rift them, Nuala."

29
EVANTHE

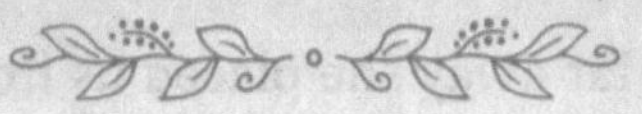

Defeated, Diaspor hands me my sword. I place it in my sheath. He's not pleased with me, and it stings. Of all the Fae I've met here, he's the one who's made me feel like I'm really one of them. He taught me how to wield my magic. To be proud of it.

"This isn't goodbye," I tell him.

"It better not be," he replies, knowing I've made him a promise that I'll fight tooth and nail to keep.

The others follow the commander to catch up with Liri, and so we are left with Nuala—Aero, Feliks, Hera, and myself. The tension is stifling as we gather our remaining items. Hera doesn't look at me, her anger seeming to be replaced by grief. I feel it too, the kind of grief that comes from losing a loved one. That's what has already happened here. One of us will leave the thicket and climb to the top of Mt. Mooring alive. The other…

"You know what to do. Each of you grab hands," Nuala mutters.

The rifter shoots me a deathly glare as she latches onto my hand. "I hope you know where you want me to land," she says.

I recall how far away she placed us from our intended location the last time she rifted Aero and me. That can't happen again.

"I know the spot, but it needs to be exact. If not, there won't be enough time—"

"Just shut up, close your eyes, and picture this place as if you're there," she interrupts.

I do as she says, transporting myself to the tree shaped like a winding river just beyond the path where the thicket meets the city. It's only a quick sprint to my stone, but I should still be shielded from the eyes of any spectators waiting to see if I arrive. I relish in the last memory I have of the place. The way the air smells of damp moss and peppery bark. How the thick canopy hovers just above my head and the dense forest floor is choked with brambles. A tingling sensation ripples through Nuala's hand to mine, and we are breaking away. Away from the Fae Realm. My heart doesn't just leap from my throat this time; it erupts, the rest of me barely hanging on. The same tangy drachma and bitter citrus flavors fill my mouth as I clench my stomach tightly in my best effort to keep from snapping in two.

We crash into the human realm with a force that devastates in comparison to the landing we took back in the Sunderline Forest. Cradling my head, I latch onto the rifter's pant leg.

"Are you trying to kill us?" I gasp.

She kicks my hand away. "That would be too gentle a death for you."

"Damnit, Nuala. I think you broke my...everything," Feliks mutters.

Moving through the pain, Aero reaches out to help me stand. The throbbing behind my skull subsides, and I look up to see the moon continuing to crawl over the sun. "I need to go."

"Are you sure I can't come with you?" Aero asks, his voice cracking.

The bond inside me is screaming to say yes. To forgo the pain our separation will bring and let him fight by my side. But that won't mend the hole inside me. It won't bring my mother's soul rest. "I need to do this on my own," I say.

Feliks latches onto Hera. "Tell me you'll reconsider, please." He falls to his knees, begging, but the Stone Holder merely pulls him to his feet and places a kiss to his cheek. Before she runs toward her stone, she gives me one last nod. "This is it. I'll see you out there."

I try to think of something to say, anything that will make this all seem right, but there are no words. Before I can open my mouth, she breaks into a sprint with Feliks running behind her. Feeling all my anguish, Aero wraps his hands around my face. "This is her choice. You need to promise me that you will come out of this. Forget the Omen. Forget the Mortia. Just promise me that you will come out of this with your heart still beating. I'm certain if you don't, mine will stop right alongside yours."

"I promise," I whisper, my eyes welling up with tears. I let them spill down my face as his lips find mine, his kiss sealing the oath.

"I thought you were in a hurry," Nuala grumbles, tapping her toes impatiently.

Wiping my tears away, I muster the strength to gather my weapons. "I have to get to Blackstone."

"How long will this battle take?" the rifter asks.

"There is no set amount of time, but most Noon-snights take one to two days. The Omen will make this one a bit different, so I can't be sure." I glance up at the sky. "The eclipse may last an hour, so you'll need to keep an eye out for vampyr. Once the sun is shining again, find a safe place to wait until I return."

Without another moment to spare, we run upon the path that takes us to the outskirts of Parea. My stomach turns at the sight, the once cared for buildings now dingier and many abandoned. Their owner's lives surely taken by Despina and her army of vampyr. I spot several spectators hiding up in the tallest buildings, their sunken faces peering out amongst the open windows. They're too afraid to come down and watch.

"Evanthe! Evanthe!" my Aunt Maria's voice bellows

out from an alleyway. She and my Aunt Cybele come barreling out, a candle in each hand.

"What are you doing here?" I ask.

"We just knew you would show, and we had to see you off. We couldn't let you go without a blessing," my Aunt Cybele says, peering around us. "Where is Sorrow?"

My heart sinks, and I open my mouth to tell her, but the words don't come out.

"She was turned, Cybele," Aero says, feeling my pain.

Her head tilts to the side, and she sighs. "I'm so sorry, Evanthe. We loved her so much. Like family."

"I know you did. She loved you both too," I reply, blinking my eyes rapidly to keep from crying.

Without another word, Maria pulls out a bushel of herbs wrapped with twine. They both tilt their candles so the flames become one. Then she presses the end of the smudge stick into the fire and begins waving the smoke through the air around me as they both recite the blessed words:

"In her strength make glad the Great Divine

May she have your alliance as her weapon

And your song as her peace

Give her victory over those who wish to do her harm

And endurance to bear the fatigue of the coming battle."

Coughing a little from the smoke, I open my eyes to find another familiar face staring back at me. Then the most godawful sensation ripples from her palm straight into my face.

"What were you thinking, girl? You're supposed to be

ending the Mortia. Not playing war games after my namesake."

I narrow my eyes at the legendary ghost. "Nice to see you too, Skira."

"Nothing nice about this," she spits.

Her brash words would lift my spirits if I weren't carrying the weight of the world on my shoulders. It was only months ago that she found me soaking wet on the shore of the Dyre Waters and made me realize the consequence of my actions and her own. Noonsnight wouldn't even exist if it weren't for her, my sharp tongued, wild eyed ancestor. But despite all that, I have missed her.

"I'm only here to avenge my mother's death and take back the throne. Then I'll be returning to the Fae Realm to end the Mortia, so you don't have to worry. Your soul won't be damned to Hades," I reply, knowing full well she's just as concerned about her own fate as she is anyone else's.

Her eyes are narrow like two slits. "You went to the Fae Realm?" She pauses to let it all sink in. "Well, I guess there's nothing we can do about this now. But you best believe I'm coming along on this Noonsnight quest."

"Fine, just keep quiet, and no spooking anyone. The other Stone Holders can't see you. I have to fight alone," I reply.

"So, she gets to tag along, but I don't?" Aero asks, feeling cheated.

I know I would feel the same way if he were about to run into battle, but Skira's ghostly presence isn't breaking any of the rules. In fact, my mother would be thrilled if the great Skira Gallanis was by my side, and a small part of me wants her there too. She's a pain in the ass, but she's helpful in a pinch. I place my hand on his chest. "She can't actually kill anyone, and we both know she won't take my feelings about the matter into consideration."

"Well, I, for one, am glad she will be going with you. You make sure she keeps her wits about her," my Aunt Maria says to Skira.

I wrap my arms around each of my aunts and direct them back to the city. "Thank you, but you really should go. I couldn't live with myself if anything happened to either of you." I turn to look at Aero. "You too."

"No chance. I'm going to be by your side until the moment I can't."

Nuala shrugs, turning to follow my aunts back into the city, but Aero latches onto her collar. "I don't think so, rifter. You can't just go running off into a city of humans. You're staying with me."

The rifter rolls her eyes but follows his order. They take their places a few steps behind me, and I turn around to face my stone. Blackstone. Smooth as a river rock and dark as the night sky that almost becomes ours. I always imagined what this day would be like—stepping onto the onyx surface. I always wondered if my mother's spirit would be here with me, but here I am, standing beside Skira's. I tense on the balls of my feet, an attempt to warm up my legs. I glance left, then right, taking in the sight of all the Stone Holders standing in their rightful places.

The stones are assembled in a line, at least a field's length away from each other, but only a few feet from where the thicket begins. The figure of Selene Kallis stands upon Hiddenstone, its shape covered in moss, blending in with its surroundings, making it difficult to see—a symbol of the Great Divine who is always there guiding us even though we cannot see her.

I shift my gaze to Athena Rokos. The one I come to claim in the name of my mother, the fallen Beta Sideris. Her shadow moves on top of Highstone, the stone that sits higher than all the others, and the stone that every current monarch must stand upon.

Then there is Hera. My friend. The one who has fought at my side, who has dressed me for my elemental gift ceremony and my bonding ceremony with Aero. Hera Terzi, who stands upon Earstone, the one shaped like an ear, so we may hear Skira's words of wisdom, and I just know she's found some way to find it humorous after all we know of the ghost now. My chest tightens.

An elder begins to climb the stairs winding up the high tower, and my heart begins to race. I try to make my mind go blank, to go to a primal place where only survival or death exist. But I can't stop staring at Hera. She's too far away to make out the details of her face, but I can tell she is looking at me too.

The elder takes her last step at the edge of the balcony, and one of the guards places the horn in her hands. I shut my eyes to keep from looking at Hera. *You can do this. You have to do this.*

Let the sky fall.

I will not tremble.

I am the stone.

The moon who claims them. For I carry the fallen.

A smattering of resounding gasps and chatter erupt from the open windows of the city, and my eyes fly open, searching for what it is they are so aghast about. My gaze whips around and finally lands on Earstone. Hera's stone. But only one of her boots remains planted upon its surface. She's halfway off the damned thing. What is she doing? She can't bow out. No one has ever withdrawn from Noonsnight. The elder on the high tower lifts the horn to her lips, and it's as if time has stopped, until Hera's boot slides off the ear-shaped stone entirely.

She turns to face me, placing one hand over her heart, and the horn sounds.

30
AERO

The low mournful sound of the horn is fitting, its last blare fading into the sky as the sun loses its battle with the moon. Everything goes dark as I watch the last of her disappear into the thicket—the thicket where we first met all those years ago. Two children who had no idea how the world would break so we could find each other once more. The land of Baros growing barren, and her land of Meraki plagued by the Omen. I just pray the reaper gives us more time. To save our people, yes. But mostly—and selfishly—to have more time with her. To see the way her nose wrinkles with the slightest bit of disgust and the way her freckles dance like stars upon the tops of her cheeks once more. Those are the things that will haunt me if she doesn't return.

The other Stone Holders gone, Hera leaps into Feliks's

arms. One part of me lifts with relief that Eva won't have to harm her friend, but an overwhelming dread is threatening to take hold of the other part. The bond begins aching inside me, telling me my mate has gone too far away, and I swallow the pain. I will take all of it, but I can't let the suffering get the better of me. She needs to stay focused. If I'm too sick with worry, it will surely find her through the bond. I need to stay strong for her, and I will.

"Shouldn't we find cover from these vampyr you speak of?" Nuala asks.

Drawing in a deep breath, I pull myself up from the ground to see Feliks and Hera running toward us. Hera arrives first and props her hands on her hips. "She's going to be alright. She'll kill Athena, and Selene doesn't stand a chance," she says, still catching her breath.

I don't know how to thank her. If she feels even a fraction of what Eva feels for this moment, it had to be so hard to step down from that stone.

"The sacrifice you just made for Eva will never be forgotten. I don't know if it's any consolation, but I'm quite certain if you two had met face to face out there, she wouldn't have been able to hurt you," I say.

She blows a strand of her hair out of her face. "Well, I'm sure she would have hurt me a little," she chides.

"Maybe just a little."

"It was the right thing to do. Evanthe is a good leader. She deserves the title. There was a time when the throne was all I wanted, but this war has opened my eyes to the burden that comes with the crown. It isn't one that I want to carry. But she can. She is strong enough."

Feliks puffs up his chest, and I can see the pride swelling inside him. He truly cares for Hera more than I ever thought he could. I try to focus on his happiness and ignore the bond trembling inside me. Nuala lets out an impatient breath. "This is heartwarming, but we need to go. I believe Evanthe's last words were to find a safe place until the sun returns."

She may be a cold-hearted wretch, but she's right. Even an hour of darkness is enough for those monsters to hunt us down. I'm sure Despina won't waste any time once she hears of our arrival. Hera nods and lifts her satchel.

"I agree. You should go to Evanthe's aunts' home. I will meet you there soon, but there's something I have to do first."

"Then I'll come with you," Feliks says.

Hera shakes her head. "No, you won't want to be there for this. I need to go check on my mother. I'm sure she's alright. I saw her watching from a high window earlier, but she won't be pleased with my decision."

My brother's brow furrows, and I know he's thinking of a way to help. But if there's one thing the women of Meraki have taught me, it's that some things can't be helped.

"Alright, but don't be long," Feliks replies reluctantly.

Hera pulls the corners of her mouth into a smile, but it doesn't meet her eyes. "I'm sure it won't take long. Don't start dinner without me. I've been dying for a hot bowl of Maria's fasolada."

The two of them embrace, and we all watch as she runs into the dark city ahead. In the distance, I can hear the waves crashing onto the shore. I close my eyes for a moment, letting the sound invade my senses, giving me hope. I take one step, then another, and we make our way through the Parean streets.

The city feels empty and unkempt. The streets that once smelled of fresh bread and gardenia, now reek of stale ale and urine. We move quietly, letting each step rock slowly from heel to toe as not to draw any unwanted attention.

"Keep your ears covered," I whisper to Nuala.

The rifter pulls her cloak up tightly and shoots me a glare. "Why do you humans hate the Fae so much anyway? Aren't they about to have one for their monarch?" she asks through clenched teeth.

"Shhhh. We'll answer questions when we get there," I reply.

Maria and Cybele's house is much the same, but four long lines have been scratched across the blue paint on the arched front door, and some of the wood has chipped away from the shutters. I ball up my fist and quietly knock.

The door opens the slightest bit, Cybele's eyes look us over, and the door swings open. "Get in, hurry. What are you doing knocking? You have to be quiet," she says with a frightened whisper.

"I'm sorry. I didn't know if you would be guarding the door with a silver pick-axe," I reply.

Maria laughs and offers to take our satchels and cloaks for us. When she reaches for Nuala's, the rifter pauses, holding tightly to the hooded cloak to keep her identity secret.

"You can remove the cloak in here. They have nothing against the Fae," I tell her.

Eyes wide, she nervously removes the hood and pulls the garment over her head. Maria inconspicuously glances at her pointy ears and quickly moves along so as not to make Nuala uncomfortable. I look around the old home. Every curtain and shutter is closed, and some of the windows are boarded up with wooden planks.

"How've you two been holding up?" I ask.

Her smile fades, giving way to the dark lines and puffy eyes that lay in its wake. A look passes between her and Cybele, one that seems to be asking if she should give us the light version or the honest one, and she settles into a seat next to the table.

"We've had our fair share of scares but have found ways to remain hidden when they come into the city. It didn't happen often after you left, but for a while, it seemed to be happening nightly."

She pauses to lift a hand to her mouth, the horrible memory seeming to make her ill. Cybele clears her throat to continue in her place. "Those who refused to prepare themselves or didn't have the means, died. Many died. Some were turned, and others fled—to where, we're not sure. But there are rumors that some were attempting to leave the island entirely, choosing to face the predators of the sea rather than spend another night here, shaking in fear. For a while, we worked together with others, finding abandoned homes to rotate between, still leaving some empty, rarely staying in the same place for long. There were a few days we stayed in the thicket, but we barely made it out alive."

The thought of them wandering the woods, being hunted by the yellow-eyed monsters, makes me furious. They might have a couple weapons, but they are twice my age, their bodies worn by the time that has passed. I remember the way those newly made vampyrs would lunge at anything with blood in its veins, their teeth snapping wildly.

"What has Athena done to try and protect you?" I ask.

Maria shakes her head. "Up until today, when the moon arrived, she has sat in her tower. It didn't take long for the vampyr to defeat all her guards. She never spared a single one of them to help the people, but worse, she never let them come inside once the sun fell. They stood outside her entrances, trembling with fear until, one by one, their blood painted the white walls."

"How did she last so long, then?" Feliks asks.

"First, she made her servants strip the guards' corpses of their armor and dispose of their bodies. When night fell, they were made to put the armor on and stand where the guards once did. Some of them fought. We could hear their shouting from here. Then, one escaped. He came running into the city, begging for refuge. Many turned him away for fear of what Athena would do to them. We opened our door, waiting to offer him a place to stay, but I was told he ran into the thicket after being denied so many times."

Wherever you are, Evanthe, do not hold back when you find Athena at the tip of your blade. Having gathered her strength, Maria gets up to warm a pot of water for tea. She pours the steaming blend of herbs into cups and hands one to each of us. "I'm sorry I don't have more to offer. It hasn't been easy getting out to gather food, and as you can imagine, the market isn't up and running anymore."

"This is more than gracious of you, Maria," I say.

Cybele blows the steam off the top of her tea and takes a sip. "So, once most of Athena's servants had died, she set out with the few that remained and started pulling more from the townspeople. Plucking them from their homes. From their families. Their wives, husbands, children left screaming and crying. None of them warriors. None of them had any such skills. We had started to worry she would be knocking on our door next, but then the eclipse began," she says.

"You can be sure that your niece will be ending her soon, if she hasn't already," I say, hoping to give them some peace, even if it's only for just one night. I wish Eva could have heard this before venturing into the thicket. Not that she needs more motivation to kill Athena, but it would be nice for her to know all the countless others she is avenging by taking her out of this world.

"Thank you for taking us in," Feliks adds.

"We would never leave a friend of Evanthe's out in the cold," Cybele replies.

Maria gets up to rinse her mug, but a soft knocking sounds at the door. Feliks leaps up, running for the door as if it was his own home. When he opens it, Hera is standing in the entrance, her eyes red and puffy. "I told you it wouldn't take long," she mutters through a choppy breath. My brother ushers her in, and Maria scrabbles to bring her a mug of tea.

"Thank you," Hera says.

Maria watches her take her first sip. "I doubt your mother was thrilled about your choice today."

Hera wipes away a rogue tear and scoffs. "That's putting it lightly."

"Well, you can stay with us as long as you like," Cybele replies.

Feliks pulls her cloak out from her satchel and wraps it around Hera's shoulders. If anyone knows the suffering a strained relationship with a parent can cause, it's him. It used to be me too, but as luck would have it, Phineas isn't actually my father. Now I'm left with an estranged sea god of a father, whom I may never really know, but my mother...well, who knows what kind of relationship we will have once she knows that I'm aware of who my real father is. She may try to have me killed. I'd like to think she wouldn't, that she loves me more than that, but if Phineas found out, he would certainly have her head.

Each of us dead tired from the journey, Maria lays out some quilts for us. "I know the sun is already starting to peer out from behind the moon, but we have become quite nocturnal in the presence of the vampyr and desperately need some rest. Help yourselves to whatever you may need."

We send them off with thanks and make our way to the library. It's a rather small home, but the library has plenty of space for us to rest a while. When we enter the room, my stomach drops. The others think nothing of it, being that they've never been here before, and Hera is so distraught over the falling out with her mother, but I know this is not what this place used to look like. I crane my neck back to look up at the soaring stacks of shelves that used to be filled to the brim with leatherbound books. Now, half of them lie in tatters on the floor beneath. I peer into the dark fireplace to see shreds of the paper and binding burnt to nothing. "They destroyed Chronicles," I say.

Hera looks up and places her hand upon the half empty shelves. "As if they haven't taken enough already, they had to destroy these too," she growls.

Too weak to fume about it, she and Feliks curl up in the corner of the room, and Nuala lies down right in the middle, upon the rug, watching me pace the room.

"Burning a hole through the floor won't do you any good. Get some rest," she says.

"Don't pretend to care," I scoff.

Rolling her eyes, she sits up and throws her hands down in a huff. "I rifted you all to an entirely different realm. A realm where Fae are hated. My magic is completely drained, and I'm exhausted. Can you just sit down so I might be able to rest a few minutes?"

She did take on a great risk in rifting us here, and if we need her to rift us back, she will need to regain her power. It feels impossible to stop moving, but I try. Crouching down in a spot beneath the window, I sit and focus on anything other than what might be happening to Eva right now. I will think of all the fond memories. I trick my bond into feeling only the feelings that will give her strength until all I can see is her returning to me victorious.

31
EVANTHE

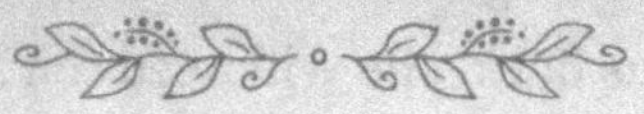

My heart hammering in my chest and my head on a swivel, I run until it feels like my lungs will give out. Every snap of a twig, chirp of a bird, and rustling sound makes me want to crawl out of my own skin. My mind knows that the vampyr can't come out until sundown, but something guttural still forces me to search for their yellow eyes amongst the brambles. The eclipse lasted longer than I remember in past Noonsnights, but I have yet to see one of the monsters. It is tempting to run for my home in the canopy of these trees, to see if everything is still the same. But I'm sure it's been ransacked by Despina or some other unfortunate souls trying to survive this mess. And I know it would be the first place Athena and Selene would go looking if they decide to go after me first.

The sun will be setting soon. That means the other Stone Holders will be distracted, looking out for any vampyr. It could be a great advantage to me. I know how to fight the vampyr, but I've never fought them in great numbers on my own, and my body is achingly sore from rifting here, separating from Aero, and running all this way. Then there is the piercing throb along my thigh. The bloom hasn't stopped glaring at me with its frigid burn since we left the Fae Realm. I reach down, adjusting the garter so it isn't sitting over the same patch of skin for too long. "If you cause me pain, I won't be able to go back and put you to use," I curse beneath my breath.

It's best that I look for a good hiding spot for the night, one that will give me cover but still allow me to see any enemies coming. As I comb the woods, I realize how strange the thicket feels. It's still my home but less vivid than I remember. It's most obvious in the way the trees wear their leaves, the once lively plumes now falling limp, hanging heavily toward the ground as if they would just rather break off from their branches and wither to the ground. The Omen has dulled the luster that this place once showed.

The last bits of light left in the sky fade away. I find a hovel at the base of a tree, where the earth is much lower on one side. Its thick roots loop up around the small underground opening, making the perfect nest to curl up in for a little while. I turn in a circle, searching for any signs of danger until I'm confident it's safe. Nestling down deep in its cavern, I try to think of anything to distract me from my discomfort. It's been so long since I've been completely alone for more than one night at a time. I quite liked being alone before all this happened. I laugh to myself. Now, here I am, my body literally writhing with loneliness in this seclusion.

"You better not fall asleep, girl," Skira whispers, her voice arriving in my ear before she appears before me.

Rolling my eyes, I tuck my weapons in beside me and lay my head back on the tree. "I need to sleep at some point. This isn't a quick battle. If I'm exhausted by the time I find Athena, it will give her an advantage. Besides, why do you think I allowed you to come here? You can warn me if someone is coming, no?"

"Oh no. Don't you put that pressure on me. This one is on you. Your little battle to fight," she hisses.

I scoff, the sound making my head throb. I must be dehydrated. I lift my canteen to my mouth, drink the last few drops, and let it fall in my lap with a limp arm. "This *little* battle was made in honor of *you*, Skira."

"It's not my fault that you all decided it was a good idea to make things even harder for yourselves after I banished those vile men. I made way for a better future. At least, that's what I thought I was doing," she says, her gaze drifting away to a far-off time.

"It seems that's all I'm ever fighting for...to right the wrongs of this place's past," I mutter. And if I defeat Athena and Selene, it will be my turn to stand in the high tower. For the first time in my life, my voice will be heard. Having every ear of Meraki would be the greatest power

I've ever known. Greater than the earth magic that surges in my veins. I could move every mound of land and bushel of trees, but none of that matters if I don't have their minds and hearts. Winning Noonsnight is one thing, but after all they've been through, I will need to defeat the Mortia to earn their respect.

My eyes fall shut, and I let the haunting sounds of the thicket lure me to sleep.

———

"Wake up, girl!" Skira's shrill voice shakes me from my sleep.

Gripping my mother's dagger, I fling up, hitting my head on one of the roots. "What's wrong? What's happening?" I ask in a hushed voice.

The ghost points into the thicket. "I heard something moving just through those trees."

I pause, searching for any sign of a threat. My body goes cold with dread, but nothing surfaces from the dark woods. "It was probably just a deer or rabbit," I say, more to convince myself than Skira.

"I think after hundreds of years on this island I know the difference between a fawn and a predator," she replies.

As if on cue, a twig snaps. My head whips toward the sound, and slowly I begin to crawl out of my hiding place on all fours, each of my hands and knees moving in a smooth, gliding motion over the forest floor like a snake. I can hear the intruder breathing, but the sound is nothing like that of a vampyr. It isn't until I pull myself up to standing behind a tall oak that I see the shadow moving toward me. It is the figure of a woman, no yellow eyes to be seen.

Moving so quietly I think I've forgotten to breathe, I draw one of the arrows from my quiver and nock it to the string. The shadow moving closer, I draw it tightly and aim. I should release it now. Shoot first, ask questions later. But what if it's just an innocent townsperson, out here trying to survive the Omen? Or Athena. I don't want it to be like this. I want to look her in the eye when I'm driving my blade through her chest, not shooting her from this distance.

"What are you doing, girl? Shoot!" Skira whispers a shout.

I will my finger to let it fly, but it won't let go. Damnit.

"Don't take another step," I say, my voice amplifying through the quiet night air.

The figure stops, but from this angle I can see they carry a blade.

"Drop the weapon," I demand.

Their head moves left to right. "Now," I growl. Slowly, the shadow lowers to the ground. When they rise, I no longer see any sign of a blade, but I know well enough how easy it is to hide a small weapon.

"Who are you?" I ask, and a hissing sound echoes behind me. It is not coming from the figure in front of me, but it is definitely coming our way.

"Selene Kallis," she says, her voice trembling.

Feeling better knowing it's not Athena, I move in closer until I can see her fully within the moonlight shining through the canopy above. Wild-eyed and frozen in place, she stares back at me. I can almost taste her fear as Hagen Elleth would be able to, its acidic bite latching onto her like a rabid dog with a bone. Her trembling hand latches onto a small dagger. The hissing grows louder, and this time, she hears it too.

"Don't come any closer," she says, her voice shaky like a leaf in the wind.

She's barely old enough to fight in the games. There could be so many more years ahead for her. She may have had the skill to earn her stone, but surviving a mob of blood-thirsty monsters is far beyond her stature. Surely she didn't plan on becoming monarch in the midst of this war against the vampyr. The girl is terrified, for fuck's sake.

"The vampyr are almost here. I will fend them off as best I can. You are going to turn around and run back home, but if I find you back out here, trying to ambush me, I will tie you up and feed you to them, understood?"

My voice is colder than I've ever heard it, and I know she hears it too.

"You have to fight me. I earned my place to be here," she says. But still I hear the tremor in her voice. She is saying what she has been taught to say, but it isn't what she really wants.

"Yes, you did. And if you want me to fight you, I will. But nothing will get in my way of that throne. I will put you in the ground if I have to, but I don't want to. I'm giving you this one chance to live."

The rustling behind me rattles through the air, reminding me that we are running out of time. "You need to make this decision now."

"Alright. May Skira be with you," she blurts out as she runs back toward Parea.

She has no idea. I search for a vantage point, but the mob of hissing monsters is too quick.

"Behind you," Skira shouts, coming into view again.

Fuck.

One set of yellow eyes launches at me, then another. I hack away at one until her head finally falls away, and I quickly find this isn't going to be easy. I may not plan on using my magic on Athena, but I'm more than fine with using it against these wretches. A male with fangs longer than I've ever seen plows through the branches like a starving beast. With the release of my fingers, the earth caves beneath him, sending him falling through the crevice. Throwing a hoard of sharp branches through the hearts of the other two coming at me, I move toward the trapped beast. His dead yellow eyes latch onto mine in a snarling frenzy. All his newly turned mind can think of is ripping my flesh open and drinking me dry. It's what makes him so deadly, yet makes him so vulnerable, because he won't see this coming. With all my might, I swing my heavy blade at his neck and take it off in one swipe.

An aching worry that isn't my own hums through my

chest, and I know it is Aero making himself sick over the whirlwind of fear and adrenaline that is being passed on to him through the bond. *I'm just fine, Aero. Don't worry,* I tell him, even though I know he can't hear my thoughts. Thank Zeus for that.

Another set of yellow eyes shines through the shadows beyond. It's going to be a long night, but I'm not afraid of these vermin anymore. It feels too good to use my magic again, and I will let it rip as many of them from this land as possible before I return to the Fae Realm and destroy their true maker.

32
EVANTHE

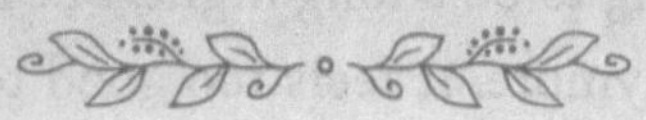

It seems I've been hunting for Athena for hours, but the sun hasn't even risen yet. After fighting vampyr through most of the night, it didn't make much sense to try and sleep through the last couple hours, so I set out after her. I nearly made it to the meadow between the thicket and Mt. Mooring, but I haven't found a single boot print. Not a single strand of her white-blonde hair. Nothing.

Stopping at a small stream, I lean over to fill up my canteen. The water is still clear as glass, and I spot a little minnow rapidly swishing his tail over the rocks at the bottom. I used to catch them for fun when I was little, usually rejoicing with each catch, their slippery bodies squirming in my hand. I'd do a dance and put them right back in the stream.

My heart sinks. All but once…

The time my mother left me to make my way across the island without a single weapon. I try to shake the memory, but it always surfaces. Especially when I'm facing something dangerous. I was starving when I caught the minnow. I tried to imagine releasing the creature, but I just couldn't let it go. I didn't dance that day. Laying it upon a large rock, I shut my eyes and brought a smaller stone down upon its head.

Once the shock wore off, I ripped it apart with my teeth, hating myself more and more with each bite but ravenously devouring it nonetheless. I had never felt badly about eating fish or meat before, but taking the life of something with my bare hands was different. And I knew, in that moment, my mother wanted me to be that vicious. That she wanted the island to teach me how to survive with nothing but the body I was born with. Although her intentions may have been pure, it tore me apart. And now I know without a doubt that it was that time with the minnow, that exact moment, that shattered my soul.

While placing my canteen back in my satchel, a flash of movement catches my eye. Not too far in the distance, I'm able to see her. Even in the last moments of night, I know exactly who it is. Her once soft, rosy hair is quite rumpled and grubby, but it's really her. Sorrow Mega. My heart leaps, and my body follows. She darts away, fast as a fallow deer. We can never be friends again. Of that I'm well aware, but I'm desperate to see her. To speak to her again. Even if she's a monster.

When it seems she has eluded me and the sun is coming over the horizon, I come to a stop—a dead stop right in front of Athena Rokos's path. The same pale strands of hair I remember twist into matted ropes around a headpiece made of chains and fall over her forehead. The black lines she painted over her face have been smudged, the greasy stains only stopping for the metal hoops in her nose and lips. She is much like I remember. But her shoulders are hunched forward, falling into the weariness that this Noonsnight has brought her way.

"After all this time, it has finally come to this," she says.

Her icy stare locks onto me as she lifts her spear in the air.

Every part of me lashes out at her. I am bringing my sword down, over and over, my hands and feet moving in a flurry. She dodges and blocks each blow with her spear. Her face growing red and slick with sweat. "You move just like your mother did," she spits.

"Then you don't stand a chance," I growl.

She throws a jab at me with the metal spike, but I bend backward just in time.

"Pity it didn't work that way for Beta," she snarls.

The sound of my mother's name coming off her vile lips sends a fresh swell of rage through me. I swing with all my might, and the impact slices the tip of her spear straight off. Her jaw drops as she inspects the jagged edge where my blade cut. Gripping my sword, I march toward her.

"Had you not taken such a cheap blow, she would still be here today," I say, my voice dripping with malice.

The treacherous monarch takes a step back and smiles.

"But whose fault was it, really? Tell me, how was it that she was so distracted, Evanthe?"

My gut twists into a ball of anger and heartache. She knew I was there the moment she drove her spear through my mother's chest. That I had run to her, barefoot in the middle of Noonsnight, because I had that burning feeling that something was wrong. That I was going to lose her too soon. I've spent years blaming myself for her death, telling myself that had I resisted the urge to warn her, she would still be here. But it wasn't my fault. I was only a child.

Shaking with fury, I begin circling her.

"I have a better question. Would you have ever made it to that Noonsnight if my father had actually loved you?" I ask. In an instant, all the beaming pride behind her eyes vanishes. *That's right. I know that he rejected you. That he wanted to stay with my mother. And you couldn't handle it, so you decided to try and take the only other thing she cared for.*

I go in for the kill. Wincing, she lifts her broken spear to block the blow. I bring my sword down with a vengeance, preparing myself for the relief this will bring. To finally put Athena Rokos behind me. But just as my blade is about to make contact, she chucks the spear aside and unsheathes her sword with her other hand. It's all a blur. Her blade is moving so quickly, so close. Too close. It slashes my leg, sending me to the ground. My thigh is searing with pain, but my first instinct is to make sure she didn't cut the garter where the bloom is stored. Finding it still intact, I lift my sword, but she snatches it right through the cross-guard with her blade and flings it into the forest.

A scheming gleam in her eye, she prowls toward me like a cellar spider who's caught a fly in her web. She stops right beside me, pointing the tip of her sword to the divot just below my neck.

"Get up, girl. You have to fight," Skira says, still keeping herself invisible as I've requested.

Athena's mouth curls into a grin. "Are you talking to yourself?" she asks, finding the thought amusing.

I try to correct her, but a wild terror stabs at my chest, clawing its way up my throat, taking away my ability to speak. This isn't the way this is supposed to happen. I might deserve to die, but not like this. Not at the hands of Athena. I listen for my mother's words of wisdom, but it's as if she's really gone now. For the first time, her voice isn't ringing in my head, and it's right when I need to hear her most. Maybe, once it's over, it won't be so bad. If I just let go, I won't have to fight anymore.

My body starts to go numb, and I lift my gaze to the sky. And before my eyes, it is covered with black rolling clouds. Ripping and roaring like a warning from the Great Divine, they even capture Athena's attention. Then the rain comes pouring down in unnaturally large drops of the warmest water the sky has ever cried. Aero. It's him. I can feel him everywhere. All the clawing in my chest fades away, replaced by an urgent warmth. It spreads through my veins like the raging storm around me with flashes of lightning striking through me.

The air lights up around us, one of the bolts of fire touching down deathly close, and Athena hesitates just long enough for me to hook my boot behind her ankle and send her crashing to the ground. After kicking her sword away with my good leg, I watch as she squirms to get back up. Just when she almost finds her feet, I knock her back down and remove the dagger from my garter. As I grip the moon-adorned handle, I know this is just how my mother would have wanted it. Pressing my boot into her throat, I lean in close enough to hear the shaky breath sputtering from her mouth, and I lift the dagger so she might see every detail of the weapon.

"I want you to know that this dagger belonged to my mother."

Lifting it over my head, I plunge it into her chest over and over until the light leaves her cold eyes, and her body lies limp beneath my weight.

33
EVANTHE

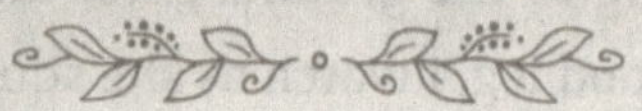

I barely remember the journey back to the streets of Parea. The storm seemed to calm the moment Athena's heart stopped beating, and as I had imagined, there were no elders waiting at the top of the mountain to confirm my victory, all of them too afraid to face the Omen—and I can't say I blame them. That might be why it's of great surprise to them all when they see me limp into city center, lifting Athena's broken spear into the air, her head sitting on top of it just as it would have been done if I were reaching the top of Mt. Mooring.

The few people scattered about drop their things and come running. They cheer louder than any crowd has ever welcomed a new monarch. Clearly, Athena had outworn her welcome on their throne. The sound of their roaring applause stretches through the city streets, calling more to join the celebration. I try not to take offense to the shocked expressions of some who must have thought Athena would defeat me. They circle around me, and I hand them the spear, letting them pass it around, lifting it to the sky. Then I hear Hera's voice as she claws her way through the horde. "Out of my way!"

Hera Terzi, my friend. No longer my enemy. My eyes welling up, I wrap my arms around her and squeeze with all my might.

"Good gods, Evanthe. I can hardly breathe," she wheezes.

I let up a bit, pulling back so I can look her in the eye. "I'll never forget what you did for me, Hera. Never."

Her lip trembles a bit, but she forces it into a smile.

"That's good, but I think we both know I'd never let you forget it."

I burst into tears, laughing along with her.

It doesn't take long for Aero to come running out from a dark alley. I feel him coming before he ever appears, and when he does, it feels as if all the world has spun to the right side up finally. I push into the crowd. They make way for me to run, crashing into his arms. He lifts all the weight of me, pulling me in tightly, and I breathe him in, the salty sage soothing my soul. This has to be better than any honorable death. Better than what arriving in the Elysian Fields must feel like. And I want to stay in this moment forever. Forget the crown. Forget the throne. Just leave me here in his arms, just like this.

"Why do your aunts have to live so far from the high

tower? I came as fast as I could when I heard the commotion," he says.

"It's alright. I knew you were on the way," I reply, letting the backs of my fingers graze along his stubble.

I can feel all the people watching us. Speculating. They will all be talking soon, saying that the new monarch is already laying claim to a potential partner. Most Stone Holders don't take a husband until their status as monarch has been made—if ever. But now that I've achieved that status, they will all be waiting to see who that man will be. Although I feel at odds letting them see me like this with him, I can't help myself. The bond has taken full control in this moment, and I don't have the strength to fight.

"Took you long enough," Feliks bellows.

Aero's smile lights up his face, showcasing a row of his perfectly arranged teeth. "Some of us were working while others were out gallivanting around town," he chides.

Then, out of the corner of my eye, I spot Selene Kallis walking through the crowd toward me. Walking in a straight line, she doesn't blink. Not even once. And for a second, I think she might be upset. But then she falls to her knees, bowing in front of me. Embarrassed by the gesture, I pull her to her feet. "Get up, Selene. There's no need for that."

"Y— You saved my life," she stutters.

"Nonsense. You saved your own life," I say, my brows pinching together.

She shakes her head as if she doesn't understand why

I'm so confused. "No, you could have fought me. You could have let those vampyr devour me, but you spared me."

The crowd gathers in tighter, mumbling whispers under their breath. This will be the first rumor to go around. I can hear them now.

The new monarch is so merciful.

No, she's weak.

She better not show any mercy to the Omen.

I clear my throat to speak loud enough for them to hear. "No, Selene. I did that so you might become part of my royal guard when I return from defeating the vampyr—that is, if you're willing."

She smiles with all her heart and nods. "Yes. Yes, of course."

That ought to take care of that rumor—for now, at least.

The elders have let me have my moment with the people, but one of them makes their way toward us. Juno Florakis. She is small and frail, but she is the eldest of the group and, therefore, the most respected. Stopping a short distance from us, she clears her throat, and I realize she is waiting for Aero to put me down. I unravel from him and follow her to the high tower, where we must climb the winding staircase. I draw in a deep breath. My leg still throbbing, I follow her to the top. She takes my hand and positions me at the ledge of the balcony. The same balcony where I watched Athena parade her servants around. Where she forced my father to feed her fruit in front of everyone, but mostly to show me the power she held. And now, here I am.

One of the other elders places a crown made of what appears to be two golden olive branches. Its lines are not perfectly symmetrical, but something about that makes it all the more beautiful. I'm sure, in the heat of things, one of the blacksmiths had to do their best to put something together quickly.

Juno lifts the crown in the air, and the crowd roars. I look into her glassy hazel eyes as she places the silver wreath upon my head, and it's in this moment that I finally hear my mother's voice. Just as she chanted for me when I returned from my journey across the island all those years ago.

Evanthe! Evanthe! Evanthe!

It's as if I'm eight years old again, and I feel her lifting me into the air, claiming me as her daughter. Then Juno's voice makes it official.

"I present you, the people of Meraki, with your new monarch, Evanthe Sideris."

A roaring cheer rips through the air. I step forward and lift my hands to quiet them.

"People of Parea, people of Meraki. It is with a heavy heart that I accept this honor before you today. I am filled with pride to be your monarch, but I can't ignore the plague that has befallen our beautiful home. Today, I give you my word that the Omen will not win this war. I will not remain here in this tower for long. I will journey to put an end to this shadow that has fallen upon our land. I will fight with every fiber of my being to defend our island, no matter the cost."

Celebration erupts in the streets. After paying my respects to the elders, they all exit the premises so I might have some time alone to get familiar with the new quarters. The moment they leave, it feels as though my legs might fall out from under me. I summon Aero and the others to join me in the high tower so we can rest before night falls.

The group scatters upon entering the grand room. Their feet shuffle slowly as their tired eyes muster the strength to take in the beautiful sight of the royal interior. I expect myself to gasp with wonder alongside them. To revel in the sweet victory that this place I once called home is mine again. But the cost has left me weak and weary.

Well aware that the tower boasts several chambers, I welcome each of them to take their pick of the accommodations. Well, any room aside from the monarch's quarters. That one is finally mine.

With a sigh, Aero hangs our satchels onto the brass hooks that are anchored to the wall beside the wardrobe. The joy that beamed from him upon my return to the city seems to have faded, replaced by the kind of worry that gnaws at your insides and turns your face ashen as his has.

I make my way to the edge of the bed and bend down to unlace my boots. Aero crouches beneath me. "Let me," he says.

Placing one hand behind my ankle, the other grips the heel and carefully removes it from my foot. He repeats the process on the other side and lifts the leg of my tattered trouser to peel off my woolen stocking, but pauses at the sight of the gash Athena left upon my leg.

"Let me find some strips of cloth and some clean water," he says, rising to his feet.

I look down at the wound. It aches a bit, but it's not that bad.

"It's nothing," I say, ushering him not to make a fuss.

His ashen face turns to stone. "No. You don't get to say that. It's not nothing, Eva. You nearly died."

"But I didn't. I'm still here, and my leg will be fine," I argue.

He shakes his head in disbelief. "What happened out there? In one moment, I could feel you throwing everything you had at Athena, in the next there was nothing. All that strength vanished. You gave up." His voice cracks, the words barely able to leave his mouth.

I recall the terror stabbing into my chest as the tip of Athena's sword was pressing into the divot beneath my neck. The panic rising as I waited for my mother's voice to find me, to save me. And the silence that followed, leaving me empty and hopeless.

"It all happened so fast. I was matching her blow for blow, but then I was on the ground. I had lost my sword, and she was standing over me. I...I was tired of fighting."

Aero runs a hand through his hair and lets it fall back onto his face as he paces the room wildly. "Do you know what that did to me? Can you try to imagine? I almost lost you!"

The words reverberate off the towering walls.

His pained face breaking me into a thousand pieces. I reach for his hand.

"I'm sorry, alright."

His eyes fill with tears as he falls to his knees at my feet.

"That's not enough. You have to promise me. Promise that you'll never do that again. That you'll never stop fighting."

Choking back a sob, my body melts from the bed and on to the floor with him. I wrap my arms and legs around him, burying my face into his neck.

"I promise," I whisper.

He draws back just enough to latch onto my gaze, and I fight the urge to wipe away my tears, letting him see the raw and broken parts of me. Without blinking an eye, he holds me through all of it. I realize now, that he always has. He draws me in tightly and clears his throat.

"No more pushing me away. You know there isn't a single human, deity, Fae, or realm I wouldn't drown in my fury if they so much as looked at you the wrong way. And if that includes the people of Baros, so be it."

The truth in his voice fills the air around us, shattering every wall I've built up over the years, and I crumble in his arms. "It's always been you. From the moment you returned to my thicket, to the courtyard of Elpida, to our bonding beside Twiltrie Lake..."

"and always," he breathes.

"Always," I swear.

I place my hand on his chest to feel the beating of his heart, its echo creating a rhythm. Its voice is a soothing beacon to my soul, entwining with his in a dance that no one else could possibly know. A magic only made for us. The only magic we will ever need. The only magic *I* will ever need.

His mouth meets mine, and a rushing tide of desire consumes me. I fling my arms around him, my body melding into his, my lips meeting his kiss with fervor.

With a growl, he lifts me onto the bed, his mouth only breaking from mine to take in the sight of me laid beneath him. His blazing gaze roaming down my heaving chest and stopping upon the gash on my leg. His face softens.

"We should tend to this," he says, his voice rugged and trembling.

His concern only makes my body ache more, but not for bandages or clean clothes. I grasp his collar and pull him down to me.

"It can wait. There are more important things to tend to," I purr.

Without another word, he gently removes my trousers and tunic. It isn't the rushed, frantic motion of lust. It is slow and tender. My hands shake as I undress him, leaving us both completely naked. Not just our bodies, but baring the deepest parts of ourselves. And I no longer feel the need to hide. Only the need to be closer to him.

The bond between us calling out, he lowers himself to

me, sliding one hand down the center of my core, bracing his weight with the other.

My breath quickens at his touch, a hushed plea for more. Reaching between us, I guide him toward me. We stare at one another with anticipation. And then he presses his mouth to mine as he eases himself inside. The size of him edging in with the sweetest pain followed by a burning pleasure like no other. Nothing has ever felt this right, this good.

He retracts and fills me once more. I gasp, my chest thundering wildly as I lose all restraint. My arms wrap around him, pressing my nails into his back. A wave inside me grows, every bone in my body crying out for more.

His hips roll with mine over and over until the cresting wave comes crashing down, obliterating all that remained of the fortress I had built up inside me. It is the storm of all storms. He roars as my body trembles, and the world I once knew is washed away, made new.

A tapping sensation wakes me from the deepest of sleeps. It pains me to pull myself up from the grand featherbed, but I find the strength. "How long have I been sleeping?" I ask, still half asleep.

"Oh, not long. But the sun is falling, and you need to make some royal decisions," Skira says.

Aero comes rushing in with a cup of hot broth and a

spoon. "I told you not to wake her yet," he snaps at the ghost.

"She's a monarch now. I don't know how you do it on that cursed island of yours, but here, in Meraki, our monarchs take care of their duties," she snips.

Grumbling to himself, he places the bowl in my hands. "The sooner we defeat the Mortia and wish her a farewell, the better."

I lift the spoon of savory liquid to my mouth. The warmth soothing my chest makes me hum.

"There's only one other thing I've seen make that sound come out of you before," Aero says with a wicked grin.

"Well, maybe you have competition," I banter, then notice the dark circles beneath his eyes. "Have you gotten any sleep since we got here?"

Pulling my leathers out from my satchel, he shakes his head. "I can sleep when the Mortia are dead."

"That's not funny," I say, giving him a warning glare.

When I pull the blankets from my body, I notice the wounds on my leg are now cleaned and bandaged. "When did you do this?" I ask.

"You fell asleep almost instantly. I didn't want to wake you," he replies.

I peel back the bandage to look closer. "Are those stitches?" I ask, bewildered.

He nods with a chuckle. I don't love the fact that I was so incapacitated that I didn't even wake while he was sewing me up, but the thought of him tending to my wounds is actually heartwarming.

"This seam is damn near perfectly straight, Aero. You may have missed your calling. Maybe you should become a seamstress instead of a sea god," I tease.

"Ha. Ha. You'll probably never hear me say this again, but put your leathers on. You need to address the guards," he says, his voice dropping an octave.

"What about them?" I ask.

Overhearing the conversation, Hera walks into the room. "First, none of them are actually guards."

They tell me how Athena has been picking away at the townspeople to defend her doors at night. How she sat inside this tower of luxury, listening to them dying out there, giving her just enough time to run away or hide long enough to last until sunrise.

"Well, of course I'm putting an end to this," I say.

Once I've pulled my leathers on, I quickly limp my way to the doors. I call them all from their posts and bring them inside the grand room. Wide-eyed, they all look around in wonder, and I realize they've actually never been inside the tower. She never even let them in once.

"It's been brought to my attention that Athena Rokos has done you all a terrible injustice. That all changes, starting tonight. You will no longer be standing guard. It is not your profession nor your obligation."

"Then who will?" one of them asks, a fearful look in his eye.

"No one. Until I clean up this mess of vampyr, there will be no royal guard."

Hera steps forward. "We will be her royal guard."

I smile at her and nod. "Yes, like Hera said, I have all the protection I need. You're all free to go back to your families. Be safe."

For fear that I change my mind, they all scramble out in a hurry. Feliks winces at the sound of one of them stumbling down the stairs. "Hope that one is still alright," he says.

Her eyes beaming with pride, my Aunt Maria takes my hand and squeezes it slightly. "You've already made your family very proud, and it's only your first day on the throne."

———

The night is quieter than the city of Parea has ever been, as if every soul inside the city walls is holding their breath for fear the Omen may hear it. Feliks doesn't even attempt to pick up his kithara. I've seen him glance over at it a time or two, but he doesn't dare make so much noise on a night like this, and I'm glad he doesn't. I remember the way sound echoes in this cavernous space. The towering ceilings make for quite the acoustics. Aside from the elders stopping by earlier to make arrangements for tomorrow, it's just our little group in this massive place.

It's strange being here in the high tower again. My mother wasn't monarch long, so it never really felt like home. It had always seemed like we were staying in someone else's home, but it was a castle in comparison to what I had known. Nuala plops down next to me with a huff.

"Can someone please explain why we aren't rifting back to the Fae Realm yet?" she asks.

"I have to attend the Granting Ceremony tomorrow. It's tradition. There are usually many more proceedings upon being crowned monarch, but due to the dire circumstances, the elders agreed to forgo most of them. Once the ceremony is over, there will be a small feast. I told them once the sun sets, we will depart. That way, we don't risk someone seeing us rifting in broad daylight. The elders think we will only be journeying across the island, looking for a way to destroy the vampyr."

Hera comes up the stairs with her hands lifted in the air. "There's a laconicum down there, and in the courtyard, there's a giant pool made for swimming. It doesn't look like anyone has been caring for it, but how amazing when you clean it up," she says, her voice far too high-pitched.

"Well, that's new. Sounds like Athena has made some changes since I last lived here," I say.

"What's a laconicum?" Skira asks.

I try to think of the best way to explain it to the ancient ghost. "It's a circular room covered by a brazen shield that can be raised or lowered to adjust the heat."

"So, what do you do in it?" she asks, her face crumpling.

"You sit in it and sweat," Hera replies bluntly.

The ghost sighs. "What a waste. All the work my generation put in so you could build rooms to sweat in. In my day, we just wanted a sturdy home with solid roof so we didn't have to sweat. What has this world come to?"

I bend over with a hushed laughter. Skira sneers at me for finding humor at her expense, but I can't help it. Here we are, wide awake in the middle of the night in the high tower, whispering to one another so as not to get attacked by a mob of vampyr, and she's complaining about a laconicum.

"It is a beautiful tower, though," Skira admits, gazing up at the arched molding.

Nuala scoffs. "It's nothing compared to the castles in our realm. I know you only got to see the Court of Ember after King Murrick's soldiers destroyed it, but it was really something before the war."

She lowers her head, and I feel sorry for her. I'm sure she misses her home. If anyone can understand that, it's me. I'm back home, and it doesn't even feel like the place I once knew. I don't argue with her. Besides, I'm sure the castles of the Fae Realm are much grander than this. I'd like to see one someday. I've seen the violent ways they can use their magic, but I've also seen the beauty that can come from it too.

Of course my Aunt Cybele wasn't about to let her get off without a retort. "Your Fae castles may be made of magic and shiny gems, but ours was built with sweat and tears, and nothing is more beautiful than that."

Nuala rolls her eyes, but to my surprise, she lets Cybele have the last word. Maybe there is a world where Fae and humans could coexist. I'm sure the day will come when the people of Meraki will find out I'm Fae. At some point, they're bound to question how I've lived so much longer than the rest of them. But by then, I could probably get away with lying about my age. I'm sure Aero will live longer than me. The gods are immortal, and he's only half human. Liri felt my Fae bloodline would be well diluted by now. But my power would say otherwise. I guess time will tell.

If we will be granted that time.

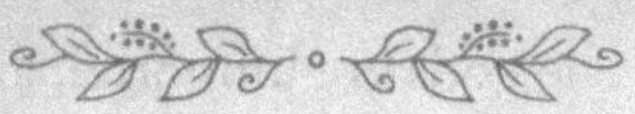

"I thought you might want to wear it today," Maria says, handing me a worn rectangular box.

I open the lid and remove the top layer of paper to find a vibrant-red material. I let my fingers graze the soft fabric as I delicately reach for the straps and lift it from the package.

"It's the most beautiful gown I've ever seen," I gasp.

"I don't know if you remember, but it was your mother's. She wore it at her Granting Ceremony, and we've held onto it in case you wanted to wear it at yours."

Cybele stands by her side, clasping her hands together, awaiting my response. The hopeful glimmer in her eye makes me choke up. Not just because of the dress—it's perfect, and I can't think of any I'd rather wear today—but because they believed in me all this time. They kept this, knowing this day would come. I've spent so much of my life bitter. So angry with the world. All the training, all the sleepless nights, so I could prove them wrong. But I didn't have to prove anything. They knew I would make it. Tears spill from my eyes.

"Well, don't ruin the dress before you even get the chance to put it on," Maria says, taking it from my hands. "Go on, out of those scrubby trousers."

I let my less-than-admirable attire fall to the floor, only leaving on my undergarments. My Aunt Cybele pinches onto a bit of my side. "Great Zeus, girl. You need to eat something. Didn't they feed you in the Fae Realm?"

"Don't you worry, I'll be eating my fill today," I reply.

Lifting my arms, she lets the red gown slide over my body. A little tucking and nipping, and it fits like a glove. She turns me to face the full-length mirror in the corner of the room, and I gasp. The off-shoulder neckline wraps elegantly across my chest, draping just below my right collarbone. The bodice hugs my figure and finishes with a daring front slit. It's a second set of skin that makes every exceptional part of me shine.

They both jump up and down, clapping their hands like it's the end of a performance and they're giving it a standing ovation. I don't know what to say. I've never cared much for fancy garments or frivolous things, but this means something.

"You look just like your mother," Maria says.

"Thank you," I say, knowing that the observation was meant to make me feel loved. No one has ever told me that

I look like my mother—because I don't, really. I look much more like my father, but Aunt Maria knows how I admire my mother, how much I've always wanted to be like her.

"It's time," Hera shouts, her head popping around the side of the door, and my stomach flutters.

Cybele places the crown of golden olive leaves upon my head and tucks a stray curl of hair around my ear. I look down at the black symbol of mine and Aero's bonding and run my fingers over it. It tingles a bit.

"They're all waiting for you, my dear," she says, scurrying away to join the others.

"I better not keep them waiting, then," I say to myself, stepping into the grand hall.

The first thing I see as I enter the sprawling room is Aero and my aunts, standing to the left of the royal throne. The massive chair is adorned with sconces and peaks that resemble the tips of spears. The group of elders wait on the right of it. Each of them is dressed in a dark-blue cloak, the color of wisdom and honesty.

Aero drinks in the sight of me, and the bond sends a wave of warmth through my core. All this time I've spent pushing him away, and here he is at my Granting Ceremony. My mind continues to advise me to take caution, but the bond is stronger, and right now I want to believe that his intentions are good.

Elder Juno Florakis reaches for a large scroll and meets me in front of the throne. "Good Elders and Royal Counsel of Meraki, we gather here today before the Great Divine and in the name of Skira Galanis." The ghost lets a wisp of herself appear behind them all, and I do my best not to break into laughter. The elder goes on. "Evanthe Sideris, daughter of the fallen Beta Sideris—"

"And of the fallen Dimitris Glazos," I blurt out, unable to fully understand the sudden urge to include my father's name. But I am just as much his as I am hers. Why shouldn't he be honored in this as well?

Not pleased with the interruption, Juno wrinkles her nose up and shakes her head.

Grasping her fingers together in thanks, my Aunt Maria's eyes well up with tears. For the first time in a long time, I feel surrounded with love. They are my family. Everyone on the left side of that throne. I would do anything for them and they me.

The elder clears her throat to regain my attention. "Are you, Evanthe Sideris, willing to take the oath before you?"

"I am," I reply.

"Do you swear on this day, and each day forward until your death, to keep the safety of the people of Meraki your utmost priority?"

"I do."

She turns to face the other elders. "Then the monarch before us, and from the battle of Noonsnight, shall go to her throne before all her counsel and pronounce the sacred oath."

I step up onto the alter, turn around, and plant myself firmly in the royal seat. The stone is cool to the touch, sending a shiver down my spine, and suddenly, the faces of the travelers and the beautiful hand-carved throne they called Agape flash before my eyes. It's been months since we saw them, but somehow it feels like it was only yesterday. I hear Petre's voice. *"No one will sit upon it. Ever."* Agape. Sacrificial love. It sounds so simple, but nothing could be more involved.

Juno shakes the scroll in front of me, pulling me back to reality. I look down at the beautifully written words and read them aloud for all to hear.

"The words I have before you promised, I shall uphold and keep to the best of my ability. So help me Great Divine."

Juno nods with approval and hands me a feather pen dipped in black ink. "Then the monarch shall sign the oath."

I watch as the wet signature turns dry, and the elder takes the scroll from my hands. That's it. I'm the monarch of Meraki from this day until I die. Now, we just have to stop the Mortia so there is an island left to rule.

The feast devoured and the elders satisfied with my initiation into the royal status, we strip from our formal attire and pull on our leathers for the war ahead. Maria and Cybele wipe their tears and send me away with another blessing. The sun has fallen, and Nuala rushes us out the tower doors so we might find a hidden spot in the thicket to rift back to the Fae Realm.

Skira drifts alongside me as we run through the dark

woods. It is eerily quiet. None of the crickets are chirping. None of the leaves are rustling in the breeze. Not a single sound. I recall my time spent alone in the thicket as a young girl. Only when a predator was present did the forest become this still. I wait for Skira to start barking orders, hoping she will break this feeling, telling me how important it is that I defeat the Mortia. But she is silent, and then I know how worried she must be. When we come to a stop, I turn to her.

"Skira, this will probably be the last time we speak to one another. I want you to know that I'm going to do everything in my power to put your soul to rest."

She places her hands on her hips and lifts her chin. "Of that I have faith, but when you return, I want you to fix this mess they've made in my name. Find a way, Evanthe. Promise me."

She doesn't have to say a word. I know what mess she speaks of. It haunts me too.

"If you didn't give me such a terrible chill, I would give you a hug," I say.

The ghost lightly shrugs. "We both know I'm not much for such emotional displays."

With a wink, she fades into the night sky, and Nuala gestures for us to grab hands. Aero latches on and then Hera. I close my eyes and brace myself for the forceful ride, but something strikes me to the ground. I try to get back up, but the wind is knocked from my chest.

Gasping, I find some air and pull myself from the dirt to find Despina and three other vampyr circling our group.

Aero blasts the larger one with a torrent of water, and the battle breaks loose. More come pouring out from the woods, and it becomes clear that Despina is sending them all toward the others, saving me for herself.

The monster salivates as she creeps closer, still wearing the same black garment wrapped in snake skins. Her yellow eyes glow with a flicker of excitement as she grows nearer. I should hate her with all my might. This is the creature that took my father's life before I had the chance to tell him how I felt, to tell him that I forgive him for Athena, and to hear from his mouth how I will need to carry the bloom. This is his legacy too. But despite all that, I just see an angry, bitter woman who sold her soul to the same vile creature I bartered with. I may not be able to hold that against her, but I can't let her kill me.

She lunges for me once, barely missing, but doesn't waste any time leaping toward me once more. I backpedal, my boots moving as quickly as I can take them, but it's not fast enough. I can see the victorious gleam in her eye. But then something flashes through the thicket and tackles her to the dirt. It's a blur of limbs and fangs until the commotion stills, and in its wake, a ragged vampyr with rosy-red hair stands above Despina's headless body.

"Sorrow!" I call out, running to her.

But she is faster than me, and like a shadow in the woods, she is gone. The clashing of blades and hissing quiets, and a warm hand finds my arm.

"Are you alright?" Aero asks, searching my body for any sign of injury.

"No," I say, for the pain seeing my dear friend again brings. "It was really her. Sorrow saved me," I whisper.

He leans over and cradles my face in his hands. "Then her soul, too, will find rest after we bury the Mortia."

I want to believe him with all the faith I can muster. If there can be a peaceful place for Skira, there has to be one for Sorrow too.

More hissing sounds in the distance. Nuala wipes the sweat from her brow and gestures for us to gather quickly. My heart still racing, I latch onto Aero and Hera once more, letting every part of me fall freely back into the Fae Realm, and the bloom begins to warm.

A heated promise of what is to come.

AUTHOR'S NOTE

Thank you so much for reading A Vow of Salt and Stone! We have one more book planned for this world, and I hope you enjoy reading them as much as I love writing them. Evanthe is near and dear to my heart as a character, and I can't wait to share the next phase of her and Aero's story with you.

If you enjoyed this book, please consider taking a moment to leave a review on Amazon and Goodreads to help other readers find and enjoy it as well. Your reviews mean everything to us authors!

And if you'd like to gain access to exclusives, news, giveaways, and upcoming releases consider signing up for my newsletter at santanasaunders.com

I would love to keep in touch!

ACKNOWLEDGMENTS

This story took months to write and many months more to polish. I couldn't have done it without the support of my family and my team.

I'll start with my husband, my sounding board, my best friend. Thank you for everything. I can't imagine life without you. And my girls, my three wildlings. Thank you for sharing me with these fictional worlds. I love you with all my heart.

My alpha reader, Emarie, this book wouldn't be the same without your notes and encouragement. You gave me the confidence I needed to take the next step.

My beta team, thank you so much for not holding back. Your honest feedback and random text messages made this story what it is today. I'd be lost without you.

My PA, Heather, for keeping the Blood and Bloom Series alive while I'm in the trenches of writing the next book. I've always struggled with sharing my stories with the world, and you do that for me in such a beautiful way.

My cover designer, Stef, you continue to take my breath away with each cover. I don't know how you manage to take the few notes I give you and turn them into the perfect visual translation.

And finally, thank **you**— for your readership, messages, reviews, and enthusiasm. You are the lifeblood of my writing journey. It's all for you and it's all because of you. I'm forever grateful.

ABOUT THE AUTHOR

Santana Saunders grew up along the Missouri River in North Dakota, where the sandbars were far-off lands and the canoes were pirate ships.

Santana went on to pursue a career in business development, and creative writing went on the back-burner. In 2019, she and her family found themselves relocating from the Midwest to the coast. Sandbars and canoes quickly became beaches and ocean. This change of scenery inspired her to return to writing.

Today, she is a U.S. based author of fantasy romance novels. When she isn't reading or writing stories she is playing at the beach with her husband and three daughters or attempting a DIY home project that will surely take weeks longer than anticipated to accomplish.

www.ingramcontent.com/pod-product-compliance
Lightning Source LLC
Chambersburg PA
CBHW011412310726
48972CB00011B/2948